J. A. BOULET

I0653026

WHICHEVER WAY THE ROAD LEADS

"1956 Love & Revolution drew me in with the summary and I must say the author as well. I will read anything by J.A. Boulet without ever reading the summary. I have loved every book that I have read by J.A. Boulet and recommend them all highly." – Nancy Allen (The Avid Reader) July 24, 2023

"I heartily recommend this book (1956 Love & Revolution) not only to those who have personal or family connections to Hungary but also to anyone who loves freedom and democracy, to anyone who admires those who fight for these ideals." – Arthur W. Turfa July 1, 2023

"Perfect blend of fact and fiction........very realistic story line surrounded by actual historical events. Tough book (The Origins) to put down once you start reading it!" – Doug Stasiuk February 16, 2023

"This book (The Wars Between Us) was a surprising find. I can't believe I never heard about the events that inspired this story, and I'm glad the author took her time to research the facts. Great book overall and is definitely a must read for history and war story readers." – Amazon Customer February 23, 2023

Also by J. A. Boulet

J. A. BOULET

WHICHEVER WAY THE ROAD LEADS

Copyright © 2024 J. A. Boulet

Published by J. A. Boulet

Book cover design: White Rabbit Arts at The Historical Fiction Company

ISBN: 978-1-7781999-8-1

This book is dedicated to my sons. May they always follow the way their roads lead.

Note to Reader

This book is a work of historical fiction. I have attempted to be accurate with many of the historical events, although some details have been intentionally skewed to fit within the story. This is a fictional saga of bravery, love and family. Even though many of the historical events are accurate, this book should be read as fiction.

J. A. Boulet May 2, 2024

PART I

NORTHWEST FRONTIER

CHAPTER 1

Jesse Eastman cradled his head in his calloused hands and wondered when he had lost his mind. He thought back to several incidents and still could not accurately pinpoint what had prompted him to make the ridiculous decision to risk his life with the Overland Astorian explorers. However, one event was obvious. The argument with his father two years ago had changed his life, for better or for worse. Jesse had never fully recovered from the sting of being thrown out of the Eastman family.

He looked up as his friend threw another log on the fire. Samuel was a tall, gangly fellow he had met last year in St. Louis when the Astorians were adding men to the team. Samuel was as close to a best friend as he'd ever met.

"Still wondering how crazy you are to be here, boy?" Samuel chuckled as the Mad River[1] sloshed menacingly behind their backs. Samuel spit and kicked a stray log with his dirty boot into the campfire. His long hair was firmly slicked back from his forehead, and the stray ends wisped onto his shoulders with every movement.

---

1   Present day Snake River, Idaho

"Yes," replied Jesse. "I'm wondering when I'm going to die, too." Jesse stood and wiped his grimy hands on his pants. The Mad River was so loud it almost drowned out the conversation at times. The closer he veered to the water, the more ominous it became. Jesse took a few steps towards the rapids and shouted towards the river. "How the hell are we going to ride those rapids tomorrow?"

Samuel grimaced and spat again. "With difficulty," he responded manically.

Jesse grunted loudly and turned back. "Hopefully, we live through it."

A burly man walked into the conversation from the main camp. "And when did you get so concerned with losing your life?" Robert McClellan shouted back.

"Hey, Robert!" Jesse sneered. "When did you start thinking you knew me so well?"

"I've known your father from way back," McClellan replied. "I saved your hide getting you onto this team."

Jesse grinned lopsidedly. "You did that, yes," he shot back. "And I may be paying with my life crossing this river. All of us might be."

Samuel interrupted. "With these tough canoes, we'll get anywhere!" he said, slapping his hand onto the side of the closest wooden vessel.

"When did you become an expert?" Jesse said jokingly.

"Way before you were born!" Samuel shot back, instantly angry and stepping forward.

Robert pushed Samuel on the shoulder. "Sit your ass down and cool off," he ordered. "Same with you, Jesse." He pointed a commanding finger at Jesse. "I know it's been a long time on this expedition, but we're getting closer. We will get to the

Columbia River, and we'll reach Fort Astoria, no matter what is thrown our way."

Jesse sat down on a rough log. Robert McClellan was one of the Pacific Fur Company partners and highly respected in the group. Along with the other partner, Douglas Mackenzie, they were two of the most experienced and trusted leaders of the expedition. And they were keeping the large group of men, women, and children alive. Jesse ran his fingers over his dark brown hair. "I trust you, McClelland," Jesse said, his brown eyes looking up. "You were mad enough to take a crazy guy like me on. I'd trust you before Wilson any day. That man doesn't know a thing about the wilderness. He's going to get us all killed."

McClellan waved his hand dismissively. "Wilson Hunt was made leader of this expedition," he replied, throwing his hands up in the air in exasperation. "Why they made him leader, I have no idea. Apparently, he has more business sense than anything. To give him credit, though, he did prove to be a valuable asset when we encountered the Indians. He secured us safe passage." McClellan gazed into the darkening wilderness, then slapped a reassuring hand on Jesse's shoulder. "And you're not that crazy, Jesse. You've just got something missing in your young brain when it comes to dancing with danger, and, fortunately, that's exactly the kind of men we need on this expedition." He turned away from the men, waving behind him. "Get some sleep, men. We'll see which way this river leads us tomorrow."

Jesse watched McClellan disappear in the bushes as the night darkened around the camp. Jesse laid down on his cot and gazed up at the night skies, feeling a shiver run through his spine.

It would be September 30, 1811 tomorrow, and Jesse imagined this was the date that would appear on his young gravestone. That is, if anyone ever found his body.

Jesse packed up the canoe with the supplies in the morning and prepared to join the rest of the team. The canoes were constructed out of the local cottonwood trees. The vessels were as sturdy as they would ever be, but he doubted they would be any match for this river. Jesse hefted the loaded canoe onto his shoulders as Samuel raised the back side. The canoe fleet had already survived one river, but Jesse doubted they would take all 60 people safely along the Mad River.

The raging rapids howled, like the devil incarnate, as they trudged through the forest. The spray from the water seemed to be increasing in intensity and was creating beckoning rainbows through the morning sun. Jesse strained to keep his eyes where he placed his feet. The ground was steadily changing to slippery mud as they neared the riverside. One misplaced foot, and the heavy canoe would be crushing him into the mud.

The humidity hung like a rain fog throughout the forest. In stark contrast to the beautiful scenery, the river seemed to be laughing at them all, touching everything with its madness. Jesse shook his head and wondered again when he had lost his mind.

It was suicide to travel in this river. The expedition had named the rapids Mad River for a reason.

"Cheer up," Samuel said, slapping the side of the canoe. "It looks like you've seen a ghost."

"Can you hear the rapids, or are you deaf?" Jesse replied almost too loudly.

Samuel laughed wildly. "My hearing is fine, boy!" he shouted back. "Don't let the river get a hold of your fears! We are hiking alongside the rapids until the Mad River settles down."

"And I suppose Hunt gets to decide when it's safe to enter those crazy rapids?"

Samuel grimaced under the canoe's weight and slipped suddenly in the mud. He spread his legs wide, trying to establish some balance while attempting to save the canoe from crashing onto him. Jesse stopped and held the front end of the canoe firmly, praying for his partner not to fall. After several tense seconds, Samuel regained his balance and shifted the canoe onto his right shoulder as Jesse exhaled a sigh of relief. "Yeah, you got me there," Samuel replied, his boots slick with mud. "Hunt doesn't know anything about these woods."

McClelland shouted from behind the group. "We will stop here, men!"

Jesse grunted from the weight of the loaded canoe as they both carefully placed it on the forest floor.

"We will attempt the river here," McClellan stated.

Jesse laughed crazily as the rapids roared in his ears. "Well!" he said loudly, wiping his dirty hands on his pants. "Remember to spell my name properly on my gravestone!"

"That won't be happening. We will get through this fine. It looks like there are only a few more raging sections of water, then it calms down ahead of us," McClellan said, pointing ahead in the distance. "We can't cross that mountainous peak in front of us by foot. Our chances are better with the river."

"The Mad River," Jesse replied sarcastically.

"Yep, the Mad River," McClellan affirmed as he stepped out of the group and assessed the entry point into the rapids. The water sloshed at his feet as the group watched him deliberating on the safest access juncture.

Jesse sat down heavily and chewed on a strip of deer jerky. Samuel and most of the group did the same. They needed some strength to tackle this lunatic river.

Samuel's face grew calm, but a sloppy grin stayed on his lips. Despite all his crazy antics, the man was a goodhearted soul similar to Jesse, just a little rough around the edges. They both chewed the jerky in silence, waiting for McClelland to return with instructions. The team had been together since the fall of 1810, leaving St. Louis and spending the winter camping at Nodaway River. They had traveled successfully 450 miles up the Missouri River in the spring of 1811 by canoes, arriving at several native Arikara Villages. Wilson Hunt had diplomatically saved the group from several Indian encounters as they had continued west on foot and horseback. Jesse was extremely grateful to have Hunt on the team for that. They would have all been dead already otherwise.

"We'll enter here," McClellan waved his hand behind him as he returned to the group. "We need to cut down some of these bushes to widen the path so we can get all our supplies through, but otherwise, it is the best we can hope for right now." McClellan waved at the mountainous passage ahead of them, which loomed like a menacing force.

Jesse nodded and swallowed the last piece of jerky. Since midsummer, the group had been tackling some of the most difficult mountainous ranges Jesse had ever seen in his life. It sounded irrational, but the river was a welcome challenge after being stuck in these mountains for three months. Everyone in the party seemed to agree.

"Who knows," Wilson Hunt added. "Maybe we will arrive at Fort Astoria before the Tonquin group."

McClellan frowned, knowing that the ship Tonquin and its crew from New York City likely had its share of difficulties sailing the Atlantic Ocean along the entire eastern side of the continent, down south and back up to the Pacific Ocean to arrive at the Fort through the west side of the Columbia

River. "They will definitely be having as many difficulties as we are," McClellan stated. "The oceans are a very different beast altogether."

Hunt nodded. "True, I'd rather be battling the land elements than negotiating with pirates and ocean currents."

Jesse stood and prepared to move the canoe to the entry point with Samuel. "I'd rather be back in New York City," Jesse whispered.

Samuel nodded. "I agree," he said. "But what we're doing is more important than you think. Opening these fur trading posts in the West means we are expanding America. It could mean some big things in the future." Samuel swallowed the last of his jerky and smiled. "We're making history, brother."

"Samuel's right," McClellan affirmed. "We are making history, and someone has to open up the West. No better men than us right now." He scraped his foot on a nearby log, attempting to rake the mud off. "Watch your steps here. It's slippery."

The group stopped as several men began cutting the bushes and smaller trees down to widen the path. Jesse and Samuel laid down the canoe and joined the fifty other men, cutting and hacking the path just enough to make it more passable. It didn't take long before the path was safe to bring the supplies through. The area wasn't perfect, but the extra lumber gave them enough material to construct another raw vessel to hold more supplies on the river.

Jesse was already drenched in sweat when the group stopped to make coffee, eat lunch, and gather courage for the bigger challenge ahead of them.

As the noon sun rose over the peak, the team cleaned up the camp. The one woman in the group washed the remaining dishes with several other boys and packed everything away securely. The woman's two children were in the middle of the group, securely protected by the larger men. Jesse was not entirely certain why the woman and her children were a part of this brutal expedition but accepted them as a wonderful distraction.

Jesse pulled his canoe to the access point with Samuel. They both stood mesmerized as they watched the vessel in front of them release into the river. The first group scrambled into the river, disappearing around the bend almost instantly, immediately engulfed by the cavernous mouth of the whitewater. Jesse glanced worriedly back at Samuel.

Their canoe was resting only a few inches in the water, but Jesse could already feel the tug of the current. He inhaled sharply and nodded at the group to get into the vessel. Jesse's canoe had the woman and her children. He felt the weight of responsibility settle firmly onto his shoulders. With six other people and a raft of supplies already loaded on, Jesse nodded to Samuel as they pushed the canoe from behind, ready to jump in as soon as the current grabbed the vessel clear of the land.

The water splashed violently against the hull at the front, the current gripping it and turning the vessel as Jesse felt sweat drip from his forehead. The canoe swayed but stayed attached to the land. Jesse bent down and tried hefting the back end of the vessel that was still stuck in the mud.

It was a cool morning, but he felt hot from exertion and fear. With one more push, the canoe shifted into the water as Jesse and Samuel scrambled in panic, barely jumping in at the last minute. The vessel careened into the Mad River with a tremendous yank of ferocious nature.

Jesse landed on his butt in the back of the canoe. Samuel landed on his right leg with his left dangling out of the canoe. Jesse clambered to pull his friend safely into the canoe just in time as the vessel careened on its own wild path through the rapids. Whitewater spray hit every occupant in the face as they all struggled to stay in the canoe. Jesse tried paddling on the left, and a few other men got their paddles out.

"We need to avoid that rock on the right!" Jesse shouted frantically at the others.

Three men in the front paddled with the fear of God in their veins, along with Jesse and Samuel paddling from the stern. The canoe pulled to the right towards the rock as they screamed at each other.

"Paddle harder!" Jesse shouted as his arms strained with the paddle, the current almost taking his paddle away.

The woman picked up a paddle and joined the group as everyone panicked in the frantic diversion of certain death. The water sprayed at all angles until, finally they could feel the canoe turn in the right direction.

As quickly as the near catastrophe happened, it was gone, and the canoe sailed around the bend, clearing the dangerous rock. The force of the river catapulted them around the bend, and another terrifying white spray of angry water loomed ahead of them. They had no time to react as the current flew the group over the top of the rapids.

The vessel tilted dangerously to the left as several people intuitively shifted to the right. The weight of the bodies saved them from a dangerous collapse as they careened past the wreckage of another canoe.

Samuel pointed and yelled. "There are people stranded in the river! We have to try and save them!"

When Jesse looked up, a man's head bobbed underneath the whitewater. "Someone grab him!"

A man threw a rope out, but it didn't reach even ten feet towards the wreckage. Jesse strained to keep the boat straight as they sailed over the rapids and hit the water hard with an enormous splash, filling the boat with water and spilling several supplies overboard.

The women and children grabbed buckets and worked in a panic to get the water out as the boat veered closer to the stranded man. Samuel held out his canoe paddle and yelled at the shipwrecked man in the river. "Grab the paddle!" The man's head bobbed up briefly, and a hand shot out. "Grab the paddle!" Samuel shouted again. The man overboard reached and grabbed the paddle, but the water was too slick. His hand slipped and wouldn't form a solid grip. The canoe tugged and then rushed mercilessly past the stranded man.

Jesse couldn't turn to look because another dangerous waterfall loomed ahead of them. It didn't look like a very tall fall, but Jesse couldn't really tell. All he could see was blue sky ahead of them and more whitewater below.

"Grab the supplies raft! It's your only chance!" Samuel shouted back to the man overboard as their own canoe rushed towards the looming waterfall.

"Hold onto the boat, people! We're going over!" Jesse shouted as he gripped the sides of the canoe firmly.

The canoe lurched to the top of the falls and, for a brief moment, teetered as the drop was clear for everyone to see. Then, the vessel fell at an angle with the bow dipping slightly down. The woman and children screamed as the boat sailed through the air and then hit the whitewater forcefully. A menacing crack sounded as the canoe landed. Jesse prayed it wasn't serious as the current pulled them along the river on its journey of madness.

The boat began to turn backward and started a slow spin. "The boat cracked!" Jesse shouted. "We need to get to shore to repair it! Paddle to the shore on the right! Paddle hard! Everyone!"

Everyone grasped their paddles and pushed the boat furiously against the angry current. They struggled as a team until, finally, the boat approached the safety of the bank on the opposite right side. A man at the front grabbed a tree and steadied the boat while he tied it to the trunk, then jumped to shore. Samuel held out a long paddle that the man grasped, pulling everyone and the boat to shore.

Jesse looked behind him and searched for the supply raft.

It was gone.

Jesse searched for the cord at the back that had attached the raft to the canoe. He lifted it through the water and pulled the length in and in until, finally, he was left with a small broken log with the tether intact. That's all they had left of the supply raft.

It must have been destroyed over the waterfall. Jesse searched the rapids for signs of the raft, but it was nowhere to be seen. The man from the wreckage was gone, too.

Everyone disembarked, dripping wet, and collapsed onto the rocky bank. Jesse heaved and tried to slow his rapid breathing down.

They were somehow miraculously alive.

Chapter 2

Zee gazed up at the September sun and felt alive inside for the first time in her life. A gusty autumn breeze lifted her long blonde hair from her shoulders. It was an unusually hot day for late September, and she felt a glow tingle throughout her body. She smoothed her hand along the horse's neck and leaned over, whispering in the animal's ear. "You are a sweet, wild child, just like me, Beauty," Zee cooed. "And you don't care what others think." Zelda laughed as the horse nodded its head in agreement. "I know, sweetie, you are the mirror of my soul."

Zelda continued caressing the horse's mane as her secret boyfriend rushed out of the stable, pretending to be working hard at pitching the hay. She grinned softly to herself and tried to appear serious, but the smile continued creeping up to her swollen lips as her father, George, galloped towards the stable.

Zee's first-ever kiss still burned on her lips, and her groin felt warm. Her senses were erratically scattered in every direction, and Zee pondered briefly about her encounter with the farmhand. She wondered if she should have thought it through a little better.

"Zelda Collard!" George yelled. "We've been looking for you all afternoon! Your mother wants you in the house!" George Collard slowed his horse to a trot as he neared Zelda.

She pulled her straw hat tightly down over her forehead and peered up, her bewitching odd-colored eyes narrowing with spunk as her father bellowed at her. Her left green eye and right blue eye simultaneously twitched as she grinned lopsidedly at her father. "Aww, Pa," she cried in her twisted American British accent. "You know, I'm not good in the kitchen! Leave me out here with the horses and cows. I can take care of the land better than a loaf of bread!"

"Listen to me for once!" her father demanded. "Your momma's not baking bread!"

Zee patted Beauty's rump and galloped a short way to get farther away from her father's sight. Her hair flowed behind her as the farmhand looked up suddenly, watching her gallop in a circle. Zelda's nicely rounded buttocks slapped on the saddle rhythmically, and the young man was momentarily hypnotized by the sight.

Zee licked her lips as the farmhand looked away suddenly, and she turned her face sideways towards her father.

George grimaced, turning his sight away from his daughter, and barked at the farmhand. "Ewart! Did you get all the water troughs filled for the cows? It's barely rained for two weeks."

"Yessir!" Ewart straightened. "Done that this morning! I'm just finishing up forking the hay and oats for the horses. Zee helped a bit, sir!"

"Zee! I told you to get to the house!" George glanced angrily behind him.

Zelda sat defiantly on her horse, then thought better of creating a scene so soon after kissing Ewart. "Sure, Pa!" she yelled and slapped Beauty's rump, galloping away towards the large house on the opposite side of the property.

George narrowed his eyes at his defiant eldest daughter and wondered what she was up to now. She never backed down that easily from a fight. He turned to his farmhand and bellowed. "Get the sickles sharpened for the wheat harvesting!" George circled his grey gelding in front of Ewart and spat in the dirt. "We'll cut the remainder of that wheat down before the cold weather hits. Some more hired hands are coming tomorrow. Zee can help bundle."

Ewart straightened. "Yessir," he said, pulling his farmer's hat low. "I'll get them sharpened now." Ewart left the barn quickly, exhaling a sigh of relief. They weren't caught, not this time. He rushed through the field to the small equipment barn and got to work, smiling.

♔

Clara Collard was 38, almost the same age as her husband. She was younger than him by only one year. George Collard had arrived in Upper Canada in 1790 and they met in 1793 when she was just twenty years old. Three years later, after the birth of Zelda and another baby, George was granted 15 acres of land in the Niagara region of Upper Canada just for being a United Empire Loyalist. He was technically only the son of a devoted Loyalist. He was too young to have fought in the war. George Collard Sr. had died in action during the American Revolutionary War and was praised as a hero by the British. George Jr. hadn't really chosen which allegiance to support in the newly formed USA. He was immediately branded as a loyalist and narrowly escaped imprisonment as a child. George Jr. fled as soon as he could, three months before his eighteenth birthday, and traveled by foot to Upper Canada.

Clara had fallen in love with him the first time they met and still very much adored her husband of 18 years. They had seven children, all daughters except the youngest two, who were hell-raising twin boys.

Unfortunately, both boys seemed to take after her wildest daughter, Zee.

"What is it, Momma?" Zee poked her head in, her matted long blonde hair poking out in every direction.

"My God, child!" Clara bellowed, twitching her nose. "Scrub down with some soap! You smell like cow manure!"

"Thanks, Mother," Zee sneered. "I love you too."

"Don't give me that smart talk, young lady!"

"Oh, I'm a lady now?" Zee replied cheekily. "Not a child?"

Clara shook her head in defeat. "Zee, I need your help with your brothers. They've gotten themselves injured climbing the fence."

"Our new fence?" Zee cried. "We just built that!"

"Yes," Clara said tiredly. "Please tend to their wounds. I need to finish baking the bread and buns for the week. You're good at being the nurse around here."

"For the animals, yes," Zee said, frowning.

"Well," Clara replied, chuckling. "I suppose you'll just have to fix up your brothers too." Clara kneaded a large lump of dough on the rough wooden kitchen counter. "Go help your brothers."

Zee stomped down the hallway toward the shouts coming from Jacob and Sam. She opened the bedroom door and found the two four-year-olds crying in pain and hugging their legs.

"I hope my fence is not broken!" Zee yelled. "I swear I'll skin you alive if you damaged it. It took Papa and I the entire year to build that."

"Zee!" Clara shouted from the kitchen.

Zelda glowered at her twin brothers. "Let's get washed up, you little troublemakers." She lifted the smaller one up onto her shoulder and grasped the other boy's hand. She looked down at the heavier twin, Jacob. "What in God's name were you doing?"

"Playing war," Jacob answered feebly.

"War is not a game," Zee responded, frowning. She placed the lighter boy on the counter near the wash bin and started cleaning the scrapes on his leg amidst howls of protest. "Sit still, Sam!"

Jacob peered up at her. "Have you ever been to war?" he asked, rubbing his mouth with the back of his grubby hand.

"Of course not," Zee replied. "I'm a girl."

"Girls aren't allowed?"

"That's right, Jacob."

"If it was allowed for girls to go to war, would you?"

"Now, what kind of question is that?" Zee asked in response.

"You're pretty good with a rifle, Zee," Jacob answered, smiling with pride at his eldest sister. "I've seen how you can shoot those cans."

"That's just practice," Zee responded.

"Practice for what?"

"Nothing and everything," Zelda stated, getting increasingly annoyed. "It doesn't matter anyway because Ma and Pa want to marry me off so I can have kids and cook bread for the rest of my life."

The twins broke into raucous fights of laughter. "You?" Sam shrieked. "Never!"

Zee laughed with them and enjoyed the time with her brothers, but she knew it was sadly true. Zelda would never be a suitable wife for any husband. She knew this with crystal clear accuracy. Her parents had tried, and it always ended disastrously. Zee was more interested in building fences, bundling wheat, and ranching. Oh, and shooting! She liked that too!

Zelda Collard would never be the woman everyone wanted her to be.

Chapter 3

Jesse surveyed the wilderness around the group to see if any of the other boats were nearby. An eagle flew overhead, jolting everyone in surprise. Jesse looked down at the wet boat and rubbed his forehead. They lost their supplies, and he had no idea how they were going to fix the canoe. They needed help.

He scanned the river just as another canoe came rushing abruptly over the waterfall.

He jumped up and waved his hands with several others. "We're here!" they shouted enthusiastically.

The canoe's occupants waved their hands in acknowledgment just as the vessel tipped over the waterfall, crashing with an awful smash into the whitewater below.

The canoe appeared almost to be submerged for several terrifying seconds, then it was over, and the vessel showed up several meters down the river, racing towards the others.

Jesse's arms fell at his sides in despair. "I guess we'll have to figure out how to fix this canoe ourselves."

Samuel nodded. "Without any supplies, it'll be nearly impossible."

"Let's take a look at it," Jesse said, walking back to the canoe with Samuel.

They turned it over and heard the bottom crack again. It was the same sickening crack they heard before. Jesse knelt down to examine the damage, running his hand along the broken cottonwood. "We are lucky to be alive," he said. "This crack runs the entire length of the canoe. It would've split the entire boat into two halves if we had kept going."

"Yes, but now what do we do?" Samuel said, exhaling with frustration.

"We try to fix it and find the others," Jesse stated, knowing that it was a daunting task without tools and tar.

⚜

"It's nighttime, Jesse," Samuel urged. "We can no longer see anything. There's not much we can do for the canoe. It's not fixable."

"No, don't say that."

"The rest of the team has gone down the river," Samuel stated. "We need food. Everyone is starving. Leave the canoe. We have other problems to deal with."

Jesse exhaled and kicked the dirt in frustration. "Why does everything in this God-forsaking Western world have to be so damn difficult?" he shouted in anger. "Every darn thing we do is wrong out here!" He shouted to the tops of the trees, and his voice echoed back.

Samuel threw a bedroll at Jesse. "Sleep it off. You'll need that eighteen-year-old energy in the next few days just to stay alive."

Jesse grabbed the bedroll angrily and clamped his mouth shut. He was just a young buck to all these weary travelers. He tried to make it in this God-forsaken Western frontier, and the wilderness kept winning, no matter what he did.

♠

The noise sounded strange, almost like someone was shuffling through his things. It must be his father getting ready to challenge him again over the little black girl, Georgina. Pa shouldn't have done what he did to her, and none of this would have happened.

The bruises on her face were swelling fast, and Jesse had no time to think. His blood just boiled over, and he struck at his father to stop the slave beating.

Georgina shrieked as Jesse's fists pounded on his father, Bob Eastman, one straight in the jaw. The right hook connected, and Pa stumbled backward onto the floor. What had he done? Jesse watched as Georgina quickly picked up the hem of her dress and shuffled in fear from the room.

Then Jesse heard another shriek. He didn't quite understand because Georgina was safe now. Then he heard the shuffling sound again.

Jesse opened his eyes and stared at the black wilderness skies.

Another shriek filled the air.

Jesse bolted up.

A large black shadow was shuffling through the camp. The woman screamed again. "A bear! Someone come quick!"

Jesse grabbed his flintlock pistol and ran to the other side of the camp as the woman began running towards the river. The bear followed in pursuit. Jesse aimed and fired. The bear jolted from the sound and changed course, running towards Jesse. He had missed!

Jesse yelled loudly at the bear, throwing a rock at it, then attempted to reload. The bear turned and darted for the woods just as a rifle boom stopped him dead.

Samuel laid down the rifle and ran to Jesse, punching him playfully on the shoulder. "You did good, boy," Samuel cried, waving him toward the dead bear. "We have some breakfast now."

Jesse laid his hands by his side, breathing rapidly, the adrenaline still coursing through his veins. He looked at the crumpled brownish fur in the distance and the smoking rifle in Samuel's arms. "Thanks, that was a good shot."

The woman ran back to them breathlessly. "Thank you," she muttered in her heavy Native accent. "You saved my life."

Jesse nodded and accepted the praise. "I would have been dead too if it wasn't for Samuel," he replied, laughing nervously. He noticed his hand was shaking and tried to quell the response, stuffing his hands in his pockets.

"Come," Samuel said. "Let's get this bear ready for breakfast before another animal tries to take it from us."

Jesse pursed his lips and blew the air out of his lungs forcefully. He grabbed his knife from the campsite and joined Samuel to butcher the bear. It was the first time Jesse had butchered an animal in his life.

The morning came quickly. The small eight-person camp was awake and grateful for the food. It wasn't the greatest meat, but everyone was so hungry that they didn't notice. The men made a small fire and roasted the bear meat on sticks, everybody devouring their portions.

The animal was smaller than they had originally thought, so they all agreed to ration the food for later. Samuel had skinned the bear and kept the fur pelt as a souvenir.

As the group deliberated on their next steps, they agreed to forsake the river and start hiking into the forest to find their way back to the Arikara villagers for help. The canoe was badly damaged and they wouldn't be able to fix it without materials. This seemed like the best option for the stranded group.

But as day turned into evening, they trudged throughout the forest, looking for any signs of human habitation.

They found nothing but animal tracks.

Jesse gazed up at the treetops as the nighttime sounds of owls and insects filled the dusk skies. "Where do we go from here?" Jesse asked aloud, wondering if they'd ever find anyone in this wilderness.

"We keep going," the woman answered. "The Arikaras may help if we trade that fur pelt."

Samuel chuckled. "She's right. We'll find the village again. The bear pelt is a good quality fur, and we need the help."

CHAPTER 4

Ewart was obsessed with her, she noticed. Something about him had changed ever since they took the kissing too far last week. It seemed that he became possessed with an internal urge to be with her again and again. Zee had submitted several times, but something inside of her knew that this wasn't the man for her. Ma and Pa wanted a good life for her, and they regularly tried to marry her off to gentlemen who lived in the surrounding countryside of Thorold and Beaverdams.

She let the reins slacken as the horse walked at a leisurely pace back to the house. Zee never rode side saddle or wore dresses. She had sewn her own britches in a fashion that was as individual as she was. Unfortunately, this was something that every gentleman despised about her.

Zee adjusted her hat and continued riding, feeling melancholy about her last tryst with Ewart. He was a nice boy, but he was too rough, and it hurt too many times. She had told him to be easy with her, but he only responded that she was too beautiful, making him lose his mind.

Zee didn't understand men. Ewart had lost his mind for her, but the town gentlemen didn't want anything to do with her. She was pretty, Zee knew. The way men looked at her with lust in their eyes was unmistakable. So, it wasn't about appearances. It was her stubborn spirit that they hated so much.

"Well, Beauty," Zee cooed to her horse. "Maybe things were meant to be. Maybe I'll always be a horse-riding, cursing female that only the worst of men want." Zelda began to cry as she said this, her inner insecurities tugging at her emotions. She pursed her lips and continued riding slowly. Her groin hurt again from the rough sex. She was so inexperienced that she had no idea if this was normal or abnormal. She mused briefly about talking to her mother but immediately abolished the thought. It would be near suicide admitting to her mother that she was no longer a virgin.

Zee exhaled and deliberated over her options. She didn't have any girlfriends. She rarely understood the country girls around here. They wore dresses and spoke like everybody was beneath their social structure. The few farm girls in the area, whom she often related to, were former black slaves, and Pa had made it loudly known that she was not to associate with them.

In the end, all she had were male friends, especially Ewart. She had grown up with him since he had started working at the farm seven years ago. Zee had never imagined that he would be her secret lover, nor did she particularly want that. It just seemed every time they were near each other, her body would instantly respond, and her brain would stop thinking clearly.

Zelda winced as the horse began a trot, and she reined in the animal, forcing Beauty to slow down again. "Easy, Beauty," Zee cooed. "I'm still hurting a bit. Remember when I delivered your baby boy last year, my sweetheart? Well, now you need to be gentle for me."

Beauty whinnied and obeyed, slowing down as the farmhouse appeared over the crest of the small hill.

♰

It was Monday finally, and Zee was in trouble. This time, it wasn't the usual trouble she faced every day from her parents and the society around her. It was something much more sinister and deeply concerning.

Zelda had missed her monthly curse two days ago.

She had awakened in the morning and rushed to the bathroom, hoping to find the spot of blood on her lacey undergarments. But there was nothing.

Zee pulled up her undergarments and sighed. She knew that she was most likely pregnant and had no idea what to do or how she would tell her mother. Most likely, the pregnancy would result in her expulsion from the family or her forced marriage to Ewart. Zee did not want either of those options.

She liked Ewart, but there were so many things she was beginning to detest about him. He was lazy and incapable of thinking about an ambitious future with her. Zee wanted a strong man who would fight for his family. Ewart didn't even know how to shoot a rifle. She wondered if she was being irrational, but something about him didn't sit right in her gut. She could never marry such a man and instantly regretted her hormonal trysts with him.

She exhaled and rubbed her forehead, pushing her long hair over her back. What was she going to do?

Zelda Collard was going to be a mother.

Zee looked up and walked back to the house from the outhouse. "What would Mother do if this happened to her?" Zee asked aloud. She knew the answer right away. Ma was a gentle, kind soul who avoided confrontations. Zee smiled as the solution became apparent.

She would tell no one and hide the pregnancy.

⚑

"How are you feeling today, sweetie?" Clara asked, placing a hand on her daughter's forehead. "You look ill. Are you sick?"

Zee grinned weakly. "I just have a weak stomach today," she said. "Must have been something I ate."

Clara's brow creased in worry. "Maybe you should lie down, Zee," she said. "Rest more, my beautiful girl. You work too hard outside."

"You're right," Zelda replied. "I'm feeling quite tired lately from all the farm work. I'll start helping more in the house like you always wanted me too."

Clara beamed with pride. "You are a beautiful woman, Zee," she said. "I will show you how to make cream pies. You'll love it." Clara ran her palms lovingly over her daughter's head. "Go warm up some water, take a short bath, and wash that lovely hair of yours." She patted Zee's knee. "I will come back and help you comb it."

"I would love that," Zee conceded. She shuffled out of the chair and walked lightly up the stairs to the small second-story hallway. Zee reached the top, then walked to the end, opening the washroom door and closing it quietly behind her. She was finally going to learn how to be a woman, whether she liked it or not. At least she didn't have to explain her absence to Ewart. Pa would do that proudly.

CHAPTER 5

If things could have gotten any worse, Jesse would have laughed. After struggling for two weeks in the wilderness, nothing was funny anymore. The mountainous regions had given way to flatter terrain but with no human activity in sight. They had traveled far from the Mad River. But how far, they did not know.

At least in the mountains, they had animals to kill for food. Here in the desolate countryside, there were only rabbits and rodents. These animals proved far too quick for capture, and a gunshot always seemed to miss the skittish creatures.

Jesse looked back as several men carried the canoe on their shoulders. They took turns carrying the canoe, and Jesse was glad because he was tired. They had eaten nothing for the last two days. They had water, but all their rations from the bear and deer kills were gone. The only animals they had any chance of killing were coyotes, but they proved to be too sly and wary.

Jesse started to shiver again. The weather had turned cold in the last month, prompting the group to walk with their blankets across their shoulders. They looked like a beggar's caravan, Jesse grimly thought.

A panic rose in his throat as he thought about the possibility that they would all die.

It was strange because Jesse didn't experience the same kind of panic when he faced the Mad River with his sixty other comrades. Now that the small stranded group was weak and emaciated, starvation placed the fear of God in his veins. Their bodies would surely be eaten by coyotes and scavenged by birds.

Jesse hugged the blanket across his shoulders and talked to himself. "Think like a man," he said softly. "Not a boy."

"What is that?" Samuel asked behind him.

"Nothing," Jesse answered loudly. "Just talking to myself."

"No," Samuel said. "I mean there." He pointed to the top of a canyon wall.

A tall column of smoke rose from behind the peak of the cliff.

"A village!" Jesse shouted as the others rejoiced with whatever energy they had left.

"Don't get too excited, my friends," Samuel stated sadly. "We have to find the strength to scale that canyon wall or find a way around."

Jesse slumped down onto the partially frozen ground and felt the wind whip through his long hair. He had tried to cut it, but the knife was brutal for cutting hair, and he was afraid he'd kill himself just trying to cut his hair. "I'm done for the day," Jesse said. "We can rest and find something to eat for energy before we attempt that cliff."

Samuel looked behind him as the rest of the group tiredly laid down the canoe and sat down with Jesse. "Okay, we'll find something," he said. "Let's rest. At least there is human activity nearby now."

"This is true," the woman replied.

Jesse laid back on his bedroll and stared up at the midday sun. Several gophers ran from holes around them. Jesse didn't even bother to try catching them. They were too swift, and expending the little energy he had left was too dangerous right now. He ran his fingers through the dead yellow hay surrounding them and wondered what they could eat. There were no berries or edible plants nearby. Maybe they could eat the hay, he thought. Then Jesse remembered the story of starving people in Africa who had eaten hay and died. He didn't know if the story was true, but he didn't want to risk it.

He crossed his feet and gazed at his leather farm boots in deep thought. A gopher poked his head out a few feet away, and Jesse lurched to try to grab it. The gopher jerked and ran away before he could even see where the varmint had gone. "Little bugger," Jesse said, cursing the gopher.

Jesse laid back in exhaustion, his mind reeling about what he could eat. They had nothing left but their canoe, their clothes, their bedrolls, and blankets. Jesse removed his boots lazily and rubbed his sore feet. He had several blisters on his feet and holes in his socks from walking so many great distances.

He peered at Samuel and saw him doing the same.

The group was worn out. They couldn't possibly scale that cliff, even on the more gradual switchback entrance. "Wait," Jesse said aloud. He pointed at the switchback trail alongside the cliff. "That looks like a trail made for humans."

Samuel lifted his head up and looked. "You're right, boy," he said. "It looks like sort of an entrance to the village on top of the hill."

"We came to Arikara from the east when we started the expedition," Jesse mused. "Then we left the village and embarked to the west." Jesse scratched his head in thought. "Is it possible that we are arriving here from the north? And that switchback trail is their own private back entrance to the village?"

"Very possible," Samuel replied. "We definitely traveled northeastward."

Jesse gazed in the distance. It was still a long distance away. They still had to find food to obtain the energy to get there.

"It's still a good distance away," Samuel stated the obvious. "We need food."

Jesse's stomach growled as he pulled off his second boot and placed it on the dead grass. He grabbed his foot and stopped, looking at his boots. "Aren't boots made out of leather?" he asked.

"Yeah," Samuel answered. "So?"

Jesse grabbed a boot and unsheathed his knife, shaving a thin slice off the top.

"What are you doing?" Samuel asked in surprise.

Jesse stuffed the leather shaving in his mouth and chewed. The rough leather was foul-tasting, but his teeth and stomach didn't argue. He chewed and chewed, then opened his mouth and tore the piece apart with his teeth.

Samuel grimaced and watched as Jesse devoured the leather strips, downing it all with a gulp of water from his canteen.

"It wasn't too bad," Jesse said, laughing. "You should try it."

By noonday, all eight of the stranded fur trader explorers had eaten portions of their boots. It was enough to give them the energy to attempt crossing to the cliff wall. They arrived at the base of the cliff at dusk and had to cross the fast-moving stream to get to the switchback trail.

Jesse sat down and shaved a few more pieces of leather off, devouring the foul food. Several other people did the same. A weak energy returned to his emaciated frame. Jesse waded slowly into the stream, cursing as the cold water soaked him to the bone. He crossed with his arms up above his head and his pack on his shoulders.

The water kept rising. He stopped, wondering if they wouldn't be able to cross. Jesse looked down and saw the water had risen to his waist, and he was six feet tall. He turned to address the rest of the group. "It's damn cold," he shouted. "But it's our only shot at survival."

Several shrieks sounded as more people entered the frigid waters.

"Keep your packs high!" Jesse shouted back. "Especially if you are shorter than six feet tall."

"What about my children?" the woman asked.

"Some of the men will have to carry them," Samuel answered, entering the cold water with the canoe above his head. Another man held the backside of the canoe, following Samuel.

Jesse hooted in delight as the water began receding around his waist, and the shoreline came closer. He made it! Jesse Eastman had survived this God-forsaken country.

He climbed onto the shoreline and laid down his pack as an arrow shot through his hat. He jumped in fright, removed his hat, and turned towards the switchback trail. A group of Arikara guards were standing there, covered in camouflage and armed with bows. Jesse raised his arms in surrender. "Please," he pleaded. "We need your help. We are from the Overland Astorian group. We have been stranded for over a month."

The natives frowned and talked amongst themselves. They shouted orders in a language that Jesse didn't understand.

Jesse pleaded with them again. "Please, we are dying," he begged.

One of the natives understood the word dying, it seemed. The large Arikara man waved his hands at Jesse, ordering him to come to them. Jesse tentatively stood up. The remaining

Overland Astorians reached the shoreline and watched in quiet resignation, except one person. The native woman from the Astorians walked up to the trail with her hands up, speaking a native language none of the explorers knew.

The large native Arikara man gestured and spoke loudly to the woman. They conversed for several minutes, speaking back and forth in a terse manner. Finally, the Arikara man's features softened, and he waved for Jesse to come closer.

Jesse walked confidently to the group as the man spoke commandingly to him in the Arikaran language. Jesse looked at him in bewilderment.

"He said that he would take everyone into the village and save our lives in exchange for the bear pelt and the canoe," the woman translated slowly.

The Arikara guard spoke again, quickly, almost jumbling over his words with passion.

"He also says that this is not a free stay. Everyone must work once they are healthy enough." The woman explained the rest of the agreement and looked at Jesse for confirmation.

Jesse looked back at the stranded Overland Astorian group. They were probably three more days away from dying, he thought. Losing the bear pelt was nothing, but the canoe would be a huge sacrifice. "Tell him we will give him what he wants," Jesse replied, rubbing his long beard. "But he must allow us to rebuild a new canoe with the surrounding trees. It is our only chance to return to St. Louis."

The woman frowned, turned to the Arikara guard, and relayed the message in their native tongue.

The Arikara man's mouth frowned in deliberation. Then, a half smile graced his face. He spoke rapidly to the woman, then turned to his group of guards, gesturing for them to grab the canoe and bear fur. They began approaching the Astorians as the native woman spoke to Jesse. "They have agreed," she translated, with a funny grin on her face. "He also said that you are stupid and young."

Jesse laughed and patted her on the shoulder. "Thank you," he said. "You saved our lives."

"No," she replied. "You did, Jesse."

CHAPTER 6

Zee pulled the long, baggy dress over her head and felt the smooth cotton fall onto her hips and belly. She looked down and frowned. The dress hung so loosely on her that it looked like a bag. Zelda turned this way and that, stretching the fabric around her swollen belly then let her hands fall.

She hated dresses.

The door creaked open slowly. "My dear," Clara cooed. "How does the dress fit? Can I come in?"

Zee sighed in exasperation. She would be forced to wear dresses until this pregnancy was over. She didn't like it, but it was the only way to hide her growing bump. "Yes, mother," she responded sweetly. "You can come in."

Clara opened the door with a huge smile on her face. "Oh, my dear!" she cried. "You look amazing! The dress is a bit too big for you, but your Aunt Karen was always on the big side." Clara squinted in suspicion. "Are you sure that you don't want one of my dresses? It would fit you much better."

Zee responded quickly, making up a lie on the spot. "No," she said, waving her arms out and turning in a circle. "This is perfect. I still want to ride Beauty, and I need a dress with a lot of room to move." She bit her lip involuntarily. Zee didn't like lying. She wasn't any good at it. The honest, brutal truth was more her style.

Clara didn't seem to notice. "Well, I am just thrilled that you are finally becoming a woman!" she smiled excitedly. "You know how to bake bread, cook pies, and now you are wearing dresses! I couldn't be happier. Your father can ask that fellow we last met if he'd reconsider marrying you again." Clara beamed proudly.

"Umm, no, Ma," Zee interrupted. "Let's not go too far with this right now. I am still learning." Zelda paused, searching for the right words to convince her mother to give her more time. "I need time to learn everything the right way and be, umm, comfortable with myself." Zee placed her hands on her hips defiantly. "Just give me more time. Maybe another year?"

"A year!" Clara exclaimed. "My child woman! A year is a long time for an eighteen-year-old girl to wait! You'll be nineteen!"

"You say this like it is a travesty!"

"It is!" Clara cried. "You've already wasted all this time on horses and doing the jobs men are supposed to be doing."

"Think of it, Ma," Zee interrupted. "I will know many skills then. I will be even more valuable."

Clara frowned in thought. "I suppose."

Zee placed both of her hands on her mother's petite shoulders. "Trust me, Ma," she said, exhaling with relief. "I will grow into the best woman you've ever seen."

Clara pursed her lips and conceded. "You win," she said. "It's your life after all."

"Yes, it is." Zee hugged her mother gently. "Thank you, Ma."

Ⓐ

The barn wasn't too far away now, and Zelda bit her bottom lip nervously again. She wondered if her parents knew of her nervous habits. They intuitively seemed to know everything about her. It was a chess game of wits to keep them both unaware of the growing pregnancy. Zee counted the months in her head again as the horse sauntered slowly to the barn. She had saddled Beauty and mounted her like normal, without sitting sidesaddle like other ladies. There were simply some things she could never do.

Ewart had sent for her this morning to attend to some of the animals. Over the past five years, Zee had become somewhat of an animal doctor. She just instinctively knew what to do. She loved those animals more than anything, but now she had a baby in her belly.

Zee lost her train of thought and counted the months again.

She was four months pregnant as of last week. Zee looked down and noticed the growing bump on her abdomen. She doubted others could see it. The baby kicked suddenly, and Zee rubbed her belly, speaking softly to the baby. "It's okay, sweetie. We will figure out a way through this. I will try to be a good momma, but I can't give up horses altogether." She patted the horse's neck slowly. "We are just altering things for a while, that's all."

Ewart walked out of the barn and rolled out a large bale of hay for the animal's feed. He stopped in shock when he saw Zelda.

She waved at him. "Just came to say hi, Ewart," Zee shouted, just in case her father was within earshot. Zee slipped gently off the horse and walked slowly towards Ewart with the reins in her hand, leading the horse to water.

"You've been gone for so long," Ewart stated, his shoulders sulking. "Nobody would tell me anything. Your father only told me you had decided to take on more womanly jobs." Ewart scratched his head and reached his hands towards her. "I called for you because you need to look at some of the cows. One of the calves appears sick, and the mother may be sick as well." He squinted at her in the sun. "You are the only one who can nurse the animals back to health." He stopped, sensing something was wrong. "Are you alright?"

Zee moved slightly away from him and looked around. "Where is Pa?"

"He's in the shop, sharpening the blades," Ewart answered.

"Let's go in the barn," Zee said, walking toward the barn doors.

Ewart followed curiously.

As Zee reached the large barn, she stepped through the smaller man door. It was a cold spring, and February wasn't about to let go of winter yet. It had snowed heavily last week. Wet, heavy snow that was very hard for the men to shovel. Zee used to help shovel, she remembered, but not anymore.

"What happened to you?" Ewart whispered immediately. "You just disappeared. I was so worried." He reached his hands around her waist and pulled Zee towards him. "I missed you."

Zelda pulled back, afraid to get too close to Ewart, before she told him the news. "Some things happened," she said vaguely.

"Like what?" he asked innocently.

Zelda mused for a way to tell him that wasn't so shocking, but she really didn't know how to be socially correct like other women. She smiled and looked down at her boots. Zee could never give up her boots for those fancy women's shoes. "I always liked my farm boots," she said, wondering if she could change the subject for a while.

"I like your farm boots too," Ewart replied, his eyebrows frowning in confusion. "I like everything about you, Zee. Please don't disappear like that again. I want us to marry one day. I want to be that man for you."

Zee looked up in shock at his words. "You really mean that?"

"Yes, I do," he confirmed. "You've deserted me for almost four months, Zee!" He shifted from foot to foot nervously. "I thought they had married you off to someone else!" Ewart eyes briefly moistened as he fought off the emotion.

"No!" Zee exclaimed softly. "I would never allow such a thing." She moved a step closer to him and grabbed his hands in hers. "But there is something I need to tell you."

Ewart gripped her hands anxiously. "What is it?" he asked. "Are you sick?"

"No, I'm fine," she replied. "Well, some days I do feel sick. But it's not that."

"Then what is it!" Ewart shouted agitatedly.

Zee looked into his eyes and inhaled sharply. "I'm pregnant," she whispered. Zee paused, running her hands through her long hair. She didn't know what else to say. "We're going to have a baby, Ewart. We're going to be parents."

Ewart felt his knees weaken as his heart hammered against his chest. "I'm going to be a father?"

"Yes," Zee answered. "Now, show me to the sick cows."

CHAPTER 7

J esse ran his hand along his shortened beard and felt the wind blow at his bare neck. The Arikara village had sharp tools to cut hair, and as soon as he had healed enough, it was one of the first things he had done.

The winter had been rough and cold, but the Arikaras had taken them all in, saving their lives.

The stranded group never did rejoin with the rest of the Overland Astorians. They heard no news of the expedition either. No travelers ventured this way during the winter. It was a long winter, and they had become a part of the Arikara village, contributing to the community with whatever skills each man and woman possessed. Even the children did work. Jesse was extremely grateful and couldn't be happier to help out. Jesse had gained all his weight and muscle back. Samuel and the rest of the group were all healed from the near-starvation journey as well. Their boots still had pieces of leather missing but it was worth it. They had their lives.

The days grew warmer before he even knew it. Jesse guessed it was May now. The stranded Astorians had deliberated about attempting to canoe downstream on the Missouri river to travel back to St Louis.

They had consulted the natives and, over the past few months, had built a new canoe. The vessel was stronger than the last.

"So, we leave tomorrow?" Samuel asked.

Somehow, Jesse had become the leader of the group. He smiled. "Yes," he answered. "We're heading back in the morning."

"Good," Samuel said. "I need a good steak and a whiskey."

Jesse laughed and slapped Samuel on the back as he stood up. "Same here, my friend."

⚓

The Missouri river was much calmer than the Mad River, Jesse mused, as the canoe with all eight passengers floated along its current. It would be a quick trip back with the downstream current pushing them along.

The Arikaras had given them food rations for the trip, homemade chewing tobacco, and some old clothes for warmth. Jesse smiled as he watched the riverside race alongside the canoe. He had never had such a close call with death so many times before. He felt like something inside him had deeply changed since he had first joined the expedition.

Jesse definitely wasn't the same man he was before, he mused. He was colder, more calculating, and smarter now.

He wasn't sure where he would be going when he got back. He thought it would most likely be back to New York City where he had originally fled to. But that was a long distance from St. Louis. He may just stay with the others or join Samuel on the next expedition.

The canoe slowed down considerably as they neared St. Louis.

The direction his life was going in was not clear, but Jesse would forge his own path if necessary. He had no choice. His father had disowned him and prevented him from contacting his siblings and mother. Jesse still didn't completely understand why the man was so angry with him. All Jesse had done was stop the slave beating. Georgina had looked well-fed and happy but something had happened that made his father overreact and lash out at her. Jesse may never know the truth.

Jesse shook his head. Family troubles were the least of his worries right now. He needed work to secure his future.

⚷

Samuel walked towards the fur trading hut with Jesse. "We'll find out what they need us to do next," Samuel said. "Maybe they will have another trip set up for us."

"Hopefully," Jesse replied. "We need work."

Samuel nodded gravely as they entered the hut.

Only one old man was at the counter trading a leather cow hide with a farmer. The group loitered quietly as the transactions concluded, every man and woman formulating a different plan for the future.

Finally, the old man looked up at the group. "What can I do for you all?"

Jesse spoke first. "We are part of the Overland Astorians team. We were stranded from the group during the Mad River attempt."

The old man's eyes widened. "We all thought you were dead!"

"We almost did die," Samuel replied. "From starvation."

The native woman in the group nodded. "The Arikaras took us in and saved our lives."

"You are lucky to be alive," the old man answered. "We thought we had lost ten people on the Mad River!" The man paused and counted. "There are only eight of you."

Jesse rubbed his trimmed beard. "We saw one man overboard in the rapids," he said. "We tried to rescue him, but he slipped away in the current."

"So that means the Mad River took only two people then," the old man replied. "Never did find any bodies. The expedition lost another nine people in the wilderness when the group split up after the Mad River. That expedition was an ill-fated journey." The old man stood suddenly. He looked down at his papers and shuffled through several documents. "That reminds me. I had a courier message for one of you. Hold on." The man walked around to the side desk, looking around in confusion. "I had it right here. A two-man courier team was just here yesterday."

"Who were they looking for?" Samuel asked.

"One of the young men on the expedition," the old man scratched his head. "Can't remember the name."

"Where did the couriers come from?" Jesse asked.

"Philadelphia."

A chill ran up Jesse's spine. That was his hometown. "Was the name Eastman?" he asked.

"Can't remember, son," the old man answered. "I have 25 customers every day. I can't recall any names." He shuffled through more papers. "Dammit. I thought I put it right here." He straightened and looked at the group.

"Did the couriers say where they'd be staying?" Jesse asked.

"Yes! That I remember. Annie's Inn on Main Street." The man smiled a row of rotten teeth. "You can find the couriers there."

Jesse stepped aside as the native woman moved forward. "If there is no further need for us," she interrupted softly. "My children and I will be going home."

"Thank you so much for your guide expertise," the man replied. "There'll be nothing else. The Overland Astorians reached Fort Astoria along the mouth of the Columbia River. They're still missing many people, but they finally arrived to join the Tonquin ship at the new Fort."

Samuel and Jesse stared wordlessly at the old man as the woman left the post with her children.

"The expedition is a success," the old man continued obliviously. "You men don't need to go all the way out there again." He scribbled something down on a piece of scrap paper.

Jesse spoke, his voice soft. "So, there's no more work for us here?"

"That'll be all, yep," the old man nodded. "You can pick up the remainder of your pay in the morning."

The remaining men exchanged glances of exasperation. They had come all this way to discover they were without direction again. Three men turned and walked resignedly away.

"I suppose that is everything then?" Jesse asked, his stomach churning.

"Yep," the old man nodded and left to the back room in search of another errant document. "Glad you're all alive! I'll report it to the Fort!"

Jesse turned with Samuel and left the trading post. "Let's get some whiskey and steak," Samuel said. "We have some money left."

Jesse nodded as they began walking down the dusty street with horses corralled on both sides amongst the water troughs. "Let's go to Annie's Inn first," he said firmly. "My family's from Philadelphia. I want to see who that message was for."

"Alright, boy," Samuel said. "You lead the way."

"Don't ever call me boy again," Jesse sneered.

The scent of steak and whiskey filtered into the air as the two men opened the saloon doors. Jesse's stomach growled cavernously and Samuel was licking his lips. They both could not think of another thing at the moment. They had lived in the mountains for almost two years, and nothing felt better than steak and whiskey right now.

Jesse pulled out an old wooden stool and sat at the bar with Samuel sitting beside him.

The barkeeper wiped his hands on a dirty bar rag. "What will you both be having?"

Samuel replied almost immediately. "Whiskey and steak," he nodded. "Both of us."

"Sure," the barkeeper replied, grabbing two small glasses and pouring whiskey straight into them.

"Make mine a double," Samuel said.

"Take it easy," Jesse whispered. "We haven't had barely any alcohol for almost two years."

"Just shy of two years, bro," Samuel replied.

"Where have you men been?" the barkeeper asked.

"Mad River territory," Jesse replied. "We were part of the Overland Astorians opening up the fur trade in the Northwest."

"Oh," the barkeeper nodded. "I heard that the British are looking at making some claims to that Northwest piece of land."

"When did that happen?" Jesse asked.

"I'm not sure when the British started thinking that American land belonged to them, but I just heard of it a few months ago. Those fur trader expeditions will be shutting down soon if the British have their way."

"You mean we almost died in that nasty wilderness for nothing?" Samuel asked, his voice rising.

"You both have honestly been gone for two years, haven't you?" the barkeeper asked.

"Yes," Jesse replied.

"Well, it's causing a lot of tensions between us and the British."

"War?" Jesse asked.

"Possibly, who knows," the barkeeper replied, wiping the bar again.

"All the more reason for having a double shot of whiskey," Samuel replied, tilting the double shot down his throat and pushing the empty shot toward the barkeeper. "Another one."

Jesse frowned. He wasn't sure what Samuel was like when he was drunk, but Jesse didn't want any trouble. "I am going to find those couriers right after we finish eating."

The barkeeper poured another whiskey shot and glanced at Jesse. "You looking for those two couriers who just checked in?"

"Yeah," Jesse replied. "Have you seen them?"

"Hell yeah," he said. "They came in here, drank too much whiskey, and got kicked up to their rooms. You won't be talking to them 'til morning. Those two will be sleeping it off." He shook his head. "Travelling across the country is a tough job, but there's no excuse for raising hell in my saloon."

Jesse frowned. "Okay, boss. I guess you're stuck with us for the night then."

The barkeeper narrowed his eyes. "Just eat your steak, drink your whiskey, and we don't have a problem."

"That's what we're here for," Jesse replied.

Samuel smiled and tipped the second shot down his throat, slamming it on the counter, grunting from the burn. "Damn, that tastes good," Samuel said. "Another one." He pushed his glass over to the barkeeper.

The man slowly filled his glass again and turned to tend to other customers.

Jesse shot down his whiskey and grinned. It did feel good, something akin to drinking cool water after living in the desert for years.

The barkeeper filled Jesse's glass and left.

Samuel stood and leaned against the counter, watching the place fill up with patrons. Several groups of men entered and sat by the far corner. The walls were dark oiled brown wood, and the tables were etched with many saloon fights, but otherwise, it seemed to be a decent saloon. There were close to twenty people packed into the saloon, and everybody seemed well-behaved. "Hell of a busy place here," Samuel said nonchalantly.

"Good indicator of decent food," Jesse said, holding his glass but not taking a drink.

They watched as a barmaid brought food to another table full of hungry men. Jesse watched as she laid biscuits and plates of salted pork on the table. She turned and caught Jesse's eye. She immediately looked away and shyly returned to the kitchen.

"Hopefully, our food is next," Samuel said. "My stomach has had enough of camping food."

The kitchen door slammed open, and the same barmaid walked straight towards them with two plates of food. She stopped in front of Jesse. "Two steaks?"

"Yes, Miss," Jesse said, smiling. "Right here." He shifted his body on the stool to make room for her to place the dinner plates in front of them. Her arm brushed against his shoulder, and Jesse felt an immediate goosebump travel over his arm.

Samuel smiled at the barmaid. "Thank you, Miss," he cooed. "What may I call you?"

"Jean," she replied. "I'm the innkeeper's niece."

"Oh, well, thank you, Jean," Samuel replied, his mouth already full of food. "You are an angel delivering food to two men who were trapped in the mountains for way too long. It tastes like heaven." Samuel rolled his eyes and touched her waist lightly again.

Jesse felt a tinge of jealousy but didn't know why. He had never met the girl before, but she was a pretty blonde.

"Enjoy, men!" Jean slipped away expertly, avoiding any more unwanted advances.

"She's a fine woman," Samuel mumbled with a mouthful of steak. "Wouldn't mind riding her."

Jesse felt another jolt of possessiveness. "She's the innkeeper's niece. Leave her alone." Jesse cut the steak and pushed a forkful into his mouth, murmuring praise. "This steak is good."

"It sure is," Samuel agreed, chewing the juicy steak. He wiped his mouth and chuckled, watching the barmaid tend to another table. "She likes you more than me."

Jesse chewed another bite of steak. "I doubt that."

They both ate in silence as the saloon filled with more patrons. Another barmaid began helping Jean as the food orders increased. Jesse chewed the rare steak and munched on a biscuit. "Mmm," he mumbled with satisfaction. "Good biscuits, too."

Samuel grabbed one and stuffed it in his mouth, agreeing.

"Are you men enjoying the food?" Jean asked, poking her head over. "Can I get you anything else?"

"Maybe some of that thigh wrapped around my waist," Samuel said, chuckling. "Steak is good too."

Jean's face dropped, and her cheeks reddened as she rushed away into the kitchen.

"Now, why would you say that to her?" Jesse asked, getting increasingly annoyed.

"Ah, don't get all defensive," Samuel said calmly. "We're cool. I won't stir the pot anymore. I know she likes you."

"She doesn't like me," Jesse stated angrily, chomping down the rest of his steak. "I just want to eat, finish my whiskey, and sleep on a normal bed tonight."

"I'm sure she'll be a nice addition to that bed."

"Stop," Jesse said warningly.

Samuel pushed his empty plate away and slammed his glass down for another whiskey. "Another double!"

Jesse glared at Samuel and stood, pulling out some coins and nodding at the barkeeper. "I'll pay my portion," he said. "I'll get a room for the night before it fills up, too."

The barkeeper took the money and gave him his change. "The inn has lots of room. Don't you worry about that."

"Alrighty then," Jesse stood, slapping his hand down on the counter. "Thanks for the meal. It is much appreciated."

"Anytime," the barkeeper replied.

"You leaving me here?" Samuel asked, his voice distorted from the alcohol.

"Yep, I sure am," Jesse stated confidently. "Come get me in the morning when you've slept it off."

"Alright, brother," Samuel leaned against the counter and tipped his whiskey back for another drink as Jesse walked past a dark-haired older man at the far end of the bar.

Jesse waved to Samuel as the stranger grabbed his arm. "You making moves on my niece, boy?" the dark-haired man asked angrily.

"I'm not your boy," Jesse answered immediately. "But even if I was, I didn't do anything other than be polite to your niece. The barmaid is the one you're talking about, I presume?"

"Well, aren't you a smart-mouthed boy?"

"I told you not to call me boy," Jesse answered, his fists throbbing from anger.

Samuel sauntered over, slamming into a few chairs. "Hey, hey," Samuel slurred. "My friend here just don't like to be called boy no more. He damn right saved all of our lives in the mountains there. This man deserves some respect." Samuel tilted over and leaned his elbow on the bar to stabilize himself. "Besides, I was the one who made moves on your pretty niece. Jean is her name, I think."

The dark-haired man stood and grabbed Samuel by the lapels, slamming him against the counter. "You are one smart assed dead man," the man sneered.

Samuel teetered and spat in the uncle's face.

Jesse knew what was coming and stopped it before it happened. The dark-haired man's fist curled, and his shoulder reared back as Jesse slammed an upper-cut punch right into the man's exposed kidney. The uncle crumpled in pain as several large men stood up at a nearby table.

Jesse put his hands up in surrender and grabbed Samuel by the arm. "He's drunk," Jesse said calmly. "Just let him pay, and I'll take him to his room at the inn. We don't want any trouble. Right, Barkeeper?" Jesse looked back at the man tending the bar.

The barkeeper nodded, wiping the counter. "The young man's right. Just let them go." The barkeeper pointed his finger at Samuel. "Pay up and get out of here."

Jesse helped Samuel throw some money on the counter, and they left with a hundred eyes on their backs. The doors swung closed behind them as Jesse curled his arm under Samuel's and stumbled to the inn's front desk.

The older lady behind the desk frowned disapprovingly. "We don't want any trouble here," she stated.

"We're no trouble, Ma'am," Jesse replied. "We've just been living in the mountains for too long. We would mightily appreciate it if we could get two rooms with soft beds for the night. We'll leave in the morning, I promise."

The older lady eyed Jesse suspiciously, then glanced over at Samuel's drunken slump.

"My friend Samuel has had a bit too much to drink," Jesse explained. "I'm sorry about that, ma'am, but I'll be putting him out of harm's way to sleep it off as soon as you give me two keys to two rooms."

The innkeeper glanced back and forth from one man to the other and sighed. "Alright," she said resignedly. "You seem like a proper man," she said, grabbing two keys under the counter. "Rooms 214 and 215. What's your names?"

Jesse grabbed the keys. "Thank you, ma'am," he said gratefully. "You can write the rooms up in my name, Jesse Eastman."

The older lady froze with the pencil in her hand. "Jesse Eastman?" she exclaimed.

"Yeah, why?"

"Two couriers need to speak with you," the lady responded with her eyes wide. "They are both drunk and sleeping in their rooms right now, but yes, they were looking for you."

"You sure it was me they were looking for?"

"Yep, damn sure it was you," the lady answered. "Your Pappa, Mr. Bob Eastman has died, son. I'm sorry to break the bad news to you, but they had an urgent message from the Eastman family, too. You must speak with them two couriers in the morning. They came all this way from Philadelphia."

Jesse felt his arms weaken and his heart quicken as a cold sweat broke out on his forehead. "Thank you, ma'am," he said tiredly, looping his arm under Samuel's armpit and hauling his drunk friend upstairs. He didn't want to even think about what the consequences of his father's death might mean.

CHAPTER 8

Zee didn't understand men. Even though she was more interested in male jobs at the farm rather than baking and being like her mother, she still could not figure out why men did the things they did.

She understood that Ewart was justifiably shocked by the news of her pregnancy but she didn't expect him to immediately propose to her.

Zee shook her head in confusion as the family sat down for dinner. She plumped out her baggy dress on her lap and sighed in exhaustion. Carrying around this baby in secret was getting more and more difficult.

"You have been looking so healthy lately, my sweet," her mother cooed.

"She's gaining weight sitting around the kitchen all the time," Papa George complained. "I hate to say it, but I need her help with the animals."

"I'll help, Papa," Zee interjected happily. "I'm just feeling a bit under the weather right now. Give me some time to get better, and you know I'll be out there with ya."

Clara frowned. "Just when I thought I had my daughter back."

"Aw, Momma," Zee cried. "I've never been too fond of baking and stuff, but what you've done with me, I do sort of like it and I will bake bread with you from now on. It tastes somehow better when I make it myself." Zee laughed as her younger siblings snickered. "What are you all snickering about?"

Her younger sister, Charlotte, spoke. "Momma's bread tastes better."

"Don't you be starting a fight with your sister!" Momma Clara cried. "Zee has been showing lots of interest in baking, and these are skills you girls all need to know as you grow up to be women. Otherwise, you will have trouble getting married."

George wiped his mouth with a cloth napkin. "Oh, that reminds me. I had one of the neighbors mention that the nice fellow who tried to court you the last time is interested in giving it another try." George laid his napkin down on his lap and bent forward. "What do you think, Zelda?"

"You don't mean Joey?" Zee exclaimed. "He was a strange man. You know that, Pappa."

"Strange, yes," George answered. "But he was mightily interested in you, Zee. He only left because you cursed at him and told him to leave you alone."

"Aw, Pappa," Zee begged. "Don't make me marry a man like that!" Zee folded the napkin on her lap and wondered how to break the news to her parents that Ewart had proposed. "Who knows, maybe there'll be another man who would be a better fit for me."

"Like who?" Pappa laughed.

"I don't know," Zee said, blushing slightly as she pushed her chair back and stood, grabbing her empty plate and Pappa's plate, too. "Maybe someone that likes bad bread." Zee chuckled and stuck her tongue out at Charlotte then exited towards the kitchen.

Pappa George leaned over to Clara. "Something has changed about that girl."

"A positive change," Clara concluded as she eyed her daughter's large, expanded rump in the kitchen. She would need to have a talk with her stubborn daughter. George was right; something had definitely changed about Zee.

⚓

"What's this all about another man that might be interested in you?" Clara asked after they had finished washing dishes. Everyone had gone to bed except the two of them.

"Do you want some tea, Mamma?" Zee asked, trying to change the subject.

"Yes, darling," Clara replied. "I'd love some tea."

Zee put a pot of water onto the cast iron stove and stared out the small kitchen window at the darkening skies.

"What's on your mind, Zee?" Clara asked, standing up and massaging her daughter's shoulders. "You seem to have a lot on your mind. You've been acting very different."

"Oh my, that feels so good, Momma," Zee murmured as she sat down heavily in a kitchen chair. "My back has been in a lot of pain from being so sick lately."

"Hmm," Clara said questioningly. "Is there something you need to tell me? You know I'm your momma, and I'll always be there for you, sweetie. Don't ever question that. I know something has been on your mind. Is it a man that you've met?"

Zee groaned inwardly. She yearned to tell someone so badly. Ewart was the only one who knew, and he swore to secrecy until they could figure everything out and tell the family in the least invasive way. She didn't want to marry him, but it seemed like she would have no choice.

Clara accepted her daughter's silence as an answer. "Well, my sweet," Clara said softly. "If you ever want to tell me, remember, I was a young woman at one time, too. I know what it's like to fall in love. Your Pappa was the most handsome man I'd ever met, and I was so nervous when I found out I was pregnant with you."

"Yeah, you told me that story," Zee replied. "He married you right after you told him."

"Yes, your Pappa is a good man," Clara stated.

A comfortable silence fell over them as the water boiled, and Zee grabbed two cups filled with tea. She poured the boiling water over the tea and added honey, sitting down beside her mother. Zee blew on the hot tea and stared out the kitchen window, deep in thought.

Clara reached across the table and held her daughter's hand. "Tell me," she urged.

Zee opened her mouth, then closed it. How could she possibly say this to her mother? All the thoughts and words jumbled in her mind. Then, miraculously, two words simply fell out of her mouth. "It's Ewart," Zee confessed.

Clara's mouth opened in shock. "Ewart?" she asked in surprise.

"Yes, Ewart," Zee whispered sadly.

"How long has this been going on?"

"Almost seven months now."

"Oh my," Clara replied. "I don't know what to say, dear. Does he love you?"

"He wants to marry me," Zee responded. "But there's more, Momma."

"What else?"

"I'm pregnant, Momma," Zee confessed.

Clara nodded. "I suspected that," she replied. "You can't hide a pregnancy from your mother."

"You knew?"

"Yes," Clara replied. "Dear, I've had seven children. I know a pregnancy when I see it. You've been sick, gaining weight, and running out of your normal energy. It's alright." Clara patted Zee's hand. "I didn't have a clue that it was Ewart, though."

"I don't love him, Momma," Zee stated, crying into her hands. It was somehow a relief to confide her secret to someone she trusted, and she was glad her mother was so sweet.

"That's alright, sweetie," Clara said, rubbing Zee's back. "We'll figure something out. When is the baby due to arrive?"

"The end of June," Zee replied, wiping her tears from her eyes.

"Okay, so we have another month and a half to prepare," Clara said. "We'll find out what is best for you and the baby then."

"Please don't tell Pappa," Zee whimpered. "Not yet."

CHAPTER 9

The early June sun warmed their backs as the horses galloped across the countryside. A dry tumbleweed rolled by in the sudden winds as Jesse reined in his horse to avoid it. They were somewhere halfway between St. Louis and Philadelphia; they didn't know exactly where. The journey was becoming eerily similar to the exploration team, except with fewer people and fewer supplies.

Jesse only had Samuel and the two couriers with him. Samuel had nowhere to go now that the expedition was over and trade was being hampered by Britain. His friend had asked to join them back to the East Coast, and Jesse was grateful to have his friend by his side.

"I bet your family will be glad to see you again," Samuel hollered as they slowed the horses for a drink at the river.

"I don't know about that," Jesse snorted. "But I suppose the argument was with my father, not anybody else. And now that he's no longer around, Momma wants me back to run the household."

"You get along with your momma?"

"Yes, always have," Jesse replied. "It's just my pappa and myself always butted heads. He would be rolling in his grave right now if he knew I was coming back."

"Your momma asked you to come back?"

"Yeah," Jesse answered. "She said in the message that the entire estate, all the property, and decisions were left to her. She wants me back to help her deal with everything."

"Estate?" Samuel asked, his eyebrows lifting in surprise.

"Yes," Jesse answered resignedly. "My father was in the importing and exporting business in Philadelphia. He's the biggest controlling donkey ass around." Jesse paused, still wondering what the family would be like with Pappa gone. "Well, he was."

Samuel shook his head in surprise as the couriers pulled their horses closer alongside them. "So, you're a rich kid?" Samuel asked, chuckling.

One of the couriers interrupted, overhearing some of the conversation. "You've never heard of the Eastman family?" he asked Samuel.

"Nope," Samuel responded. "Living in the bush for too long." He pulled out a tin of chewing tobacco that the Arikaras had given him. It was the strangest mix of energy he'd ever tasted. "Do you want some?" he asked Jesse.

"No," Jesse replied. "I've never tasted anything like that before in my life until we lived with those Arikaras. That stuff was useful for energy in the mountains. Maybe you should save it when we really need it. I think we're only halfway there."

The taller courier glanced from Jesse to Samuel. "That stuff is strange. Do you swallow it?" he asked.

"Nope," Samuel answered. "You just chew it and spit it out, Ted."

"Why?" Ted asked.

Jesse laughed. "For energy, I suppose."

"Why did you choose to join an expedition in the mountains, Jesse?" the shorter courier asked. "The Eastman family is one of the richest families in the US."

"Long story, Barney," Jesse answered inconclusively, gazing out over the countryside. Another massive tumbleweed rolled across the dusty countryside, and the sun was high in the sky, baking the skin on his arms.

Barney walked quietly with his horse. "I suppose it doesn't matter," he responded. "I was just asking, that's all."

Jesse eyed him suspiciously. "Why are you riding back with us to Philadelphia? Your courier job was done. You delivered the message."

"The Eastman's offered a large incentive," he answered. "To bring you back alive."

"I should have known," Jesse concluded.

"Your family cares about you, at least," Barney replied.

Samuel put the chewing tobacco tin away and pulled his hat down, watching the two men talk. "Why didn't you ever tell me?" Samuel interrupted.

"Tell you what?"

"That you were a rich kid."

"I'm not rich," Jesse stated. "My father was rich, and he was a mean, callous person. Nothing will fix your soul once you have that kind of money. Besides, you would have thought of me differently. I didn't want to be treated like the son of Bob Eastman."

Samuel nodded as he walked his horse to the river with the others. "Makes sense," Samuel replied. "Sometimes it's better to learn who the real person is before discovering where they came from."

"Exactly," Jesse said, watching his horse drink water at the river. The other horses did the same as the couriers filled their canteens. Ted and Barney were rough, travel-weary men who were accustomed to trekking long distances. "Let's rest the horses here," Jesse instructed. "We can have some grub and coffee."

The two couriers nodded and began gathering wood for a small fire. "We'll set up here then, Mr. Eastman?" Ted asked.

"Don't call me Mr. Eastman, Ted," Jesse stated. "I'm Jesse. Call me that."

"Yep, alright, Jesse," Ted replied.

The other courier, Barney, smiled, showing his rotting teeth. "We'll get some grub cooked up for ya all."

Jesse didn't particularly like these two couriers but knew his family had paid them handsomely to find him and bring him back home. He appreciated that Ted and Barney were risking their lives to travel such a distance but he still felt a cautious type of wariness toward the pair. They both looked like they were just let out of jail. Their clothes were filthy from weeks of traveling, and their breath smelled like rotting fish. Jesse watched as the pair sparked the fire, and the flames jumped to life. The fire crackled and spit orange tentacles, barely recognizable against the sun's hot rays.

Samuel turned to one of the couriers and spoke quietly to him briefly. Jesse caught the exchange but couldn't make out the words that were transpiring between the two. He wondered if Samuel had an ulterior motive to join them all to Philadelphia. Jesse sat down on a log by the fire and exhaled wearily. He shouldn't be so suspicious. Samuel didn't even know Jesse was part of the Eastman Empire until just a few hours ago. Or did he? Maybe Samuel knew all along. Jesse looked down at his half eaten boots and grimaced at the memory. No, Samuel was along for the ride because he had nowhere to go, Jesse concluded.

He accepted a tin cup of strong coffee from the courier and sipped it gratefully. Ever since his family history became known to everyone, he was becoming wary of trusting anyone now. Money did strange things to people. Jesse Eastman knew this all too well. He had grown up as an Eastman, after all.

Another week in the hot sun was wearing on his resolve as the food supply began dwindling. Jesse rode his horse second, with Ted leading. Samuel was third in line, and Barney took up the rear.

Jesse and Samuel were still another week away from Philadelphia and reaching the starving point again. He was encouraging the group to move on faster, but the horses needed rest, too. There was no point in pushing the horses too hard and losing a horse.

The group had just entered the rolling hills of Pennsylvania and chose to follow the winding rivers to get through the mountainous region. The trees and shrubs surrounded them on all sides, forcing them to ride in a single line. Jesse's horse whinnied as they became engulfed in the forested area. He kept a firm hold on the reins.

The sun was setting behind the rolling mountains, and the forest was darkening. It was a beautiful sight, but Jesse's stomach growled instead. They had been living off two slices of jerky per day and strong coffee. Nothing was beautiful about that, Jesse thought.

"We'll set up camp here by the river," Ted stated as the tired group slowed their horses to a small clearing.

"Looks like this was a campsite," Samuel commented.

"There's even an old firepit," Jesse stated, pointing.

"Perfect," Barney said, pulling his horse's reins to a halt by the used cold ashes. He disembarked and started unloading the supplies, removing a small axe to cut up deadwood for the fire.

Jesse and Samuel tied the horses to a tree as they began to whinny again. "Shh." Jesse cooed. "What's got you spooked, Pretty?"

"Who calls their horse Pretty anyways?" Samuel said teasingly.

"None of your business," Jesse barked. "She's a big white mare, and she's damn pretty, don't ya think?"

"We were lucky to get whatever horses we could get back in St Louis, so I'm not complaining," Samuel answered, pulling out his canteen and filling it in the river.

"Hey, what's that?" Ted barked.

All the men turned their heads towards the grassy pathway as the horses whinnied again. Jesse frowned. "Something has gotten the horses nervous," he said.

"What is it?" Barney asked, curiosity getting the better of him.

"Stay back, you numbskull!" Ted barked, grabbing a stick.

The grass moved slightly as Ted pointed to the pathway. A tanned, dark brown striped reptile slithered through the grass and began crossing the path.

Barney was the closest and grabbed a stick to chase away the snake that steadily approached the horses.

"Watch out, it looks like a copperhead!" Ted barked.

Jesse grabbed the small axe and crept towards the snake, which was edging closer to the horses. Barney leaped onto the pathway and poked his stick at the pit viper. The snake immediately curled around in surprise, lashing out at his attacker.

Barney yelped and jumped away, landing on his butt. "He bit me!" he howled, grabbing his right leg and screaming in pain.

"Stay where you are!" Ted yelled. "He won't come at you again. Copperheads are poisonous, but you'll still live!"

Barney screamed in agonizing pain, writhing on the ground.

Ted approached the snake with a long, pointed stick and stabbed at it multiple times, then backed off expertly. "Come on, you pit viper," Ted cooed. "One good stab and you're dead." The snake curled around the stick, fighting. Ted stabbed the snake again, missing. "Let me at ya, you bastard." Ted jabbed again and caught the snake in the belly, pinning the snake on the path as Barney continued to howl in pain. The snake tried escaping violently but was trapped.

Jesse walked forward calmly and lifted the axe, aiming at the snake's upper body. "You picked the wrong campers," Jesse snarled as he swung the axe onto the snake's head and severed the head an inch below the reptile's jaw. "You are dinner now." Jesse wet his lips. "I'm not eating my boots again."

The copperhead's body continued twitching as Jesse grabbed the decapitated snake. Samuel rushed forward and held the end straight as Jesse fished in his pocket for his hunting knife. He found it and started slicing the skin expertly down the length of the reptile.

The snake's body jumped several times as Ted stopped watching the gruesome scene and rushed to Barney. "Are you okay?" he asked.

"No!" Barney shouted in pain, clutching his leg. Two bloody puncture wounds were reddening on his lower calf.

"It's okay, you'll live!" Ted shouted. "Copperhead's poison won't kill you. I'll get something to keep your leg up."

Barney shouted in pain again as Ted moved his leg.

Jesse looked up at the two couriers briefly, then continued slicing the remainder of the snake's skin off as Samuel held it steady. Jesse grabbed the inner snake meat and pulled the skin away, yanking with his left hand while stretching the skin down the body with the other. The snake meat pulled away from the skin as Jesse wet his lips. His stomach churned.

"Gotta take the guts out, bro," Samuel reminded him. "And cook that viper fully."

Jesse nodded and curled his fingers inside the middle gap, pulling the center guts and organs away from the meat, similar to the skinning, but pulling the innards away from the meat now. A long string of guts and organs peeled out of the snake meat, and Jesse threw it on the ground, bringing the precious meat to the firepit. "How's Barney doing?" he asked.

Ted finished tying a rough sling to a branch. "He's looking a bit light-headed, but he'll survive," Ted replied. "No major swelling yet, so we'll see. Time will tell."

"I'll get the wood," Samuel said, lifting the axe and stomping into the bush.

Jesse was so hungry he wanted to eat the snake raw in his hands but stopped himself. He suspected that snakes needed to be cooked thoroughly before it was safe. The head was cut clean of the body, and that was where all the venom was, so he was certain it was safe to eat the body.

Samuel returned with firewood and started the fire quickly, hunger urging him on. He grabbed the metal grate from the sacks and placed it above the fire. They both waited impatiently until the fire heated the metal enough. "That should be hot enough. Put it on there," Samuel instructed.

Jesse placed the snake meat on the cooking grill, hearing the delicious sizzle as the meat touched the hot surface.

"Cook it for a good ten minutes," Samuel stated. "Make sure it's fit for eating."

Jesse smiled as the two cooked the snake together, flipping it over once while Ted tended to Barney.

After the full ten minutes, Jesse removed the curled-up, seared meat from the grill, ripping off pieces for Samuel and the two couriers.

"You men sure know how to survive in the mountains," Ted commented, eating the meat delicately.

Jesse ate the snake meat and savored every bite. "Samuel and I have had a bit too much wilderness experience," Jesse replied, laughing and licking his fingers. "Snake is good!"

"It sure is, brother!" Samuel said, chuckling as they ate their spontaneous dinner.

The morning was humid and hot in the rolling mountains of Pennsylvania. Jesse shifted in his blanket and then abruptly awakened. He was half-afraid of another snake attacking them and hungry enough to wish for another one. Jesse opened his eyes and watched the clouds in the light blue sky slowly drifting above him. Jesse heard a moan and bolted up.

He turned to Samuel and saw that his friend was fast asleep. It seemed like he was the only one awake.

He stood and heard another moan. Jesse walked over to Barney as the courier groaned in pain. "Hey, Barney, are you okay?" he asked.

Barney grimaced and clutched his leg.

"Let me see that," Jesse said, pointing towards the injury.

Barney winced and nodded, the pain obviously overwhelming his senses.

Jesse bent down and inspected Barney's leg. There was a large red patch of swelling from the ankle all the way up to just below his knee. He lifted Barney's leg gently from the support sling and laid it down on the ground. He noticed that someone had tied a tourniquet above the bite. Jesse wasn't an expert on snake bites, but Barney's limb looked pretty bad, and his forehead was sweating. "Who tied the tourniquet?" Jesse asked.

"I did," Barney groaned. "It hurt too much. I had to do something."

"I'll wake up Ted and see what he says." Jesse walked over to the other sleeping courier. "Hey, Ted, get up." He shook Ted's shoulder lightly.

"What?" Ted mumbled lazily and curled away from Jesse.

"Barney's not doing so well."

"What's wrong?" Ted asked, rubbing his eyes and lying flat on his back.

"His leg is swelling something horrible. He tied a tourniquet onto it during the night."

Ted sat upright. "Why did he do that?"

"The pain."

Ted cursed and stood up stiffly, stretching his legs. "What the hell did you do, Barney?" he shouted at his comrade. He stomped over to his friend and looked down at the swollen leg. He untied the tourniquet and threw it on the ground. "That's only for cobras, you numbskull. For copperhead bites, you just wait it out." He placed two fingers on the swelling and pushed down as Barney yelped. "I told you before! You don't die from copperhead poison. But you can sure lose a leg if you do something stupid like this!"

Barney groaned and lost consciousness.

Ted cursed with a string of colorful profanities and walked over to Jesse. "I need you to help me save his life. God dammit!"

Ted rummaged in the sack, pulled out the axe, and stumbled into the bush, collecting deadwood. "We need to get the fire going now!"

Jesse joined him and collected a large stash of firewood.

"Let's get this fire raging hot," Ted yelled.

Jesse hurriedly grabbed several logs and began splitting them with the axe.

Ted placed the wood and branches in a pile and started the fire.

"What are we going to do about Barney?" Jesse asked, confused.

"We need to cut off his leg."

Jesse grimaced and added more branches to the small fire.

"We need that fire hotter than any fire you've ever seen." Ted grabbed the axe and cleaned the blade with his shirt. He sharpened the blade methodically on a stone, inspecting the blade periodically and swearing at Barney.

Jesse worked at adding logs until the flames were three feet high and watched Ted approach the fire with the axe. Jesse wasn't looking forward to what was going to happen next.

"What's going on?" Samuel asked tiredly, awakening from the commotion.

"Barney's sick, in a bad way," Jesse answered. "Ted says we have to amputate his leg, or else he'll die."

"Oh shit," Samuel stated. "Anything I can help with?"

"You can hold him down," Ted replied. "He'll wake up from the shock momentarily, and I need him steady."

Samuel grimaced. "I can do that, I suppose," he answered, watching Ted turn the axe over in the fire. "That axe won't be good for amputation. It'll just crush the bone. Do you have a saw?"

"I have a small saw, yes," Ted replied.

"Let's use that," Samuel said firmly.

"Okay," Jesse said, rushing to the pack thrown on the ground.

"It should be in there!" Ted yelled.

"I found it!" Jesse said, grabbing a small saw and handing it to Ted.

Ted inspected it, turning it this way and that. "It should be good enough." He placed the saw on the stone and tried his best to sharpen the small teeth, but it was futile. He wiped the blade with his shirt, then straightened and held the saw above the fire, sanitizing the teeth as best as he could. Finally, after several minutes, he spoke gravely. "Okay, let's do this."

Jesse and Samuel followed Ted towards Barney's unconscious form. "Hey, Barney," Jesse barked. "You need to wake up for us so we don't give you a heart attack." Jesse shook his shoulder. Barney didn't react.

"Just hold him down!" Ted shouted.

Samuel pinned Barney's arms down as Jesse held the man's hips down to prevent him from bucking. Ted tied the tourniquet tight near Barney's knee, then lifted the saw and started cutting. The flesh seared as the hot saw cut through skin and bone.

Immediately, Barney jolted awake and almost got out of the two-man grip. Jesse fought to keep the man's pelvis down, and Samuel put all his strength into immobilizing Barney's arms. "Keep sawing!" Samuel shouted.

Barney howled in agony as the saw hit bone again, then he lost consciousness and went limp.

Ted continued the laborious task of amputating his friend's leg as the blood squirted out from the severed edges.

Jesse felt sick and tried looking away but had to focus on keeping the patient's hips still.

After a long, agonizing minute, the limb finally fell onto the ground. Jesse grabbed the towel and blotted the stump as Ted rushed to the fire, grabbing a large branch. He pulled it out of the fire. The end of the branch was a glowing red poker, and he returned to Barney's limp form. Ted placed the hot poker along the stump cut as the nauseating smell of burning flesh filled the air.

Jesse let go of Barney and gagged. "Holy, that smells bad!"

"Just think of how it feels," Ted yelled back. "Good thing he's out." He continued searing the wound until it was all cauterized.

Both Samuel and Jesse returned to the fire to make coffee. "Well, good morning," Samuel said cynically.

"Nothing good about it," Jesse spat back.

The next morning wasn't much better, or the several mornings after that. Jesse had lost a lot of weight and was weak again. His head swam with dizziness from lack of nourishment. They were able to kill a squirrel once, but it wasn't enough. They all had nicks and scratches everywhere along their bodies, and they hadn't bathed in a few days. The river was long behind them, and the hustle of Philadelphia began to form around the group. Curious onlookers stared at the rugged team of dirty travelers. Barney stayed on the horse, his right leg a stump. His eyes were bright and focused, though. He had recovered quickly after the amputation. After a day of sleeping, Barney had awoken in pain. Samuel had given him a whiskey flask, and by day two, Barney was well enough to ride.

But their jerky rations had run out the next day, and they had starved for two days before catching the squirrel. They gave Barney most of the food to aid in his recovery. Jesse was exhausted, and for once in his life, he looked forward to seeing his family. He chuckled and knew that wasn't true. Jesse had always loved his siblings and his mom. It was always his father that formed the thick wall between himself and his family.

Bob Eastman was no longer alive now, Jesse told himself. The realization of it felt surreal. Jesse had never imagined his father would ever die. Parents were supposed to live forever, it seemed. He knew it was not so; it just seemed strange that it would happen to his family. And especially a man like Bob Eastman.

Jesse lifted his chin. After spending two years in the woods, he learned that nobody was indestructible.

They walked through the crowds, leading Barney and the horses through the busy market areas. Food drifted from several stalls. Samuel immediately stopped, purchasing cooked ribs and biscuits. They ate ravenously and licked their fingers. They all felt an immediate surge of energy and continued towards the Eastman estate.

It was still over a four-hour walk to the port area where his father's estate was situated. After three long weeks of traveling, Jesse was impatient to get there. "Let's keep going," Jesse stated. "I don't want to stop now." He climbed upon his horse. "The crowd is breaking up. We can ride again."

The group meandered slowly through the thinning crowd until the streets were clearer, and Jesse urged his tired horse to a faster trot.

The sun was hot and baked the backs of their necks. Philadelphia had changed since he was here last. Jesse had spent a year in New York City after being kicked out of the Eastman household. He hadn't been back to Philadelphia in over three years and never thought he would ever be allowed back.

Jesse felt a comforting nostalgia while they rode through town. There were good times as a small boy. His childhood was easier than most, and he was often envied by the best of people. It wasn't every day that a child had the luxury of growing up in a wealthy household. But Jesse had never known anything else until New York City, of course. He had to find work and become his own man, all in the blink of an eye. It was a difficult turning point in his life, but he was glad, in a strange sort of way, that it had occurred. Otherwise, he wouldn't be the strong man that he is now.

Jesse wondered how his mother and siblings looked like. His closest brother, Billy, was only thirteen-years old when Jesse had left. Billy would be sixteen-years old now! Jesse chuckled and wondered if his younger brother would be unrecognizable now.

The slave girl, Georgina, would be close to Jesse's age now. Her day of freedom at twenty-eight years old would be coming closer, Jesse thought. The young mulatto girl was born only six months after Jesse was born. She had become like a sister to him. Jesse shook his head. That was why he had defended her fiercely from his father. He liked the girl. She was quiet and reserved, always cleaning and cooking within the household. He had grown up with her and sometimes they had even secretly played together.

Jesse didn't understand why his family still had slaves. Most of the slaves had already been freed, and only a small percentage of families still had them in Philadelphia. Of course, an estate the size of the Eastman's would need multiple workers, but they had the money to pay regular household staff, so he didn't quite understand why Bob Eastman refused to let go of Georgina.

Jesse never understood much of why his father did the things he did.

A rolling hill stretched before them as the landscape changed dramatically. The Eastman estate loomed intimidatingly in the distance. The lawns were manicured, and the gates at the front were closed. Jesse wondered whether his key still worked. He fished in his pocket and found the old skeleton key. He rolled it in his hands as the group slowly approached the large iron gates.

Jesse reached the gate first and climbed off his horse. "Hopefully, this works," Jesse said out loud. He inserted the key into the lock, and it miraculously clicked. The iron gate creaked loudly as Jesse pushed it open. He walked confidently with his horse onto the estate grounds with the caravan behind him.

A few groundskeepers stared at the group as they approached the massive front walkway of the large house.

Jesse handed his reins to Samuel as he stepped up the wide front steps. Before he could ring the loud chime, a small, dark-haired Irish lady opened the front door and ran outside to him, hugging him fiercely. "Oh my Lord, Jesse!" Ellen Eastman exclaimed. "You are here! You made it back alive!"

Jesse felt hundreds of emotions cascade from his mind and hugged his mother back fiercely. "Momma," he said simply, the emotions clogging his words.

"Jesse," she replied, her tears cascading down her cheeks. "I was so afraid that you were dead."

"Nope," he chuckled. "I'm alive but barely. Just the journey back nearly killed us all."

Ellen frowned and held him out at arms-length. "You need time to recuperate," she said lovingly, peering around Jesse at the caravan members. She noticed the couriers. "Ted and Barney! Thank you so much. You will be rewarded for bringing my son back alive!"

Barney spoke first, pointing at his right missing leg. "Jesse made it back better than I, Mrs. Eastman. We are all lucky to be alive."

"I will get the stable hand to get the horses," Ellen said. "All of you, please come on in, and we will see to it that you are all taken care of."

Towards the end of the week, Jesse felt his usual energy finally returning back to him. The entire family and several servants banded together to help the starved and harried group of weary travelers. A doctor was called in for Barney, and the physician also checked all the men in the group. Starvation had hollowed their eyes and stripped their bodies of fat and muscle. Jesse still had black circles under his eyes, and his limbs were still very slim, but he was feeling much better.

He had reunited with his brother Billy and his younger siblings, Joshua, Katie, and Bridget. His younger sisters brought him soups and stews for his sensitive stomach. His brothers played chess with him and walked around the grounds with him regularly.

Jesse sat down tiredly in the large sunroom. He would have been happy just to sleep and eat for the entire week, but seeing his family was beyond lovely.

Georgina was excited to see him also. He watched as she entered the garden sunroom, holding a breakfast tray of biscuits, eggs, coffee, and a newspaper.

"You are looking better already," she said, placing the tray down on the small end table.

Jesse turned his head and smiled. "Everyone has helped immensely," he said, opening the newspaper and biting into the boiled egg. As he read the headlines, his eyes narrowed into slits. "Our country has declared war on the British?"

"They have?" she asked.

"Yes, look!" he said, holding out the newspaper for her to read. He noticed the blank look on her face and remembered that she didn't know how to read. "It says that the United States has declared war today on Upper Canada over the Royal Navy blockade of US Atlantic trading. The British cannot stop us from trading." He slammed down the newspaper. "This isn't good. I came back home, and now our country is at war."

"That's terrible news," she said, still standing.

"It really is!" Jesse exclaimed. "Maybe this means we can finally find a way to increase our exporting business. If we win, that is."

"I hope the two countries will be able to find a peaceful solution," Georgian said sincerely.

"I hope so, too," he replied, waving for her to sit down.

After several seconds of silence, she glanced around, then sat down, crossing her fingers. "How was it like in the mountains?" she asked in a quiet voice.

"It was rough," he answered. "But beautiful at the same time. It's hard to describe."

"I've always wanted to see the mountains."

"You have?"

"Yes," Georgina replied. "I have not gone anywhere other than Philadelphia. I would love to see other places."

"You will be able to soon," Jesse stated. "You are turning nineteen soon."

"It's still another nine years before I turn twenty-eight."

"Well," Jesse said, grasping her curled hands. "I will see what we can do about that."

"You would?"

"Of course, I would," Jesse replied. "You've been like a sister to me my entire life."

Georgina grew quiet and stared at her toes. "Yes, I feel the same."

"Slavery will soon be a thing of the past here in Philadelphia."

"You think so?"

"Yes, I know so," Jesse responded. "I will begin helping my mother starting this week with the estate. I will talk to her about it."

Her eyes widened. "I would have nowhere to go, Jesse," she said. "I have no family. My mother died when I was young, and my father, well," she coughed briefly. "He was never found."

"I will suggest that we begin paying you then," Jesse added. "You can stay here."

"Alright," she replied. "I suppose if you are in charge of the Eastman household and you freed me, I would stay."

Jesse frowned. "My pappa was cruel to you." He watched her eyes lose focus and cloud over. "He was always yelling at you." Jesse paused and wondered why his father had paid so much attention to her. It was harsh attention, but nevertheless, Bob Eastman usually didn't bother too much with the slaves. "I never understood why Pappa was so intense with you. I'm glad I stopped him from beating you. I would've done it a hundred times over. It was worth every punishment I received."

Georgina looked up into Jesse's eyes and began speaking, then stopped.

"What is it?" Jesse asked, sensing her sudden, uncomfortable demeanor.

"It was a huge sacrifice for you," she said softly. "Thank you."

"If I had to repeat it, I would," Jesse said. "You were always like a sister to me. I grew up with you, Georgina."

"Yes," she replied quickly. "You were a brother to me, too."

Jesse watched as she continued curling her fingers over one another, the anxiety within her obvious. She had a familiar gracefulness to her arms, just like his sisters did. He always thought that was funny. "What is it, Georgina?" Jesse asked. "Is there something you want to tell me?"

"Well," she said hesitantly. "Now that your father is no longer here. He would have killed me if I said anything."

"Said what?" Jesse asked, sitting straighter.

"My mother," she started, then paused, swallowing hard. "She told me something on her death bed when I was only six-years old." She glanced up into Jesse's eyes. "I have never forgotten what she said."

"What did she say?" Jesse asked, completely confused.

"My momma said," Georgina said quietly, almost whispering. "She said that my father was not a random man who disappeared. She confessed that my father was her slave master."

Jesse picked up a biscuit and bit into it then stopped chewing, as the realization of Georgina's words hit him.

"Yes," Georgina said softly. "I am your half-sister, Jesse."

PART II

1812 WAR

Chapter 10

"I never asked for this war!" George Collard exclaimed angrily. "My father fought with his life and lost. I had no safe place to live in the United States afterward. I came here with nothing but my shoes, hat, and my clothes. I built a decent life in Upper Canada. I thought I was safe from all this." George gestured into the air in resignation. "I didn't ask for this, Clara."

"You don't have to go," Clara replied emotionally.

"I have to, Clara," George responded. "I have no choice. Do you want us to lose everything we've worked so hard for?"

"No!" Clara exclaimed, reaching out for him and hugging him fiercely. "I don't want to lose you. You're the most important thing to me. How can I deal with the farm without you? My sweetheart, don't go." Clara sniffled her tears back as her forehead touched his chest.

George wrapped his arms protectively around Clara, holding her tight. He swayed with her for several minutes as the room grew quiet. George kissed the top of her head and did not look forward to leaving, but he knew that he must. "Sweetheart," he said softly. "I will survive. Don't worry about me. You must stay and keep the farm operating with our children. Zee knows a lot about the farm. Ewart can help, too."

"No," Clara whimpered.

"I must go," George responded, kissing her head several times. He felt torn between his need to protect his country and leaving his wife. She was his rock, the only person in his life he could always trust. Clara was his one true love, and it felt like he was ripping his heart out, leaving her. "The Americans are already taking over some households near the border. Our house is far enough away that you should be safe, but we must stop them from advancing. Do you understand how important this is, Clara? The last thing we need is for the United States to take over our land in Upper Canada and take our livelihoods with it. I won't let that happen, Clara. I've worked too hard for all of this." He waved his hand around the room to encompass the forty acres of Collard farmland. "Heck, I'm still working hard on the land. We'll be clearing another five acres of land for corn next year. I can't just allow it all to be taken away." George bent forward and grasped her chin, pulling her face up to meet his. Her eyes were wet, and her lips quivered. "Listen to me, darling. I will be fine. Don't worry about me. My father fought in the Revolutionary War. My cousins and uncles did, too. We are not men that go down easy. I will survive this. We will survive this."

Clara blinked as the hot tears blurred her vision. "How can I live without you?" she asked, her voice cracking with emotion.

George wrapped his large frame around her, engulfing her in his embrace. "Darling," he cooed. A thought entered his mind, and he realized with increasing clarity what this was really about. "It's not just about the farm, is it?"

"It's not entirely about the farm," she confessed, her eyes casting down.

"It's about our love for each other, isn't it?"

"Yes," she sobbed, gulping in her words as a torrent of tears escaped. She cried into his chest heavily for several minutes.

Clara sniffled, feeling like all the energy was escaping from her body and mind. "I don't know how to live without your love."

He smoothed her hair along her back and kissed the top of her head again. "My love will always be here," he patted his heart. "It's not going anywhere."

"You might die," Clara whimpered.

"I'm not going to die," George replied.

"How do you know?" she asked incredulously. "You don't know that!"

George swallowed. She was right. There was no way he could guarantee his life in the midst of a war. He didn't intend on dying and couldn't even fathom how that would affect her. "You're right. I cannot know for certain," he said. "But my love for you will prevail. I know this. I will come back when I can or send word to let you know that I am alive and well. Whatever I need to do, I will, Clara. You must believe me."

Clara blinked and looked up at George. "I believe you," she said slowly, her words betraying her heart.

"I know it's hard," George cooed. "But I will be back again. Wait for me, Clara. We will harvest the corn next year."

Clara swallowed, knowing it was a lie. Their lives would never be the same again. "I will wait for your return, my husband."

"It'll be alright, Momma," Zee said as she rubbed her mother's shoulder soothingly. "This war won't last forever. Dad will be back."

"I hope so," Clara responded. "He just left yesterday, and it feels like he's been gone forever." Clara looked down at her folded hands on her lap. She hadn't done much around the house since George had left. Her heart felt like it was shattering silently inside her chest.

"We'll be fine," Zee repeated reassuringly. "There is a lot to be done on the farm. It'll keep us busy." Zee looked down at her swollen belly and the oversized dress that hid it all too well. She wondered how they would manage or if they could even continue operating things like they had been. Zee wasn't able to do anything physical for the farm anymore. The late stages of pregnancy kept her confined to the house. She wondered when the baby was going to come. It must be any day now, she thought.

"Busy," Clara said thoughtfully, her eyes focusing outside as she noticed Ewart picking up a bale of hay. "It will be impossible without your father."

"Don't say that," Zee replied. "You have seven able-bodied children."

Clara rubbed her eyes in stress, then looked up at Zee. "And you'll be giving birth any day," she stated. "I've already lost my best farm girl. Now I wish you were outside doing your father's jobs instead of inside all the time."

"I will be back outside as soon as I am able," Zee replied. "You know that."

"Giving birth is tougher than you may think."

"Going to war is tougher," Zee replied. "I'd rather be giving birth." Zee smoothed her dress and sat down beside her mother. A thought crossed her mind. "Did you tell Pappa?"

"No, of course not," Clara responded. "We will figure out what to do when the baby comes."

"Okay, Momma."

⚓

Ewart shoved the pitchfork in the hay and hauled the bale into the barn for the horses. He spun around as several children from the house surrounded him.

One of them spoke up, the smallest girl named Elise. "Momma told us to come out and help you as much as we can."

"I need to clear the bush to prepare for the spring corn planting," Ewart stated, looking at the children with a mixture of amusement and bewilderment. "I have some scathes and several tillers. Which one of you can be put to work? You girls have never even been in a field before, and your brothers are too young. Where's Zelda?"

"She's still feeling sick," Charlotte, the older sister, said. "She's been eating too much and getting quite fat. I don't know what is wrong with her, but momma says Zee should recover soon."

Hanna interrupted. "Momma shooed us out of the house and told us to help you as much as we can."

Ewart paused, looking at the children with a perplexed frown knotting his brows. "I don't know how much work I can give you all. It's hard labor."

"Momma was very strict," Charlotte added. "She told us not to come back until the day has ended." Charlotte shifted from foot to foot. "We will do whatever we can. I can help with the baling and the horses."

Ewart frowned. "I suppose," he said slowly. "I can go out and start clearing the bushes." He handed the pitchfork to Charlotte. "I will show you all how to do the baling, and then whoever is the fittest can try to help me with the clearing."

The younger children smiled and giggled. Charlotte frowned at her siblings. "You all better behave," she said. "I'm only your sister, but Momma will skin you alive if you don't help."

Elise grinned. "I am behaving!"

"We'll see," Charlotte replied.

Ewart stomped to the hay fields and showed the children what to do. His hands were filthy, and he was exhausted from the extra work. Without George or Zee, the farm work had quickly become overwhelming. He appreciated any kind of help, but was still worried why Zee was nowhere to be found lately. "Okay, watch and learn because we need to get this done before the rains start."

The quiet house was pierced by Zee's groan. She lay on her straw bed, praying for the cramping pains to subside. It had started in the morning. It was already afternoon, and the abdominal pains were only getting worse. Momma had cleared the children out of the house, started boiling water and gathered the tub for a cleansing bath. There were towels strewn everywhere, and the house was a mess.

"Stay strong, my sweetheart," Clara cooed. "Once the baby comes, it will all be over, and the pain will subside." She grabbed a towel, laid it under Zee's bottom, and rushed into the kitchen to clean her hands in the hot water once again. "We can do this together. Everything will work out fine. Don't worry."

A film of sweat creased Zee's forehead as another cramp ripped through her abdomen. She shouted and curled over, grasping her large belly. She had pillows propping up her head and back. Zee's legs were spread, with the dress covering her naked lady parts. A large wet stain spread across the floor beside her bed when her waters had broken. She was scared and fearful but immensely grateful for her mother's experience and devoted love.

"Push," Clara instructed. "Every time you feel that cramp." She peered under the dress and positioned a large pail of warm water nearby. "I will catch the baby, don't worry. Your pappa helped deliver all of you when I was in labor. It will be fine."

Zelda groaned heavily, pushing with all her might. She felt a strange movement inside her belly and spread her legs further apart. "The baby's coming, Momma!"

Clara held her hands out near Zelda's opening and prayed silently. "Keep pushing!"

Zelda exhaled out forcefully and pushed again with all her strength. "I feel the baby moving!"

"Good, keep pushing," Clara said, her hands slightly shaking.

Zee exhaled rapidly, and then the pain slowly subsided. A quiet calm descended upon the two as Zelda breathed a sigh of relief and relaxed back onto the pillows. "I'm so thirsty, Momma."

Clara stood up and raced into the kitchen to grab a cup of cool water. She moved quickly and returned to the bedroom, handing the tin cup to Zelda.

Zee grasped it gratefully and sipped the cool liquid until it was all gone. She wiped her forehead and exhaled. "When is the baby going to come?" she asked.

"The baby comes when it is ready," Clara answered. She grabbed a large hair brush and started combing Zelda's long hair soothingly. "Just focus on relaxing when you can and pushing when you have the urge."

Zelda moaned as the brush calmed her nerves. Her mother hadn't brushed her hair since she was twelve-years old, and it felt wonderous at the moment.

Clara continued combing Zee's hair and started humming a lullaby as the minutes turned into hours. Intermittent labor pains racked Zelda's body, then subsided repeatedly as the clock chimed 4 o'clock. "We only have a few more hours before the children come back home, Zelda."

Zee's eyes widened. "Okay, I will start pushing again."

"Only when the cramps tell you to, sweetheart," Clara cooed. "If we could, we would just tell this baby to come out now."

It seemed the baby heard. An intense cramp rippled through Zee's body. She squirmed back with her arms straight out behind her and pushed with all her strength. Zelda screeched as the baby slid out into Clara's hands.

"The baby is out halfway!" Clara shouted. "Gentle pushes now! Gentle!"

Zelda fought against her urge to push hard and gently pushed down as the infant cleared the birth canal.

"He's here!" Clara shouted gleefully as she grasped the infant and cut the cord.

"It's a boy?" Zee shouted back.

"Yes!" Clara laughed. "It's a boy!"

Clara washed the newborn infant and then handed the baby to Zelda. "Feed him," she urged.

Zelda pulled the infant to her left breast and plopped her hard nipple into his mouth. "Well, hello, Xavier," she cooed with love. "You are one fine little man." Zee laughed with joy. "My baby boy."

Clara smiled broadly. "We did it, my sweetheart!"

"Yes, we did!"

The group of exhausted children entered the house one by one and wondered why dinner wasn't prepared. They were all starving and depleted from being in the hot sun all day.

"Momma!" Charlotte called. "We're back!"

The floorboards creaked as Clara walked through the hallway into the kitchen with a tiny bundle in her hands. The children all looked at her in confusion. "Say hello to your new baby brother, Xavier."

CHAPTER 11

Jesse stood at the desk while his mother continued writing her ledger notes detailing the estate's assets. He noticed a movement outside on the front pathway, and a disappointment settled heavily in his heart. Several men approached the household with a small military attaché behind them. The doorbell chimed.

Jesse knew what it was concerning before he had even opened the door.

Jesse yanked open the door.

The military man in the front spoke loudly, holding a draft notice in his right hand. "Mr. Jesse Eastman? Your name came up as a draftee for the 1812 war. Do you wish to hire a substitute for the 1812 draft? I have brought along many suitable candidates."

Jesse exhaled. He knew his decision would irk his mother and the entire family. Jesse felt that after surviving the western frontier, he was more suitable for war than anyone else. He frowned at the collection of seven men. "Who brought you all here?" Jesse asked. "Regardless, there is no one to hire. No substitute is required."

"What do you mean, Mr. Eastman?"

"I am going to war myself," Jesse stated firmly. "Thank you for your devotion to our country. You can all enlist yourselves voluntarily." Jesse grasped the document, closed the door firmly, and leaned against the door, sighing.

His younger brother, Billy, saw the entire exchange. Billy sat on a step on the grand front staircase. "You're going to war?" Billy asked a tone of astonishment in his voice. "Mother is not going to like that. Who's going to run the estate?"

"Well," Jesse replied. "That's what you'll be here for. You are sixteen. The draft only applies to men eighteen to fifty-three years old."

Billy snorted. "What do I know about the estate and father's business?" Billy stood and combed his fingers through his short hair. "I know more about guns than you do. I should be in this war, not you."

"Sorry," Jesse stated confidently. "I'm the only Eastman from this family joining the war. You have no idea the things I've learned during the Astorian expedition. A lifetime of experience." Jesse let his hands fall to his sides. "You're the one staying, Billy. Besides, I have organized most of the business assets, and the company has changed over to us now. There will be little left to do, but manage it now."

Billy stared down at Jesse from the staircase as their mother, Ellen, appeared in the foyer.

"Who was at the door?" she asked, watching as the military group marched away outside. Her eyes moved to the document in Jesse's hand.

"Nobody," Jesse responded, holding his left hand up with the document. "I've been drafted to the war. I'll be leaving tomorrow, Mother. Billy will take over for Pappa's estate while I am gone."

George Collard grimaced as he lifted the cannon balls and placed them in a stack near the mounted garrison gun at Fort George. The large cannons were very difficult to move and required a team of strong men to operate and maintain them. The heavy machinery, weighing several tons, was mounted on a cart, but the trick was to move the cart. By land, it was very slow and labor-intensive, so they left the five garrison guns where they were. There was a shortage of these heavy cannons in Upper Canada, and George knew they were vital to any war.

The summer had been cruel and slow for George. He had sent word back to his family in August that he was alive and well, but that was over two months ago now. The October winds had cooled the hot, humid summer at Fort George, and he lived his life in his barracks home under the command of Sir Isaac Brock.

Any day now, Brock was awaiting an American attack on Fort George. The commander said it was the most apparent and accessible point of attack for the United States Army.

The Fort lay atop a hill across from Fort Niagara, USA. All the Americans needed to do was cross the Niagara River. The waters were much calmer in this area. The river dumped into Lake Ontario within sight of the shoreline. It was a beautiful area and George often thought about relocating his family here after the war was over. If it ever would end.

The British, under Brock's command, had taken the Detroit River. Brock had returned to Fort George expecting the Americans to retaliate here. Before that, many of the battles were fought on ships along Lake Erie and over several rivers in a struggle to control the shipping routes the British were so keen on taking away from the Americans. The most recent Battle of Lake Erie was a win for the Americans, capturing six vessels of the British Navy. Unfortunately, the wins and losses were see-sawed back and forth between the U.S. and the British.

George shook his head and thought it was a pointless war with an easy solution. All the British had to do was allow the Americans their trading routes, and the war would be over.

But war was never fought with clear heads, George thought. Many people hypothesized that the true reason for the 1812 war was an expansion of American territory. While that may have been true, George could also understand that choking America's ability to ship goods and trade was a clear reason to fight. But on the Canadian side, many of the men, white and freed blacks, would fight to the death for their family and land, including George.

He looked up at the rising sun and was thankful that the war had not reached them yet. Life wasn't too bad at Fort George. They had comfortable buildings for their sleeping and eating areas. The militia had to sleep in crowded buildings with cots strewn everywhere, but they were warm, and the food was good. The higher-ranking officers had better housing and dining buildings, but that was to be expected.

The black soldiers, Runchey's Company of Colored Men, a Canadian militia of free blacks and indentured servants, were segregated from the white soldiers. In fact, George was surprised to see the group of approximately 40 colored men when he had first arrived at the Fort. It was an uncommon sight, for sure, but George felt it was a positive sign of the times. Slavery was something that should have been abolished entirely in America, but he knew it was still a contentious subject in his home country. A subject that could cause a murderous rage in certain folks. Better to leave the issue of slavery to the government, George thought. Upper Canada had accomplished just that and signed promising legislation in the 1793 Act to Limit Slavery. George wondered when America would follow suit.

George and several other soldiers looked up at the smoke billowing out of the cookhouse. Breakfast would be served soon.

The food was much better than George had expected, even for his group of militia members. There was a separate cookhouse for baking bread and the daily meals. Sometimes, the aroma would waft over with the wind and instantly start a craving inside his belly, as it was doing now.

It was nothing like home, but it was much better than he had expected. George started walking, with several other soldiers, towards the building right beside the cookhouse. It was the dining building, and it was quickly getting crowded with hungry men.

George wiped his dirty hands on his pants as he quickened his steps, nearing the dining building's front door. A woman rushed out of the nearby cookhouse with a pail of refuse and dumped it in a larger bin. George smiled at her and nodded. Not too many women were at the Fort, and seeing her made him instantly miss Clara. Maybe he would ask if he could see his wife, even for a short visit. George's heart leaped excitedly from the thought of seeing Clara again. It had been a long four months.

George's militia unit was training nearby when they overheard the Major Generals conversing. Sir Isaac Brock stood near the ammunition storehouse with several key commanders, discussing the war.

"I can't explain it either," Sir Isaac Brock said, waving his hand in frustration. "The Americans will retaliate for Detroit! I know it! We are ready and waiting." He removed his hat briefly and scratched his head. "Fort George is the closest and easiest target for the United States Army. It doesn't make any sense. We're just sitting here watching the American boats deliver more supplies."

"What do you suggest we do, Sir?" Major General Roger Hale Sheaffe asked, knowing the political answer but wondering what Brock was really thinking. Sheaffe had been stationed at Fort George while Brock was at the Detroit siege. Roger Sheaffe had been given the task of negotiating an armistice with the American forces on the opposite side of the river from Fort George. The short-lived armistice had since ended, and the American army was substantially reinforced now, as they routinely witnessed with the constant boatloads of supplies. Sheaffe had a long, solid career in the British military but sensed that he wasn't much liked by his subordinates, unlike the charismatic Brock, whom everybody seemed to love. Sheaffe thought his decisions were more crucial and calculating, often with good results. He supposed that he was just stricter and more disciplined than Brock.

Brock gazed out over the descending dusk settling on the fort. "We wait for the Americans to make their move," Brock answered. "Orders from Prevost are to remain defensive. If I had my way, we'd attack right now."

Sheaffe tried to keep the frown from his face. He often disagreed with Brock, but Sheaffe was still a valuable asset, and he knew it. He agreed with Lieutenant General Prevost to remain defensive. The escarpment was Upper Canada's natural defense. Once the British crossed it, they would lose that advantage.

"Well, let's wrap things up for the night," Brock said commandingly. "We will see what tomorrow brings."

Jesse ate the slop he was given and sat down on a log, in Lewiston, on the American side of the Niagara River. The plan was to attack at dawn. He didn't know much more about the strategies, but a separate attack at Fort George was supposed to be carried out simultaneously. Although, somehow, those plans had been thwarted. General Van Rensselaer was angry and frustrated at the insubordination of his other general, Smyth, who was somewhere between Lewiston and Buffalo now.

"The man clearly has no scruples," Van Rensselaer commented viciously. "If I had more time, I would court-martial that miserable General! Smyth should have stayed as a lawyer! He never responds to my summons. I commanded him to be at Fort George, but his force of seventeen hundred soldiers couldn't make it through the mud?"

"To be clear, sir," Lieutenant Colonel Winfield Scott stated adversely. "That was the same storm we had to trudge through. We almost lost our supplies in the mud, too."

"But we didn't!" Van Rensselaer shouted angrily. "And that is the point! Smyth's force is incompetent, and they struggle to follow simple orders."

Scott knew not to say another word.

Jesse watched the exchange between the two leaders. He was part of a hastily organized team of untrained militia. The detachment he was currently with didn't even have an officer. The leaders were discussing who would be in charge of the large group of unorganized militias. Personally, Jesse thought Colonel Scott was the stronger of the two leaders, with a strong, indomitable presence. Standing six foot five inches tall, he was physically more intimidating than the other leaders. But it was the Colonel's mind that commanded respect. Jesse had heard that Scott had studied to be a lawyer before the war. Something about the man led Jesse to believe that he would reach great heights.

Jesse looked down and finished eating the slop of beef stew on his tin plate. He washed the plate in the river and placed it in his pack. Jesse was frustrated at the lack of organization and eavesdropped on the commander's discussions as much as he could.

The war was not going as planned, as far as Jesse could make out. Detroit had surrendered following the surprise attack from Brock, but the Americans had several victories with the Navy ships on Lake Erie.

"Do we wait for Smyth?" Scott asked, stepping slightly away from the enraged General.

"No!" Van Rensselaer yelled. "We will be rolling in our graves waiting for that insolent pig to join us!"

"We proceed without him?" Scott asked quietly, waiting for the confirmation.

"Yes!" Van Rensselaer commanded. "We attack at 3 am."

Jesse marched to his tent and groaned, mentally preparing himself for the terrible day he would most likely experience tomorrow.

♔

Brock bolted upright in his bed. He rushed to the window, peered outside at the dark dawn, and wondered what had awakened him so abruptly. Then he heard it.

Volley fire in the distance.

It was a murmur in the distance, and Brock thought for an instant that he had imagined it from his dreams.

Then, the field guns and mortar opened up.

Brock sprang out of bed and pulled his vest on hastily as several others at Fort George were also awakened. Brock secured his rifle, ran outside to the highest point, and looked in all directions. He darted his eyes across the river toward Fort Niagara on the USA side. There was no activity, no Americans crossing the Niagara River, nothing. There was clearly no immediate attack being undertaken on his position at Fort George. Then he heard the field guns and mortar again. He glanced to the south and could not see much through the dawn skies. It was too dark.

But it was definitely an American attack. Those field guns wouldn't be going off otherwise. The booming sounds echoed farther away toward the direction of Queenston.

"What are you doing, Van Rensselaer?" Brock squinted his eyes and whispered towards the American border as several other commanders joined him on the hill.

The men all looked at Brock bewildered, seeking explanations.

"It looks like a diversion," Brock stated loudly.

Then they all heard the heavy 18-pounder fire in the distance.

"That doesn't sound like a diversion," Sheaffe stated calmly.

Brock mused over the apparent battle in the distance. He weighed his options carefully and removed his hat, scratching his head. "I will go on horseback with a few men and investigate," Brock announced. "Keep this fort armed and ready, Sheaffe!"

Jesse was stationed with a team of militias on the American side, awaiting instructions. The orders never came. The commanders, Van Rensselaer and Scott, were already in the boats crossing the Niagara River. Once the commanders arrived on the Canadian side, the British 18-pounders opened up on them. After that, Jesse could barely see past the gunpowder smoke clouds. It was mayhem. Many boats were struck down or drifted down toward the lake on the swift currents. Hundreds of militiamen on the American side had not been given proper instructions. Some had received ridiculous orders, and many men failed to comply.

Jesse was caught in the middle of all the indecisiveness. He weighed his options and decided to creep toward the shoreline, unnoticed, and investigate.

The early dawn darkness made it extremely difficult to see. Jesse squinted and tried to make out what was happening.

In astonishment, he saw Van Rensselaer's boat reach the Canadian shore. The commander stepped off and suddenly went down on the shoreline. Jesse cursed, wondering if the commander was shot. Jesse's eyes scanned upwards, analyzing the troop's movements.

The escarpment rose 300 forested feet uphill from the shoreline. The village of Queenston was near the shoreline, but the British detachment was on top of the hill. He scanned the escarpment for the object of the American capture, a redan, that stood somewhere halfway up the escarpment. It did not appear heavily armed with British forces. Several American soldiers scrambled up a hidden path to the clifftop gun. Jesse wondered if they'd get to the top. It didn't look impossible, but it definitely looked challenging. Many more American soldiers joined the group, and they were very close to the clifftop gun emplacement when things started changing.

The British opened fire towards the Lewiston side. Jesse instinctively ducked and lay down behind a large rock outcrop. Then the earth shook with return American fire from the 18-pounder guns on the US side. Jesse straightened to watch as the attack progressed. He glanced at the others still awaiting orders on the American side and scrambled back to the group, grasping a long rifle. Nobody paid much attention to him. Several militiamen began arguing amongst themselves.

"We are under state orders, not federal!" one man shouted.

A chorus of agreement rose through the hundreds of militiamen on the American side.

"Nobody is even giving us orders!" another man shouted. "Completely unorganized! Van Rensselaer has abandoned our group."

"Actually, I think Rensselaer has been hit," another man commented.

Jesse crept from the men and returned to his position near the outcrop. He stood in the mud, positioned his rifle forward, aimed towards the Canadian side, and waited.

Brock rode his horse hard as three aides galloped to catch up. The sounds of war grew louder and louder. Smoke was rising from the river as the dawn broke the darkened skies. The horses panted as they neared the 49th Regiment while the men were engaged in battle against the invading Americans. At once, the group noticed Brock and began to cheer.

"They're attempting to capture our redan!" a soldier shouted with a shrill voice, reloading his rifle.

Brock galloped to a higher point to view the position of the redan halfway up the clifftop. He groaned as he watched several Americans take over the 18-pounder gun. Brock turned to the mass crowd who had inadvertently followed him. "Send a message to General Sheaffe at Fort George to send troops immediately!" he shouted as his eyes scanned the area. Blood pumped in his throat as he waved energetically to the men. Several soldiers ran towards the detachment to deliver the message. Brock stared at the remaining group awaiting orders.

"We're going to take back that redan!" Brock shouted. He galloped away on his horse, pulling out a sword, and led the charge. A troop of men followed him on horseback and foot, hastily rushing to catch up.

Jesse could see more clearly as the dawn began to break and the sun began to lighten the skies. He watched the battle unfold and calmly lowered his weapon. It was too far across the Niagara River to shoot at anything with accuracy and he may inadvertently hit some of his own comrades.

Jesse mulled over what to do as the morning sun rose over the American countryside, casting eerie golden rays across the escarpment. He noticed a boat preparing to leave and made a rash decision. He leaped towards the shoreline with his long rifle and jumped into the boat at the last minute.

He wasn't going to stay put with no direction and watch this war.

He was crossing to the Canadian side.

Jesse clambered from the boat on the Canadian side as the British began firing down on the boats as they reached shore.

He immediately ran to the bushes. Several of the New York militia fell before his eyes. Jesse exhaled rapidly and tried to calm his racing heart. He was alive, and that he was thankful for. Whether it was luck or skill, he was grateful that his life was spared.

Hundreds of other militiamen followed him into the bushes. Jesse heard a skirmish and poked his head through some branches, aimed at a red uniform some 50 feet away, and fired. The British soldier stopped and flew backward. Jesse blinked. He had never killed another man before, and his mind didn't know how to react. He lowered his long rifle and reloaded calmly in the shelter of the bushes, then sat wearily on a rock.

It could have been a man the same age as his brother or his friend Samuel, just wearing a British red coat. Jesse stood with the rifle and aimed through the bushes again. He didn't even know if he had killed the British soldier or not. Then he heard a yell from the area as several British soldiers carried the body away.

Jesse grimaced and froze in the bushes. He watched the soldiers drag the man's body away, and an instant remorse filled Jesse's mind. The bushes moved behind him as several of his fellow militiamen stealthily climbed up the mountain. Jesse followed and started climbing the escarpment.

ⵢ

The morning turned into afternoon, and Jesse was tiring. He had reloaded his long rifle countless times and shot many men now. He didn't even know how many. He stood and peered down onto the shoreline battle as he saw a tall British commander in a redcoat holding out his sword. Jesse cursed as the lead ball failed to load into the soot-coated bore. He threw the rifle down and searched amongst the bodies and debris.

He found a British musket and rummaged on the ground for the dead soldier's ammunition cartridges and balls. He laced the ammunition pouch around his shoulders and pulled one out, biting off the top and loading it into the pan. Jesse swung the handle to the ground and dropped the musket ball down the barrel, shoving the ramrod in. When he was done, he stood tall, clearing the bushes for a few seconds. Chaos assaulted him immediately, all at once. American and British soldiers were shooting rapidly at each other, the noise reverberating in his ears. Gunsmoke filled the air in pockets of constant shooting. Horses were collapsing, and men were falling. Jesse tried to clear his mind and focus but all he could manage was to aim and fire at the tall British commander.

He didn't even have enough time to check if he had hit his target when a barrage of fire assaulted him. He ducked back into the bushes and scrambled up the cliffside.

It didn't take him long before he caught up with the other militia men as they attempted to scale the cliff. Jesse's boots slipped in the mud, and he felt himself sliding back down. He cursed and grabbed a large tree branch for leverage. His left foot kept sliding in the mud, and for a terrifying second, he thought he was going to fall down the escarpment. He grasped the tree branch and pulled himself up as another American soldier peered down at him.

"Jesse? Is that you?"

Jesse peered up as the man held out his hand and hoisted him to the higher ground near a fortified barrier. Jesse had to look twice to make sure he wasn't imagining things. "Samuel?" he cried. "Is that you? I had no idea you were in the New York Militia!"

Samuel laughed and slapped Jesse's back roughly. "Tarnation! We sure got separated during the draft!" Samuel replied, smiling broadly. "It's nice to see your sorry ass is here, though! I trust you with my life more so than any of these corrupt city slickers."

Jesse chuckled and wrapped his arm around Samuel's neck, pulling him into a headlock. The two sparred for an agonizing minute before they realized they both might tumble down the mountain or simply be shot. Jesse released the hold first. "Hell! We have a war to win, brother!" Jesse said, pointing through the bushes. "Isn't that the redan?"

A holler ricocheted through the bushes as several groups of soldiers and militia joined the small group of Americans who had already taken possession of the redan. Jesse scanned the bushes, then climbed up to the point. He gazed down at the commanding view of Lewiston across the river and the smoke rising from all the musket shots.

"We did it, Jesse!" Samuel shouted as he joined the assault in progress and fed ammunition into the black 18-pounder.

The cannon expelled the ammunition with a force that made their ears ring, sending the volley onto the battle below.

An American soldier shouted excitedly at the new group. "Brock has been shot!" he cried. "Someone saw his body being carried away by the British!"

Jesse's heart fluttered. "The British General? Brock? He's been killed?"

"Not certain!" the man replied. "But he definitely wasn't moving."

Jesse blinked and looked down below at the chaos. "Do they know who shot him?"

"Nope, we're still trying to figure it out," another soldier answered. "Some militia man in the bushes just stood, aimed, and fired, then disappeared. Whoever it was, it was a good lucky shot!"

Jesse's heart thumped loudly in his chest as he contemplated the consequences of shooting down the British commander. He filtered through his memory and tried to piece out the series of events. He had just blindly shot at the red coat. The man was tall and had a sword in his hand. Jesse had ducked back into the bushes so quickly that he couldn't be certain if it was a fatal hit or not.

"You look like you've seen a ghost, Jesse," Samuel teased. "What's up?"

Jesse swallowed. His mind raced through all the possibilities. The war wasn't over, he thought. There wasn't any advantage of revealing his uncalculated shot to anyone. Killing a General was serious. "Nothing," Jesse replied. "Just glad we finally got to the objective."

"It's more than that!" Samuel exclaimed. "The British General is down! We're winning!"

♔

George Collard saddled his horse quickly and joined the 41st light company with Sheaffe in command. They were bringing a load of weapons and ammunition with them to Queenston Heights. The Company of Colored Men was traveling with them as well.

The horses galloped through the countryside urgently, trying to cover as much distance as possible. Once they neared Queenston Heights, Sheaffe commanded a slower approach. They approached while the British Canadians were under a full American siege. Sheaffe led his men towards the remaining British detachments on the hill. When they arrived, a war whoop sounded, and the incoming group was welcomed wholeheartedly.

A captain approached Sheaffe angrily. "Brock is dead," the captain shouted. This news enraged many of the 41st soldiers, including George. Everyone loved Brock. An angry murmur grew amongst the soldiers as they turned to watch another regiment join the group.

This new group was very different from the 41st soldiers and militia. It was a large unit of several hundred Mohawk warriors. They joined the group situated near the top of the heights. "Two of our chiefs have been killed!" A massive war cry erupted from the Mohawk warriors upon hearing the words spoken. Several warriors began running to the bushes in an instantaneous emotional counterattack against the Americans.

Sheaffe attempted to calm the emotional responses. "Halt your men!" Sheaffe shouted authoritatively. "We will plan this properly! Don't be fools. We can still win this fight!"

George watched as the commanders quieted and listened.

"What's the American's position?" Sheaffe asked.

"They've taken the redan!" a soldier answered passionately.

Sheaffe cursed softly and leaned towards one of the commanders. "Let's see the layout of the land and where the Americans have taken control."

The captain led Sheaffe into a bunker, and they examined a rough map. "Here," the captain pointed. "And here. The Americans climbed the escarpment to the right of us and were able to take command of the redan. They have Queenston down below, and it sounds like they are looting the town."

Sheaffe groaned. "Let's think about this strategically." He looked at the map and ran his finger around both sides. "We attack the Americans from the side flanks. If successful, we will be trapping them where they stand. This detour will also benefit us, serving as a shield from the American artillery." Murmurs of agreement chorused throughout the group in the bunker. The commanders drew lines at landmarks on the rough map and returned outside as Sheaffe spoke to the captains of each unit. They listened as Sheaffe took the lead and detailed the planned attack.

Sheaffe left the bunker and approached the 41st regiment, sharing the details. George thought it was a sound plan and instantly had a renewed appreciation of Sheaffe. After the flanked attack was shared amongst the hundreds of soldiers and militia, the crowd of men began to relax noticeably.

"Where was Brock taken?" Sheaffe asked the crowd calmly.

"His team fell back through Queenston to Durham's farm," a commander reported. "Another Captain was injured badly, too. Macdonell was taken to Durham by the troops along with Brock's body."

George was standing with his unit, very close to the commanders, as a murmur of excitement rippled throughout the men. He nodded and looked to Sheaffe for more instructions.

"We strike at 4 pm," Sheaffe announced.

⚔

Jesse felt trapped on the clifftop with the redan. They had unspiked the 18-pounder and tried firing at the village but found that the cannon had limited field of fire away from the river. It was a heavy piece of machinery that was extremely difficult to move without the proper equipment. The weapon weighed in excess of 3,000 pounds. The good news was that Queenston was captured, but the hill above them was still in British hands, and it was never a good thing to have your enemy on top of a hill looking down on you.

Jesse grabbed Samuel's arm. "We'd do better in the bushes," Jesse whispered. "The redan has been captured. There is no use for us to be here now."

Samuel motioned Jesse to the side. "I heard Scott was in charge now," he stated in a low voice.

"Our group currently has no clear orders," Jesse responded.

"True," Samuel said. "What do you suggest?"

"We can bring a team of militia with us and hide in the bushes, firing at the Canadians as they come down the hill," Jesse replied, pointing backward to the pathway edging down the hill.

"Let's do it," Samuel said.

CHAPTER 12

They had been waiting in the bushes for over an hour now, and Jesse was getting worried. There was little movement from the British on the hill. Jesse hadn't even fired five rounds since they set up with approximately fifty other men. As they moved through the heavy overgrown shrubs, they realized many other American militia were also hidden, and their hopes increased.

They spoke to the other men and found out they had also crossed to the Canadian side, much later than expected, but they did cross. Hundreds of other militias still refused to cross, but the ones that did were reinforcing the American's position. It was unclear whether Colonel Scott knew of the late arrival of the militia.

Jesse waited patiently, aiming toward the hill. A chilling sound unexpectedly echoed through the valley. Jesse straightened and felt the hair on the back of his neck rise in warning.

Another Mohawk war cry whooped down the hill as a massive group of angry Canadian Mohawk warriors attacked their right flank. There were so many of them that Jesse was momentarily frozen as he watched the warriors jump and shoot downwards at the village of Queenston. Then, the sound of immense gunfire erupted on their left side as a trained battalion of British soldiers flooded the other flank.

Jesse looked to the top of the cliff, and from where he was situated, it was impossible to climb straight up.

Samuel nudged him in the bushes. "Stay still," he whispered. "They can't see us."

Jesse loaded the musket quietly, trying to remain as still as possible. The team of Mohawk warriors crashed through the tangled shrubbery, and the war cry was eerily savage. Jesse aimed the musket and froze.

Samuel put his hand up to stop him. "Wait," he said. "Something's happening. Let's watch how this plays out before letting everyone know our position."

Several boats had just left to the American side for reinforcements, and the shoreline was filled with Americans waiting for the return boats.

"Are we retreating?" Jesse asked in astonishment.

Samuel frowned. "I don't know, but it looks like we don't have any boats," he answered. "We're trapped."

Then, a white piece of cloth waved in the air, very close to where they were. Only 50 feet away, Colonel Scott stood, waving a large white piece of cloth in surrender.

"No!" Jesse cried in a hushed tone.

"Scott doesn't know we're here," Samuel said disappointedly.

Jesse cursed under his breath. "What do we do?"

Samuel groaned. "We have no choice," he said regretfully, placing his musket down on the ground. "Our Colonel has surrendered."

Jesse cursed and watched as nearly 500 hidden militia men began standing in surrender from the bushes. Scott's face registered surprise as well as regret.

Jesse and Samuel put their weapons down and stood slowly with their hands in the air.

Ⴔ

It wasn't long before the British and Canadian forces had rounded up all the surrendered Americans. George had been astonished at the total number of Americans. There were over 900 Americans being held as prisoners of war. There were no such facilities to house them all, so they were kept in churches and hospitals. Many of the wounded were not even being treated due to a lack of doctors and space. George heard that a temporary truce was negotiated by Sheaffe to allow Van Rensselaer to send surgeons across to aid the many wounded American soldiers.

It was a hard-earned narrow win for Upper Canada, George thought as he patrolled through the packed church of American prisoners. The British had captured all the surrendered weapons, including a 6-pounder gun and the colors of the New York Militia.

George felt lucky that he was unharmed. He scrutinized many of the American soldiers who looked so similar to himself and felt goosebumps rise on his arms. George was American, after all. He shook his head and mumbled to himself as he passed several young men lying exhausted on the church pews.

"Sir, is there anywhere we can get water?" Jesse asked, sitting slowly upright. His feet and back ached from climbing all day. The post-adrenaline crash had left his body weak and fatigued.

George Collard peered down at the group of young men and grabbed his canteen from his belt. "I will send for water immediately," George said quietly. "But you can have this for now."

Jesse tentatively grasped the canteen.

"Take it," George urged. "It may be another hour before we get organized enough to start feeding you men."

Jesse took the offered canteen. "Thank you," he said with a parched mouth.

George nodded and continued his patrol as the young men shared the small canteen. He wondered why this war was necessary. He shook his head and headed to the front altar, yelling at several younger boys brought from the town to help. "Find a way to get water and food to these Americans!"

⚓

After two weeks of being held prisoner, Jesse was fidgety. They were carted from building to building, and even Colonel Scott had been returned to the US as part of a prisoner exchange. Van Rensselaer resigned immediately after the Battle of Queenston, and everyone's morale sank.

"This war is crazy," Jesse stated.

Samuel nodded as he scooped a mouthful of Shepard's pie in his mouth. "I agree," he said. "I was in it because of the British trade restrictions. The British can't stop our trading. The fur trade, the western frontier, everything we had worked for with the Overland Astorians would be for waste."

"I agree," Jesse replied. "I feel the same. The British cannot get away with stopping our trade." He spooned the delicious Shepard's pie in his mouth. "Their food is good, though!" Jesse laughed. He spooned the remainder of the dinner in his mouth and wiped his lips with the back of his hand. "This war has got to end soon."

Samuel nodded. "Something's going to change," he said. "Winter is coming soon, and we'll be stuck in Canada doing nothing if something isn't done soon."

Jesse narrowed his eyes as several American commanders walked by, sitting farther down at a table together. "I wonder what our next move is going to be."

Samuel finished eating and stacked his plate on top of Jesse's. "I don't particularly enjoy being a prisoner."

"Neither do I," Jesse replied.

George dipped the ink in the well and wrote the last few lines of the letter:

I can't wait to see you, darling. I will be requesting some time off to see you; hopefully, my commander will grant it soon.

I am alive and well at Queenston. They will be sending me back to Fort George in the upcoming weeks, and hopefully, afterward, I'll be able to go home for a few days and kiss your wonderful lips again.

Darling, don't worry. I will be back home soon. I love you so much, Clara.

- George Collard, November 20, 1812

He inspected his words and smiled happily. He was worried about Clara and wondered how the family was getting along without him at the farm. He loved her with a passion and missed her greatly. Time never seemed to dull the love he felt for his wife, as he saw happen in so many other marriages. Clara and George had barely spent more than a few days apart since they had first met. She was everything he had ever wanted in a woman, and he often felt like the luckiest man alive.

Until now.

He yearned to see her again. His fingers ached to touch her body, her breasts, and her inner thighs again.

George leaned back and imagined what it would be like to see her again. It had been a long six months, much too long for a husband in love with his beautiful wife.

He missed his daughters and sons, also. His heart broke for them every day when he awakened and realized he was still trapped in this war with no end near.

George inhaled deeply and exhaled. He looked around for Sheaffe and spotted the commander near the command post. George was beginning to hate this war, but he knew he had to do his best to secure his freedom in his new country.

Sheaffe leaned imposingly against a large wooden pillar. George didn't like the man; he was always obstinately strict with the troops. It seemed to have gotten worse since the Queenston battle, George thought.

"Major General," George spoke strongly. "Could I have a word with you?"

"Certainly, Sgt. Collard," Sheaffe responded stiffly.

George held out the letter. "This is an important letter to my wife. Could you see that it gets to her?"

"Certainly," Sheaffe answered, grabbing the letter and passing it to a lieutenant.

"There's something else," George stated.

Sheaffe didn't respond, just nodded for George to continue.

"I would like to visit my family," George said, trying to keep the pleading tone out of his voice. "I have a wife and seven children."

Sheaffe narrowed his eyes. "We will see," he replied. "I need you back at Fort George tomorrow."

George's face fell in disappointment. "Yes, sir."

Sheaffe nodded. "The armistice ended this morning. Did you not hear the American cannon fire?" Sheaffe frowned, obviously displeased by the early morning change in the war and oblivious to George's plea. "We need as many soldiers as we can muster. As for your family visit, we will discuss it in January. It depends on which way this war turns out. I can't give you any promises."

"Thank you, Sir," George replied. He was being formally dismissed. George watched Sheaffe stomp back into the stone armament. George's hope fell, and his heart ached. He may not be seeing his wife and the thought made him angry at the world. He wished the British would send in another commander soon. Sheaffe may have saved Queenston, but nobody liked him, including George. The loss of General Brock was an American victory in so many ways.

CHAPTER 13

The baby boy was already seven months old and crawling everywhere. Zee enjoyed being a mother. Every day, she would secretly breastfeed the baby multiple times, wash him, and care for him. Her siblings were too young and self-absorbed to notice any significant changes other than they all had a baby brother.

Nobody was told that Xavier was Zelda's baby, and Zee was okay with the slight lie. It was better than being branded an unwed mother or, worse, being forced into a marriage with Ewart. She rarely enjoyed spending time with him anymore. He was loud, lazy, and incompetent in running the farm.

Zee had spent the late summer and early fall harvesting the wheat and preparing the fields for corn. Soon after delivering the baby, she had headed back out to the fields, trying to recover the farm from the absence of her pappa.

And Ewart was no replacement.

He had been errant on several of the duties, so Zee had to hire several young boys from Beaverdams to help with the bush clearing. She was angry at Ewart for not taking it upon himself to become a leader in the family. Even worse, there was news that he may be drafted for the war soon. He wasn't keen on going to war and loudly proclaimed his resistance.

Zee argued with him almost daily now. She was astonished at the change in her attraction to him. She no longer saw him as the sexy farmhand. That image had been crushed with the recent efforts to maintain the Collard Farm.

It was sad to think, but she would be happy if Ewart was forced to leave for the war.

Zelda had cut her long hair up to her shoulders and stuffed her shortened hair into her fur hat. It was a long, cold winter, and today was the snowiest day of the season. The snow had blown down in a blizzard and buried everything in sight, covering all the land. She could barely open the front door because of the wet snow. She pushed on the door and cursed as her mother woke up.

"It was quite the storm last night," Clara stated. "How bad is it out there?"

"Four feet of wet, heavy snow," Zee responded. "It's too heavy to move it all. I will try shoveling the front porch. We will wait for the rest to melt."

"Call Ewart to help," Clara offered.

"That man is useless!"

"Now, Zee!"

"Momma," Zee replied. "He barely helped me clear the bush for the new corn field last fall. I had several ten-year-old boys help me, and we did a better job than a fully grown man!"

Clara frowned at Zee's outburst.

"You know I'm right," Zee shouted. She grabbed a shovel and began pushing open the door. "Ewart is no replacement for Pappa."

Clara's eyes instantly watered at the mention of her husband.

Zee turned around when she heard her mother sniffle. "I'm sorry, Momma," Zee said softly, putting down the shovel and embracing her mother warmly. "I know how much you miss Pappa. I shouldn't have mentioned him."

Clara felt the tears erupt from her eyes and hugged her daughter tightly. "We've received no word," she cried. "He could be dead. He was at Queenston. That's all I could find out."

"Momma, don't cry," Zee consoled. "Pappa is still alive. They would have notified us otherwise. Don't worry, Momma." She rubbed her mother's shoulders. "We will make it out of this. We just have to stay strong."

Xavier's cries filled the back bedroom, and Clara pulled away as Zee's eyes darted to the bedroom. "I will get the baby, sweetie," Clara said. "You continue shoveling. You are the closest this family has to my beloved George. We need you."

Zelda picked up the shovel and watched her mother retreat to the bedroom. Clara's shoulders were slumped, and her eyes lost focus as she bumped into an errant kitchen chair and toppled it over. "Momma!" Zee cried. "Are you okay?"

"I'm fine," Clara said, brushing her hands along her dress and picking up the toppled chair. "I just miss your father so much."

"I know you do, Momma."

⚓

Zee had finished clearing the snow off the porch and looked out across the white winter land at the guest cabin where Ewart lived.

"Ewart!" she shouted, hoping her voice would carry across to the small house.

The wind blew harshly over the open field as the sun disappeared behind a snowy cloud. Nothing moved at the cabin.

She tried shouting again. "Ewart!" Zee yelled. "We need your help!"

The wind was the only response.

Zee looked down at her leather boots, and they were darkened wet from the shoveling. The field was too large to cross without significant effort, and she was already exhausted from moving all the snow off the porch. She sat down heavily on the porch swing and sighed, looking up at the snowy skies.

She would go to the guest cabin later once the snow melted a bit.

Clara stirred the hot soup rhythmically and sighed. The war wasn't ending anytime soon, and it seemed like pieces of her heart chipped away every morning when she woke up without George. He had said that he would send word, but nothing so far. No letter, no message, nothing.

She grabbed a wooden ladle and began preparing the bowls of chicken soup for the family.

Her daughters and sons were in the kitchen fixing the dinner table. Zee had left to check on Ewart at the guest cabin. They hadn't heard from him for several days. He had his own small kitchen and food supplies, so they weren't worried, but the family needed his help to clear the snow that had begun to crust over with ice.

Clara turned as the baby began to fuss in the wooden highchair. She crushed the chicken and potatoes in with the soup for the infant. He was a big, healthy baby, and Clara was relieved that her children didn't ask questions about their new baby brother.

Charlotte and Betty laid the tablecloth down and began placing the bowls of hot soup on the table. "Where's Zee?" Charlotte asked.

"She's gone to the guest cabin to rouse Ewart," Clara answered just as several footsteps sounded on the porch. "That sounds like her now."

The door opened, and Zee stomped the snow from her feet, then stepped in with a murderous scowl on her face.

"What's wrong?" Charlotte asked.

"Ewart's gone," Zee said angrily. "He left a note saying that he could not be forced into fighting this war." She snorted in disgust. "He even asked our forgiveness for leaving."

"Ewart's left?" Clara asked in surprise.

"Yes," Zee answered, her eyebrows knitting into a frown. "The swine has gone."

CHAPTER 14

J esse arose from the blanket on the floor and stared up at the church ceiling. It had been a cold winter, and the sun was straining to shine through the clouds. They were still being held as prisoners in Queenston, and Jesse had enough of living like this. His entire reasons for joining the war were being halted by this prisoner camp. Jesse fumed and wondered why he felt so ornery today.

He mused over it and couldn't coherently organize his thoughts, but one stood out in his mind.

His countrymen should have attacked Queensland to free them all by now. Jesse felt resentful and had enough of waiting for the counterattack. He stood and aroused Samuel.

"I want to leave," Jesse whispered.

Samuel opened his eyes groggily. "What?" he asked sleepily.

"You heard me," Jesse stated, standing over his friend. "Get up."

"I was sleeping!" Samuel grumbled and reached into his pocket for the last stash of chewing tobacco he had saved from the Arikaras. He placed a small wad in his mouth.

Jesse watched Samuel chomp on the chewing tobacco. "That stuff is probably rancid by now," he joked.

"Anything is good if it passes the time here in this winter paradise," he replied, his tone ladled with sarcasm.

Jesse scratched his rough beard and watched Samuel stand. "I'm not staying here," Jesse whispered.

Samuel narrowed his eyes.

"Yeah, you heard me."

Samuel exhaled heavily and started walking towards the makeshift breakfast table. "Well, we might as well get some good grub before the long day ahead."

Jesse chuckled and slapped him on the back. "Spoken with words of truth," he laughed.

🜛

Before lunch, Jesse and Samuel slipped out unnoticed. They had taken their American clothes and balled them up in a sack stolen from a group of British soldiers in a heated discussion. They luckily found a spare British red coat in the pack and a white British shirt. Jesse donned the red overcoat, and Samuel wore the white shirt. Nobody paid two British soldiers much attention as they animatedly discussed the war and walked out of town.

Jesse didn't think of filling the pack with food, but there wasn't time. They left quickly and chuckled when they reached the heavily treed countryside.

Samuel's smile turned to a frown. "You never thought of what we were going to eat?" he asked incredulously.

Jesse grimaced. "No."

"Well," Samuel replied, exasperated. "We need to find a way to kill some food then."

Jesse peered at the countryside. "It's not like we haven't been in this situation before."

Samuel nodded. "You're right about that," he replied, slumping down against a tree. "Let's rest awhile and find some food."

The countryside was mostly deciduous trees that were filling out with May leaves after the harsh winter. The ground was soggy but void of snow. The grassy hills were somehow still green, and the days were already growing hot and humid.

Jesse wiped a bead of sweat from his collar and took off the red coat, stuffing it in the pack. He relaxed back onto the large tree shirtless and instantly heard a rustle. A squirrel jumped out of the tree and ran along the log in front of them.

Samuel jumped forward as Jesse rummaged in the pack. He chuckled as he pulled out a large knife, something that looked like it had been used in a military kitchen. He showed Samuel. "At least we have something," Jesse said, brandishing the knife and turning it side to side. He tested the blade, and it was definitely sharp. "We might have to use this." Before he could say anything more, a lynx jumped from the bush and pounced on the squirrel, surprising them both. The medium-sized grey cat briefly fought with the squirrel, then quickly dragged the squirming catch away in its mouth.

Samuel and Jesse watched the lynx and squirrel disappear from sight as they both tried to register in their minds what they had just witnessed. It was a quick prey and predator scene that was so random and close up they both had little time to react. The lynx was fast!

Jesse started chuckling, and Samuel joined in.

"If we could only learn to hunt like that cat!" Samuel laughed.

"Maybe we don't have to," Jesse said, pointing at a lump in the bushes. A brightly colored red sleeve appeared in the forest as Jesse cautiously approached the site with his knife ready.

Samuel quietly crept with him.

The winter's old leaves coated the forest floor, and as they approached the crumpled form, it wasn't entirely clear what it was. Until Samuel picked some leaves off with a branch, revealing a dead British soldier. The body was partially decayed and missing parts. The lynx had most likely eaten much of it.

Jesse turned and almost vomited. The gag in his throat refused to stop, and he had to take three mouthfuls of fresh air to calm down his revulsion.

Samuel clucked his tongue. "Well," he said sadly. "Nobody found him in time." He approached the site and reached down beside the soldier, pulling out a musket.

Jesse swallowed down his bile and searched the site for a pack, anything. A few feet away lay the pack, but it was torn open by the lynx and had been ravaged many months before. Jesse threw it down as Samuel turned over the body, finding the ammunition pouch.

Samuel removed the pouch from the body and walked back to the tree. He yelled over his shoulder, "Find the ramrod, Jesse."

After several moments of searching, Jesse recovered the ramrod and joined Samuel at the tree.

"We're going to clean this weapon and get it operational," Samuel said in a dark tone.

Jesse looked up at the tree and then peered into the thick forest where the lynx had disappeared into. "Maybe we should leave this area. It looks like we've stumbled on the lynx's den."

"We'll move back to a safer position," Samuel said, fiddling with the gun. Then he looked up sharply towards the bushes. "But we're going to ambush that lynx when he comes back, and we'll be having wild cat for dinner."

Jesse and Samuel started a small fire to roast the lynx meat. It had taken the entire day of patiently staking out the site but the cat had returned as expected. And the musket fired well. It had taken Samuel several hours to clean up the dirty gun, but it had worked.

Jesse had never tasted lynx meat before. It tasted gamey but still palatable, almost like deer meat. They chewed on the rubbery meat and extinguished the fire as soon as it was fully cooked, packing the rest away for the remainder of their trip.

Samuel motioned with his head. "We should get away from the fire before we get noticed." He hoisted the gun over his shoulder as Jesse stood with the pack. "Which way do we go now?"

Jesse nodded his head to the right. "Towards Fort George."

Samuel's eyes widened. "That's suicide, brother."

"Not really," Jesse motioned with his hands. "I overheard a few New York Milita stating that the Fort was originally in the Queenston attack plan."

"So, what do you suggest?"

"We lie in wait, keep camouflaged, and watch the Fort," Jesse said. "If Scott does come back, we'll put our old uniforms back on and join the attacking team."

⚔

George arrived back at Fort George several weeks ago and quelled his anger at Sheaffe. He rarely spoke to the commander and just did his job, vowing to get away to see his wife one way or another.

But today was different. He had found out that the letter was not delivered to his family. He had found it in the items they had brought back to Fort George. He yelled emotionally at the Sergeant in charge and was immediately reprimanded.

His duties were now in the horse stable and tool house, cleaning the muck and dirt out of the stalls. George held in his seething anger but refused to let it consume him. Nevertheless, every day, he awoke with a burning hatred in his heart. The sergeant had now become malicious towards him, and George kept away from the commander's housing units.

George heard the door slap open and looked up. A fellow sergeant named Thomas stepped into the barn. George braced for trouble, but the man's expression was odd.

Thomas stepped forward. "George Collard," he called out.

"Yes, that's me."

"I have something for you." Thomas held out an envelope.

George's eyes watered with emotion and hatred. He looked at the envelope and immediately knew it was the unsent letter. "What do you want?" George asked. "I know it wasn't sent, and I have been demoted because of someone else's error."

"I'm not here to discuss that."

"Then why are you here?"

"I'm here to return what is yours," Thomas answered, throwing the letter on the iron workbench.

George stared at the letter as if it might come to life. He lifted the letter and ran his fingers along the still-intact seal. His hands shook briefly, and he tried to stem the emotions bubbling within his heart. He hastily stuffed the letter in his pocket.

Thomas stared at him, then looked behind him. "Don't tell anyone. As far as the Sergeant is concerned, it was taken out with the trash."

George saluted the much younger man. "Thank you, Sergeant Thomas."

Without another word, Thomas exited the horse stall, slamming the door behind him.

CHAPTER 15

J esse peered out from the tree line surrounding Fort George. They had been in the wilderness for over two weeks now, so they didn't have to camouflage themselves anymore; nature took care of it for them. They were filthy from head to toe, and their stomachs were growling with hunger again. They had finished the last of the lynx and the other small wildlife they had managed to kill.

It was early dawn and the fog was lifting off the Niagara River. Jesse had crept closer to the river and heard the water sloshing loudly in the morning dawn. He strained to see the ghostly movements in the distance.

"Samuel!" he whispered. "Get up! Get up now!"

Samuel stirred and rolled over quickly, scuttling over to Jesse's position.

Jesse gestured his hand to the mouth of the river, where it joined with the much larger Lake Ontario.

Samuel's eyes widened, and a smile crept on his lips as he watched the movements on the water. "They've finally come."

Jesse grinned as hundreds of boats and scows approached the shoreline. "Let's get our old uniforms back on."

They quickly changed and shifted closer to the country-side, away from the river, waiting to see what happened next.

As the morning fog lifted, cannons fired from the large ships as hundreds of Americans stormed the shoreline. The counterattack was such a surprise that a mass exodus of British soldiers began fleeing over the walls of the Fort, running on foot into the countryside east of where Jesse and Samuel were hiding. They loaded the musket and waited, watching in astonishment as the Fort was being effectively ambushed.

Jesse aimed and shot an armed British soldier dead. Samuel scrambled to raid the dead man's weapons. Samuel instantly loaded the weapon and aimed at more armed British soldiers, shooting them dead in their tracks.

"Wait!" Jesse yelled, holding his hand up. "They are fleeing!"

Samuel looked up and joined Jesse in the safety of the tree line. "They are!" Samuel whooped in excitement.

"Let them go," Jesse commanded, slightly lowering the rifle.

Just then, the bushes rustled, and a large, burly British soldier in his nightclothes bolted into their view. Jesse instantly aimed the musket at the older man. "Halt!" Jesse shouted.

The man froze twenty feet away and raised his arms over his head.

"Come closer!" Jesse shouted commandingly.

The man stepped cautiously toward the tree line. He had a strange resignation mixed with purpose on his face. Within moments, they were face to face.

"Put your weapon down," Jesse shouted.

The man laid his rifle on the ground. "Don't shoot," the older man pleaded. "I have a wife, five daughters, and two sons. My family needs me."

Jesse narrowed his eyes at the man. He noticed something familiar about the British soldier. "What's your name?"

"Private George Collard," he replied, frowning. "I used to be a Sergeant."

Jesse frowned and assessed the soldier. "You look familiar. Were you at Queenston?"

"Yes, I was guarding the prisoners for a while."

Something dawned on Jesse, and the memory became clearer. "You were the Sergeant who gave us your canteen of water."

George squinted his eyes at the two dirty men. "I did do that, yes, for a group of weary Americans." George swallowed. "Were you the men I gave the canteen to?"

"Yes, we are," Jesse answered, keeping his focus on the older man. Something looked familiar about George Collard. His jawline and mess of dark hair looked oddly American. His eyes were blue, and he was a large, broad man, definitely not somebody you'd want to take any chances with. "Where are you from, Private Collard?"

George kept his hands up in surrender. "I'm from Philadelphia," he confessed, hoping that Jesse would lower the weapon and not shoot him.

Samuel interrupted, chuckling. "You're American? You look like you're on the British side if you haven't noticed."

"I left the United States," George answered, trying to spill all the details out before they could decide whether to shoot him or not. "It wasn't safe in the United States for me anymore. You have to understand, at the time, Canada had welcomed me and gave me a parcel of land."

"You escaped from Philadelphia?"

"Yes, I met and fell in love with a Canadian woman. We married and had lots of children. We became farmers." He stopped briefly, lowering his hands slightly in an animated expression. "My family needs me. Don't shoot."

Jesse narrowed his eyes. "I think I remember the Collards in Philly," he said, trying to remember the foggy details of his childhood. "They were loyalists, I seem to remember."

"My father was a loyalist," George stated.

"Are you?"

"I'm just a family man who doesn't want to lose my home, family, and everything I've worked for in Upper Canada. Nothing more."

Jesse lowered the gun slightly. "Go home, George Collard."

Samuel kept his hands on his musket, ready to raise the weapon in case George tried something. But all he could see was relief and gratitude flooding over the man.

"Thank you, Sir," George said, his voice wavering with emotion. "What name should I address you as?"

The wind blew through the trees behind them as an uncomfortable silence settled on the men. "Jesse," he responded finally, his brows knitted into a frown. "Jesse Eastman."

George's eyes widened. "The Eastman family?" he asked incredulously.

Jesse grunted in resignation. "Yes."

"You shouldn't be fighting in this war," George replied, his eyebrows lifting in surprise. Everybody in Philadelphia knew of the Eastman Empire. "You shouldn't be fighting in any war, for that matter, Mr. Eastman."

Jesse squared his shoulders. "On the contrary, I am one of those men who should be here." He assessed George's large frame and determined features. "It looks like you might be one of those men too."

"I don't want to fight in this war," George said calmly. "I just want to see my wife and family again. The Collard farm is suffering without me. They haven't seen me in almost a year." His voice trailed off as he gazed into the distance.

Jesse nodded in the direction George was looking in. "Go see your family," he said, letting his weapon fall to his side. "Get out of here, George."

George walked slowly south, then turned into the forest. He yelled back. "Much gratitude, Mr. Eastman!"

Jesse smiled as he watched the older man disappear into the woods. He felt a welcoming warmth settle on his shoulders. Jesse Eastman had done something good today.

Samuel grinned. "You were right about one thing," he said. "We are the kind of men who should be in this war." Samuel slapped Jesse's back. "Let's go join our comrades at Fort George."

CHAPTER 16

Zee smiled as she watched her baby fall slowly asleep in her arms. A surge of motherly hormones warmed her heart, and she felt the glow permeate her entire body. Xavier's mouth opened briefly and let out a satisfied sigh, then his eyes rolled back with tiredness, and his head flopped onto the crook of her arm.

Zee chuckled softly. "You really like this when I rock you to sleep, don't you?"

Xavier opened his mouth once again, and a small grunt escaped his lips.

Zee began to sing softly, soothing the boy into a deep sleep. He had fussed so much today. It seemed he was much more interested in exploring with his new skill of walking everywhere. He was still only a year old, but his strength and determination were clearly from Zee's genetics.

"You are definitely a Collard, my sweet," Zee cooed as the sun fell into the night sky, scattering rays of pink and purples across the fields. Zee felt a moment of exasperation as she studied the unkept fields. She was trying her hardest, but it was extremely difficult to keep up with the planting of the corn and wheat. She had hired more of the neighborhood boys, but that was all the labor she could find. Most of the able-bodied men were off to war, and towns only had women, grandfathers, and children left.

Zee let out a long sigh and murmured to the baby. "How am I supposed to be a mother and a farmer?" she asked softly. "How am I supposed to replace Pappa and Ewart all by myself?"

Xavier grunted and placed a tiny hand on her breast.

"I wish all I had to do was to raise you and bake bread now," she said, chuckling at the irony. "But now I am needed every-where at once." She stared at the grandfather clock, watching the large hand tick to the top as the expected chime filled the house. "Your grandma isn't doing well, Xavier. She forgets things all the time now and sobs multiple times a day." Zee frowned and pursed her lips together. "I don't know what to do about your grandma. I'm trying, but it seems like everything I do is never enough." The clock stopped chiming, and Zee gazed past the clock through the window at the yellow fields. "We need Pappa back."

Xavier nuzzled his head into her chest.

Zee looked down at her beautiful baby boy and smiled. "At least I have you, Xavier. You have changed my life." Zee kissed him softly on the head.

Her smile slowly turned into a grimace as the weight of the world crushed upon her shoulders. "I don't know if Pappa will ever be back." Her eyes moistened at the thought of losing Pappa. "He is at war, Xavier." The thought touched her heart as a tendril of fear slipped through her veins. "And the Americans. I don't know where they are, but they may raid our home too. What will we do if that happens? Where do we live?" She quietly assessed the situation and found no readily available solution. Then, a cruel thought crept back into her mind. She spoke it aloud. "Men die at war, Xavier. Pappa can die."

A sudden realization dawned on her. "If Pappa never comes home, the farm is my responsibility." She swallowed hard. "Your grandma would die without Pappa. She's dying already without him." Silence filled the front room as she heard her mother stepping lightly down the hallway. "I would have a family of seven at the impossible age of twenty," she whispered to Xavier.

Zee's left green eye followed her blue eye as she glanced into the archway, waiting for her mother to appear. She continued waiting patiently and began to feel alarmed when Momma didn't show up in the archway. "Momma?" she hollered.

The slight sound of a slipper sliding against the rough floorboards made her ears strain to hear more. Then, the sound of her mother's body collapsing in the hallway filled her panicked heart. She leaped from the rocking chair with Xavier in her arms.

🜨

George crept through the woods all afternoon and stopped overnight, slumping against a tree. Without a horse and avoiding another American capture, it could take him another day or two to reach his home. But nothing could stop him now. He was freed unexpectedly, and his first mission was to reunite with his family. Another opportunity like this may never come along again, he mused.

George patted the letter in his breast pocket as a good luck charm when he heard a skirmish of firepower erupt behind him.

He ducked into the bushes and glanced behind him with caution. He knew it was the Americans heading inland. They were intent on occupying more territory.

A chill crept down his spine. He felt an urgency like none other to return home to protect his family.

⚔

Jesse and Samuel joined the Fort George occupation. They were astonished and pleased to see General Scott in command of the successful invasion of Fort George. It seemed the British had made a grave mistake in agreeing to return him in that prisoner exchange. Jesse scanned the water and was amazed at the hundreds of boats shored alongside Lake Ontario. He had heard that the American Navy was performing quite well during the war, with multiple wins.

It definitely helped to dampen Jesse's doubts about the American Army's losses during this war. It wasn't always just about one team's efforts. It was a whole, rounded war.

But something else was happening. A change was in the air, not in the war, but inside his own heart.

After freeing George Collard, he felt a significant shift in the way he viewed things, and he sensed that Samuel felt it, too. He began to see the war as almost a continuation of the Revolutionary War, and not many Americans wanted that anymore. Collard was an American himself! So many of the Upper Canada soldiers on the British side were either loyalists or part-American. It felt like the Americans were in battle with their own kind again.

The soldiers had sat down for a well-anticipated dinner at the dining house. The amenities within the walls of Fort George were better than anything Jesse had experienced since setting foot in Upper Canada. Many of the Canadian women and children were left behind when the British army fled from the fort. They were put to work in the cookhouse immediately and served up a hot dinner for the occupying Americans. Leaving the women behind was a useful British mistake, especially for the Americans. Jesse watched a few young women serve the food.

His eyes wandered to their ample buttocks. The men were all warned by the commanding officers to keep away from the women, so they knew their boundaries. But nevertheless, like all men of war, their testosterone was high, and they fought off the sexual urges valiantly.

Jesse had sex with only two women in the past, but it was so terribly long ago that he wondered if he would even know what to do now. It was when he had lived in New York City, a time that seemed so distant and surreal now. Between the Overland Astorians and the events leading up to the war, Jesse's life had been in a constant circle of turmoil. He would never dream of inviting a woman into his crazy life. But that didn't mean he didn't think about it. Jesse thought about females more than he cared to admit. His body would respond immediately in ways beyond his control.

A young woman glanced at him briefly, and Jesse immediately glanced down. He didn't need to get reprimanded, and, furthermore, the food looked too delicious.

The chicken stew had swirls of steam rising from the bowl, and the bun served with it was warm from the oven with a slab of butter melting on it. Jesse's stomach growled and almost felt painful. Jesse picked up the bun and stuffed it in his mouth like a starved animal. He gulped water to wash it down and then started on the chicken stew. He completely forgot about women for a moment and just focused on his immediate hunger for survival.

He finished his stew and watched as the mess hall filled with soldiers. Samuel walked in and sat across from him, smiling.

"We made it back," Samuel said.

"Yes, we did," Jesse said, devouring another bun from the basket on the table. They were finally back within the American lines, and it was a huge relief, almost like a homecoming.

"I just heard that our unit is going out tomorrow to occupy more territory," Samuel said somberly. "We better get as much food in our bellies as we can."

Jesse groaned and gulped water. "Not again."

"Yep, again," Samuel responded, staring at the young woman as she placed a bowl of chicken stew in front of him. Samuel nodded gratefully and devoured the food.

⚓

The bleakness of dawn came early as the unit assembled. Jesse was hastily promoted to sergeant, and they were sent out with several other units to begin occupying more territory. Jesse wasn't clear why he was made sergeant so quickly other than they needed more units to spread out and had fewer people to command them. The objective was clear. Take as many towns as possible.

Jesse's unit advanced southwest as the other units approached Queenston. The countryside spread far into the distance as his team tried staying hidden within the tree line, covering as much distance as possible. They walked the entire morning since they had left the fort at 4:30 am. Their feet were sore, and they had barely stopped all morning. The afternoon sun beat down on their heads as they approached a small hamlet.

The unit stayed back within the tree line, assessing the area. A small collection of red coats dotted the streets. Most of them seemed unaware of the imminent American invasion.

Jesse raised his weapon and aimed at the first red coat as his entire unit did the same. He held up a stop hand as everybody held their breath for the signal. Several tall two-story houses lined the streets, and a few women and children sauntered by. Jesse lowered the weapon as several others did the same.

He inhaled sharply and waited until the families had cleared the area. His heart hammered wildly in his chest, and his ears began to ring. Jesse exhaled and continued surveying the scene. The town was only a hamlet. There was one main street, which was barely one block long, with a store and a small restaurant on one side. The other side of the street had family homes. Jesse gulped. He didn't want to kill any families. He just wanted to overtake the town, that's all. The store would be the best place to start.

The store was a square stone building built with the light grey quarry rocks common in this area. It appeared that the British soldiers were picking up items at the store for their units. They probably weren't even stationed here.

Jesse watched as the three British soldiers walked away to their horses, packed the purchases into a wagon, and then mounted their horses. Several agonizing seconds passed while the street was emptied. Jesse held up a stop hand to his unit. He wanted the red coats to leave. The fewer deaths he could manage, the better.

Finally, the British group left the area. The street was deserted.

Jesse waved to his team as they crept into the town with weapons raised. A woman walked towards the store and froze, staring in bewilderment at the American team. Jesse yelled at her. "Go back home! Quietly!"

She turned around and ran away from the store with her hand over her mouth. The unit advanced towards the store.

Before Jesse could react, an elderly man opened the front door of the store with a rifle in his hands. The gun recoiled, and a bullet slammed into one of his soldiers. Jesse fired instinctively at the man's head. The storeowner's body jerked back towards the door, spraying it with blood as his body slid lifelessly down to the ground. Jesse rushed into the store with his team as Samuel helped up the injured comrade.

Then, a woman shrieked behind them.

Several armed civilians came out of the nearby houses and started shooting. Samuel struggled on the street with the injured soldier, then slammed down beside him as a bullet ripped through his shoulder. He huffed heavily as the pain seared through his body, and his face collapsed into the dirt of the road. Samuel blinked, then felt his eyes lose focus, and the blackness of his mind took over.

⚓

Jesse screamed viciously and pointed his weapon through the window, smashing the glass and firing at the houses across the street. The elderly man across the street fell as Jesse's bullet tore through his midsection. The American soldiers launched a steady barrage of firepower across the street for several seconds. Then, just as suddenly, everything went quiet as gun smoke filtered up into the sky. Jesse's heart felt like it was about to burst from his chest.

"Bring our men in," he commanded, nodding at two American soldiers. "We will provide cover fire." He nodded at the others as they positioned themselves in the windows. As soon as the door opened, the American unit opened a steady barrage. The two men ran into the street and dragged the two downed men inside safely. They slammed the door as Jesse ran to the bodies and placed his hand on Samuel's wrist. "He's alive." His heart lurched with hope. Jesse could not lose his closest friend. Not now.

He grabbed the other man's wrist and pressed hard. Nothing. He pressed his fingers on the man's throat to feel for a weak pulse and nothing. The man was dead.

Jesse stood grimacing. "One dead and one injured. We need to stabilize Samuel. Wrap his shoulder." Just as he was finishing his sentence, a barrage of bullets smashed into the stone storefront. Jesse pounced to the floor and lay down, creeping towards the window and removing the pistol from his hip holster. He peered up and was astonished to see the small team of British soldiers returning to the store, shooting at the windows. Jesse fired the pistol, praying that it actually made contact, and then loaded his rifle quickly, aiming into the chaos of smoke. A red coat was at the door! As soon as it opened, Jesse's unit opened fire, riddling the man's body with bullets. The door swung back closed, hanging on one of its hinges.

Jesse's mind swirled as he tried to assess how many more red coats were outside. The smoke began to clear as he saw one more crouching by a horse trailer. The other two appeared to be hit. Jesse fired his rifle as his team continued barraging the lone soldier.

A young boy appeared on the porch of the house across the street and opened fire at the Americans. The soldier to Jesse's left suddenly grunted loudly and fell to the ground. Jesse cursed.

Then, the red coat caught an American bullet and flew backward, falling hard on the street. A return barrage of bullets assailed the American team as another boy appeared on the porch across the street.

Jesse groaned as he reloaded and aimed at the first young boy. He whispered a silent prayer and shot the boy.

The street quieted down as the younger boy jumped towards his brother, screaming. He dropped his weapon, cried loudly, and hollered. "No!"

Jesse could hear nothing else except the ringing in his ears. The smoke settled as a heavy cloud of silence settled upon the massacre. Jesse turned to check on his team. Tears moistened in his eyes as he willed the emotions to leave his body. He crawled over to his remaining soldiers. "Acknowledge me if you're unharmed."

"Here!" several men saluted.

Jesse looked down at the bodies. Five men were down, including Samuel and the first man. The man who was beside Jesse at the window was now dead. Jesse exhaled and removed his cap, running his hand through his hair. He immediately turned towards the street and assessed the danger. The younger boy was still crouched over his brother on the porch, and the British soldiers were unmoving on the ground.

"We're crossing the street to disable that young boy," Jesse said. "Once he gets over his grief, he will start shooting again. We are not killing another boy." Jesse pointed at two men. "Both of you, let's go. We'll go out the back, just in case."

The three-man team rummaged through the store until they exited out the back. Jesse crept against the wall of the building to the front, holding his rifle up. He looked both ways and could see no activity. "Come on," he motioned to the others and ran across the street to the house.

Jesse stomped up the stone steps as the young boy turned around in fright. A moment of anger crossed the boy's face, and then he stood bravely. "Shoot me then. What are you waiting for?"

"I'm not shooting you," Jesse said.

"That's what you came here for," the boy answered. He was no older than eight years old. "You killed my brother."

"I will be the judge of that," Jesse said. "I'm going to approach your brother now to see if he's still alive. You will surrender to my troops." Jesse nodded to his men as the two soldiers grasped the boy's arms.

Jesse knelt down beside the boy and placed two fingers on his neck. A steady, strong heartbeat pumped back. He searched the older boy's body for the wound and found his side bleeding. Jesse grunted and picked up the injured boy. "We need to find a doctor," he said, addressing the younger brother. "Where is the doctor in town?"

"There's no doctor here," the boy replied. "There's a farm outside of town. They fix animals, but not humans."

"Good enough," Jesse said. "Lead our team to the farm. We're going to try to save your brother and my injured team members." He turned to his two men and spoke to the private on the right. "Go back and assemble our team. Grab those horses and that wagon." Jesse pointed to the British horses corralled at the far end of the street. "We're taking the team to a makeshift field hospital."

♔

George heard the guns behind him and in front of him. He felt surrounded. George prayed that he would be able to make it alive to his home. He couldn't stop now. George was well within occupied American territory now. He could feel it.

He had been traveling for two days now. His hair was stuck with sweat against his back, and his boots were caked with mud. George had removed his uniform earlier and stuffed it in his pack, walking shirtless in the heat all afternoon. It seemed the sun was growing hotter and hotter every day. He was so close now, and his hope urged him on. He would see his Clara again!

He estimated that he was within the town's boundaries.

George watched from across the field and then scurried through the neighbor's field. He scrambled for over an hour through shrubs and open fields. The sun beat down on his bare back as George yearned for a cool drink of water. He knew that his canteen was empty, but his home was within sight now!

He entered the forest and scanned the trees for the blue paint markings that he had done himself ten years ago to mark his property. His eyes scanned left then right, finally noticing a blue mark in the distance. He ran to it and smiled as he finally stepped onto his expansive property. It was still another 15 acres to the house, but he felt a rush of gratitude wash over him. He was finally home again!

CHAPTER 17

Zee held a cold rag on her mother's forehead. She had picked up Clara and carried her to the sofa with Charlotte's help. They both stared at their mother. "Momma!" Charlotte shouted. "Please wake up."

Zee bent over and laid an ear on her mother's chest. "Her heart is beating strong," Zee said, grasping her mother's hand. "We need to arouse her again. Please go to the kitchen, Charlotte, and grab some more cold water and a bowl of soup. Momma hasn't been eating well since Pappa left." Charlotte ran into the kitchen as several muffled sounds rumbled in the distance. Zee froze, straining to hear.

Charlotte returned several minutes later with the items, placing them on the sofa table. "What's that noise outside?" Charlotte asked worriedly.

Zee grabbed the towel and dipped it in the cold water, ringing it out. "I don't know," she said, trying to remain calm. "We'll try the cold water again and if that doesn't work, we will have to risk a ride to Welland to call on the doctor to visit."

Charlotte looked at her with a mixture of fear and adolescent maturity. "I will stay here with Momma then?"

"Yes," Zee agreed, placing the cold towel on her mother's face. She covered Clara's nose, chin and neck briefly with the cold cloth, hoping it would shock her mother awake.

Zee quickly removed the towel as Clara jerked awake. "What happened?" Clara mumbled, her eyes blinking rapidly at the ceiling. She turned her head and looked at her daughters with a confused look.

"You're sick, Momma," Zee said soothingly, grabbing the bowl of soup. "It's alright, you're okay now. Please eat some soup right away. You haven't been eating." She held up a spoonful to Clara's lips. "Eat," she instructed.

Clara opened her mouth, accepted the warm soup, and swallowed. She gulped another spoonful and another. Color began returning to her face as her daughters lovingly fed her. When she finished, Clara sat up. "I don't know what happened."

"You fainted again," Zee replied. "This is the third time you've fainted in just the past few days, Momma. You have to start eating better."

"I don't feel like eating," Clara said sadly. "My appetite is gone."

"But you must."

"Yes," Clara replied slowly. She looked across the room at the comfy chair George always occupied. It was his favorite chair, and the family began referring to it as Pappa's chair. "My George."

Zee grimaced. "He's alive, Momma, don't fret."

Clara began crying softly and laid back on the sofa.

"I will get the doctor to come look at you, Momma," Zee said softly. "Is that alright?"

Clara didn't respond. She just kept crying.

The muffled sounds in the distance grew closer as Zee weighed the risks of venturing out. "I think it's safe to leave and get the doctor," Zee stated, looking at Charlotte's worried face. "Welland is farther west from the war than even we are. I heard the Americans were attacking from the north and the east."

"Attacking?" Clara cried worriedly, sniffling.

"Don't worry, Momma," Zee said calmly. "We should be far enough away from the conflict. Nobody would want to bother with this small little town."

Clara's eyes widened, and she started crying again. "My sweet George," she whimpered. "He's in danger."

Zee grabbed her coat. "Take care of Momma. Make sure she is drinking. I will be back tonight." She turned to approach the front door when a heavy set of urgent boots stomped onto the porch.

"Who is that?" Charlotte asked in alarm.

Three loud knocks hammered against the large wooden door.

"I don't know," replied Zee, her face falling into a worried frown as tendrils of fear and confusion raced up her spine. She shoved her feet into her leather boots and grasped open the door.

CHAPTER 18

The large stone house was perched on top of a slight gradual incline. It had a large grand porch spanning the entire front width of the house and two strong stone pillars on each side of the front stairs.

Jesse felt the blood from the boy's injuries moistening the front of his army uniform. His biceps screamed from the exertion of holding the boy for so long. The unit had trekked through the town and into the surrounding farmland, some on horseback, and some had walked. Jesse refused to let go of the boy in his arms. He was going to do whatever it took to save the boy's life. He would not let him die.

Jesse placed a foot on the first stone step and held onto the boy tight. He had wrapped his undershirt around the boy's waist tightly back in the town in an attempt to stop the bleeding. It had worked initially, but after walking with the boy in his arms for almost twenty minutes, the boy's gunshot wound was bleeding again. Jesse grunted as he stepped up the remaining three stairs to the porch and glanced beside him as his unit assembled around him.

He approached the front door and nodded for a teammate on his left to knock.

The large man rapped his knuckles three times urgently on the wooden door.

There was a moment of silence, and Jesse worried if it was all for naught and nobody was home. Then the door opened hastily, and he almost exhaled in relief.

A beautiful, odd woman stood in the doorway. One of her eyes was green, and the other was blue. She had shoulder length blonde hair and had her boots on, ready to leave.

Jesse swallowed and glared into the woman's bewitching eyes. "You have to save this boy!" Jesse commanded, his voice unnaturally stressed. Jesse was close to losing his best friend and this young boy in his arms. He had no time to be nice. Jesse stepped into the large home.

The woman blocked the doorway.

"If you don't step aside, I will force you to," Jesse snarled, surprising himself at his ferocity. "I have two men dead, three seriously injured, and this young boy needs a doctor." Jesse pushed his way into the house as the woman stepped aside. The home was expansive. He walked into the front room and noticed an older woman on the sofa, holding her head in her hands. She was blonde-haired as well and most likely the mother. Several children stood frozen in the hallway. "Look, we are here because we need your help," Jesse stated. "We mean no harm. There is no doctor in town."

The injured boy's brother rushed from behind Jesse's side. "Zelda!" he shrieked. "I had to tell them to come here. Tommy is going to die! He was shot. This is Sergeant Jesse Eastman. He brought Tommy here from the massacre on Main Street."

"Eric?" Zee cried, approaching the smaller brother and placing a caring hand on his shoulder. "That's Tommy?"

Eric nodded with tears in his eyes. "Yes, please save him, Zelda."

Zee bent over close to Jesse's arms and smoothed a lock of hair away from the injured boy's eyes. Tommy's eyes were closed. She laid on a hand on Tommy's forehead. Only a few weeks ago, she had hired both Eric and Tommy to help with the crops.

With a start, Zee realized that she was standing extremely close to Jesse. She looked up with a mixture of confusion and anger, meeting the eyes of the sergeant. "Why are you saving Tommy's life? You are American. You came here to kill us all."

"I did not come here to kill families and children," Jesse stated abruptly.

Zee frowned and pointed to the kitchen table. "Lay Tommy on the table," she said commandingly. "Charlotte!" she shouted, turning around in search of her sister.

Charlotte ran to her side as the rest of the fifteen men entered the house. Two men were on makeshift stretchers.

"Boil a large pot of water!" Zee yelled. "Bring me some cloths too. I'll find mom's needles and threads for stitches." She turned to help Charlotte hoist a large pot of water onto the stone stove. Zee's mind was racing with pure adrenaline. While Charlotte disappeared down the hallway to grab the cloths, Zee ran over to her mother. "Momma!" she shook her arms lightly.

Clara was nearly catatonic on the sofa, covering her mouth with her hands.

"Momma!" Zee yelled. "Where is your sewing kit?"

Elise, the youngest sister, shouted from behind them. "I know where it is!" she yelled. Elise rushed out of the room and returned several minutes later with a sewing box.

"Good!" Zee said. "Thank you, Elise." Zee approached the kitchen and rolled her sleeves up, washing her hands thoroughly. She watched the sergeant lay the boy gently on the table and turned to address her other sisters, Betty and Hanna. "We need all this equipment clean. Needles, cloths, everything. Put another pot on and throw a few kitchen knives in there, too, in case we need to cut out any bullets."

Jesse stepped back from the table and felt his arms relieved of the dead weight. His fingers felt numb, and he was grateful for Zelda taking control. "Thank you," he uttered, speaking his thoughts out loud. "I have two other injured men that need your expertise as well."

Zee turned her head towards Jesse, her sweaty hair falling over her eyes. "Sergeant Jesse, right? That's what Eric said."

Yes," he replied, offering his bloodied hand in a handshake. "Sergeant Jesse Eastman. And you are Zelda?"

"Zee," she replied. "Zee Collard." She straightened stubbornly. "I'm not a doctor, Jesse."

Jesse felt a chill run up his spine. "Collard?" he interrupted suddenly.

"Yes," Zee replied quickly. "Why? Do you know of the Collard farm?"

"I have heard of the Collard farm, yes," Jesse stated, instantly wondering what had happened to George Collard. Did the father make it back home? Was he hiding in the house somewhere? Jesse glanced around and opened his mouth to ask, then closed it abruptly. "I'm pleased to meet you, Miss Collard." He wiped his bloody hand on his pants and offered it in a handshake again.

Zee narrowed her eyes at the strange, young, handsome man. "Well, Sergeant Eastman," Zee replied, shaking his dirty hand tentatively. "I cannot say that I am pleased to meet you."

Jesse didn't know how to respond to that. She was definitely a beautiful woman and obviously strong-willed, too. He kept his mouth shut, wondering how she was going to proceed. His mind reeled in a hundred different directions. He needed this woman to save lives.

Zee frowned at Jesse. "You and your team can help with the injured. Bring them all in the front room and kitchen. Lie them down and assess where the bullets have entered. Remove their clothing and use some sheets to cover them." She turned away from him and yelled down the hall. "Charlotte! Bring some clean sheets, too!"

Jesse nodded appraisingly at Zee. She was unquestionably a woman who would get things done, he mused. "I will do what you say, Zee." He turned and faced his unit. "Lay down Samuel and the two others! Right over there!" Jesse pointed to the open area beside the older woman on the sofa. He walked into the front area and glanced bewilderingly at the mother. "Zee! Get your siblings to take your mother away from here. She looks like she cannot handle much else right now."

Zee looked up, pointing at her twin brothers. "Do as the sergeant asks! Get Momma out of here! Take her to her bedroom!"

Clara glanced up with a confused look on her face as the young boys held her hands. "Momma," Jacob said, tugging on her hand. "Come with us to the bedroom."

"What is going on?" Clara asked suddenly, finally snapping out of her daze.

Zee yelled. "Mom! Go to bed! We've got it under control." Sweat dripped off her forehead as she bent over the young patient's body and pushed her fingers gently against the wound, searching for the bullet.

A moment of silence fell inside the room as Jesse motioned the men to lie down the injured patients in front of the mother.

Zee glanced back up when she realized her mother hadn't moved from the sofa. "Momma! Go with the boys! Now!" she screamed, her voice pitching into a shrill.

Clara stood upright as if a lightning bolt had struck her. "Alright! You don't have to shout!"

Zee frowned at her mother and nodded towards the hallway, motioning for her mother to follow her orders without saying another word.

Jacob and Sam led Clara to the back bedroom as the three injured men were laid out on the floor. Blood streaked the floor as Jesse kneeled over Samuel and removed his friend's clothing. The blood was soaked through Samuel's shirt. Jesse removed it carefully, rolling Samuel over to the side as he cut off the uniform from his friend's body with his knife.

Samuel groaned.

"Hey," Jesse whispered. "You're alright, brother. Hang in there. We're getting you all fixed up."

Samuel's eyes fluttered open briefly. "What?"

"Don't worry," Jesse said, grasping Samuel's forearm in a gesture of male affection. "You're going to be alright. It looks like you were hit in the shoulder. It laid you out good while all the fighting took place. That bullet probably saved your life." Jesse laughed.

Samuel chuckled. "I've never heard that a bullet slamming into my shoulder could save my life before," he mumbled, his voice thick with pain. "But at least I'm alive."

"Don't get up," Jesse stated, laying a restricting hand on his chest. "We'll get that bullet out."

"I don't think the bullet is in me," Samuel responded. "It probably went clean right through me."

"You sure?"

"I've been hit before," Samuel replied. "It doesn't feel like I have a bullet lodged in me. But I can't say whether my shoulder joint is okay. I can't move my shoulder at all." Samuel tried moving and winced. "Hurts like a bugger."

"Pain is a good sign," Jesse said. "It means you're alive and kicking. I'm just going to take a look." Jesse gently unwrapped the bloodied sling his men had hastily secured on. The massacre assaulted Jesse's mind briefly, and it felt like the event had happened yesterday or a year ago, but it hadn't. It all happened not even an hour ago.

Samuel winced as the bandage came off. "How does it look?"

"I'm not a doctor," Jesse replied. "But it looks like you need a lot of stitches to close up this wound. That bullet tore through a good-sized chunk of your muscle." He turned to grab one of the sheets the younger children had placed on the floor. Jesse ripped a piece off and wrapped it tight around the wound as Samuel whistled in pain. "It's okay, Samuel. Hold on. I'm almost finished."

Samuel laid back and winced, groaning loudly. "Okay, that's enough of that."

Jesse stopped and watched his best friend exhale against the pain. Jesse inspected his work and deduced that the sling was repositioned better now. The bleeding was reduced, so that was good. He looked up and glanced at Zee as she was preparing to do surgery on the young boy. Jesse prayed silently in his head.

"Sergeant Jesse," Zee hollered. "I need your help once you've secured all those other injured fellers."

Jesse nodded and patted Samuel's arm. "You'll be okay. Rest for a bit, Samuel." Jesse stood and approached the next man. "I'll be there in a moment," he answered Zee.

Two soldiers laid down the next injured man gingerly. Jesse knelt beside him and examined his body for the wound, removing the man's shirt, coat, and pants. He had several wounds. One bullet was lodged in his forearm, a piece of his ear was blown off, and another bullet looked like it was buried in the man's thigh.

The soldier was unconscious. Jesse's men helped to remove the officer's boots and socks. Then, they tightly wrapped a tourniquet over the man's leg and forearm. Jesse assessed the patient and decided to wrap a tight bandage around the patient's head to cover the ear wound. It was bleeding profusely, and the man was turning pale. Jesse tried to work as quickly as possible. When Jesse was finished, his soldiers draped a thin sheet over the severely injured man.

Jesse stood and felt a rush of dizziness come over him. He grasped the wooden entryway.

"Charlotte, get Sergeant Jesse some water!" Zee yelled. "Immediately!"

Charlotte quickly poured fresh water into a tin cup and ran over to Jesse.

Jesse nodded thankfully and took the cup, gulping down the cool water. He walked gingerly to the kitchen table.

"Are you alright, Sergeant Jesse?" Zee asked.

Jesse sat down at the table and placed his hand on the boy's knee. "Don't worry about me, just save this boy."

"I can't save him without your help, Jesse." Zee frowned. The sergeant was almost sickly thin, and she noticed his collarbone sticking out from his shirt. She searched the room for her sisters. "Hanna, bring Sergeant Jesse some of that chicken soup. I need him alert."

Hanna rummaged in the cupboards for a bowl, then ladled the soup into the ceramic bowl and brought it to Jesse.

Jesse's stomach growled, and he realized for the first time that he had very little to eat all day. He only had a porridge breakfast and had starved for almost a week before arriving at Fort George. Without another word, Jesse spooned the warm soup into his mouth hungrily and continued until he had devoured it all.

"Looks like you were mighty hungry," Zee stated, grinning softly. "Now, could you come over here and hold both flaps of his skin together while I stitch Tommy's side up? I have removed the bullet already."

"Certainly." Jesse stood.

"Wash your hands first," Zee instructed, pointing to the sink behind her.

Jesse wandered over to the sink and was appalled at the state of his hands. He had blood all over himself. Jesse removed his overcoat and inspected his chest just to make sure it wasn't his own blood. When he was satisfied, he scrubbed his hands with the tallow soap. The basin turned a bright red as the blood rinsed clean from his hands. Jesse lathered the soap into his hands another time to remove all the blood and dirt. When he was satisfied his hands were clean, he dried his hands and returned to the table.

Zee glanced directly at his naked chest, then abruptly looked away. "You are good and clean now?" When Jesse nodded, she pointed to the boy's bloodied side as she dabbed it with a cloth. "Keep these two sides together for me, and I will continue to dab the blood away while I stitch."

Jesse grasped the boy's side, pulling both sides of the skin together as instructed. As Zee began to stitch the wound closed, he caught a whiff of her womanly scent. It was a heady mix of sweat, animals, and flowers. He glanced at her fingers as she weaved the stitches through the boy's skin. "Will he live?" Jesse asked.

Zee exhaled as she concentrated on the next stitch and paused, her hands briefly shaking. "I'm not a doctor, Jesse," Zee stated. "I have only worked on animals before and my own family. I can only do what I know to do. I can't promise that Tommy will live."

"Well, whatever you know is more than any of us right now," Jesse replied.

Zee nodded and continued stitching the wound closed. Tommy was a good, hardworking ten-year-old boy. He had helped with clearing the fields for the corn crops at the end of last summer. His younger brother, Eric, had helped along with five other boys. Zee wouldn't have succeeded in planting the corn this May without them. Tommy had even come back to help with the seeding. She owed it to the boy to save his life.

She didn't feel the same about the other injured soldiers bleeding in the front room.

"How does it look?" she asked Jesse, stepping back from the stitched wound.

"It looks good," Jesse replied, inspecting her work. "You do better work than you think."

"We'll have to keep an eye on it and make sure we keep the area clean for the next week," she said, frowning and placing a hand on Tommy's forehead. "That is if he makes it through the night."

"He must," Jesse stated.

"What makes you so intent on saving his life?" Zee asked. "Your men shot him. Didn't they?"

Jesse looked directly at her. Her right blue eye twinkled as her other green eye stared into his soul. "We had to. Tommy was shooting at us from his front porch. One of his bullets killed one of my soldiers. We had no choice but to stop the barrage of bullets. We tried not to shoot him fatally," Jesse explained. "It was not an easy thing for me to do." Jesse stumbled on his words and was disappointed that he inadvertently confessed.

"You're the one that shot him?" Zee asked incredulously.

"Yes."

"Why save his life then?" she asked. "Why walk with him in your arms all the way to bring him here?"

Jesse sighed. "I don't kill women and children. I'm not a savage." He straightened and helped Zee lay the sheet over Tommy's body. He glanced into her strange eyes. "I'm a human being."

Zee looked into his eyes for several silent moments, then finally broke the gaze. She walked over to the basin, washed her bloodied hands, and then dried them.

"I need you to work on my two injured men also," Jesse commanded, speaking over her shoulder.

Zee was silent. She knew that she was in no position to refuse but would not voluntarily concede either.

Jesse approached the sink and washed his hands vigorously with the soap. He exhaled with relief that she hadn't refused. He dried his hands and looked up when a small baby's cries echoed from the end of the hallway. Jesse noticed Zee's head instantly snap up. "Is that your baby?" he asked.

She hesitated for a brief second, uncomfortable with telling a lie. "He's my baby brother," she answered. "I must go see him." She started down the hallway as Clara showed up with the baby in her arms.

"He's hungry," Clara said. "I will feed him. Don't worry, Zee. You have lots of other things to do."

Zee glanced from her mother to Jesse. "I didn't agree to become a doctor for injured Americans."

"No, you didn't," Jesse said. "But you must. One of the injured soldiers is my closest friend. I cannot lose him."

Zee grunted undecidedly. "So now I must care about your feelings?"

"I would hope that you are a human being like myself."

Zee raised her chin and looked towards the front room. "Which one is he?"

"His name is Samuel," Jesse answered, pointing. "He caught a bullet in the shoulder, although he says it went clean through him."

"Just stitches, then?"

"Yes."

"And the other injured man?"

"He has three wounds," Jesse stated solemnly. "Leg wound, arm, and his ear. He's lost a lot of blood."

"Okay, we will start with him then."

"He may not make it," Jesse replied.

"Well, let's see him," she stated, walking over to the injured men on the floor.

Jesse walked with her, motioning Zee towards the severely injured man. He was lying prone on the floor with his head flopped to the side. Jesse knelt down and placed a hand on his wrist. His face twisted into a dark frown.

"What is it?" Zee asked, grasping the man's other wrist. She felt up and down his wrist, pressing hard into the man's arm. "There's no pulse."

"He passed while you were both stitching up Tommy," another soldier said, standing up off the sofa.

Jesse knelt down and slowly covered the body entirely.

Zee watched Jesse and began appreciating his gentleness, along with his swift, commanding behavior. "Is this Samuel?" she asked, pointing at the man lying on the floor with a sling on his arm.

"Yes, I'm Samuel," he responded, sitting up. "It feels like the bullet went through me cleanly. It knocked me out for a while, but I came to."

Zee knelt down to Samuel. "Can you get up? We can help move you to a kitchen chair while I examine the wound."

"Sure."

Jesse instantly rushed over and helped him stand, then snaked an arm under Samuel's good shoulder. "Come on, brother, I got you."

"You are brothers?" Zee asked.

"No," Jesse answered. "But close enough. We've lived throughout the Northwest and back."

"The Northwest?"

"Long story," Samuel replied, wincing as he stumbled to the kitchen chair and sat heavily.

"Put your elbow on this hallway table," Zee said, grabbing a small, narrow table and dragging it to Samuel.

Clara watched from the kitchen, mesmerized. She spooned oat porridge into Xavier's mouth as the house turned into a hospital. When Zee neared the kitchen, the boy opened his arms and smiled when he saw his mother.

"Xavier!" Zee cooed. "Aren't you a happy boy today?"

The baby giggled and yelled out. "Ma!"

Jesse glanced at Zee as she temporarily hid her face. "Sometimes he thinks I'm Momma."

Jesse laughed. "He's a cute boy."

"He is!" Zee replied. "He's already learned a few words!" Zee beamed like a proud parent.

Jesse patted the boy's head. "Wish we could be as happy as you, Xavier," Jesse chuckled.

Zee unwrapped the sling and started examining Samuel's wound. "This will hurt a tiny bit," she said. "I'm going to prod the wound to see if there is still a bullet in there." Zee pressed the sides of the wound in a circular motion. Samuel winced several times, but Zee held his arm firmly still.

"You're good at this," Samuel said.

"I'm better with horses, cows, and goats," she replied, chuckling.

"You should have been a doctor," Samuel stated.

"I'm better at farming," Zee replied. "Now, hold still." She grasped his arm and blotted the blood away, grabbing a clean towel with soapy water to cleanse the wound. "I'm cleaning everything up, then I'll stitch it closed. You should be fine, but you won't be able to shoot anybody with that right arm for a while." Zee finished cleaning the wound. "That's a good thing. This war needs to stop. It's taking too many good men."

Jesse watched Zee tend to Samuel and kept his eye on his remaining soldiers. One was looking out the large side bay window. "What is it?" Jesse asked loudly.

The soldier turned around quickly. "I saw some movement by the barn."

Jesse straightened. "Take someone with you and approach with caution," he commanded. Jesse turned to Zee. "Are you expecting anyone?"

Zee shook her head. "No, nobody has been around for a while, and the corn crop has been planted, so none of the workers should be outside," she replied. "Don't shoot any more boys! It could be one of my young helpers. There are no men left because of the war. My horses are in the barn. Don't you harm them!"

Jesse chuckled. "You heard the woman," he said. "Don't shoot, just investigate."

George Collard watched the house quickly being taken over by a small squadron of Americans. He cursed to himself as he hid behind the wild raspberry bush. It was in full bloom and thorny, too. A few thorns had torn his jacket, and he tried to crouch as low as possible to avoid detection.

George could feel his heartbeat in his ears. He was seconds away from reuniting with his wife, and the Americans had stormed the house before him.

George wanted nothing more than to run into the house with guns blazing but knew that it would most likely be a suicidal attack. There were at least seven men, all armed. They were carrying an injured boy and another small boy had followed.

He had watched the entire scene play out before him, and it took all of his willpower to stay hidden.

George pondered over his next move. He had to somehow at least get the letter in Clara's hands. His heart broke inexplicably upon thinking about her. He sat momentarily powerless and let the emotions consume him. Tears of frustration began to fall from his eyes and silently ran down his cheeks.

He was so close! He is home!

If he entered the house, he would die or be taken prisoner. And that wouldn't help anyone.

Suddenly, he heard a baby cry. It was a faint cry at this distance but undeniably a baby's cry. His mind swirled in confusion. There's a baby in the house? Clara wasn't pregnant when he left. It made no sense.

George grunted and stayed in the bushes longer until he could be certain that no one was looking out of the side bay window. He knew this side of the house gave a clear view of the raspberry bushes and the barn. George estimated the distance to the barn was twenty yards from the raspberry bush. During the circumstances, it was a long distance, but he could make it in a minute if he ran swiftly. But that would most likely alert someone to his position. He could crawl in the grass, but that would make him an easy target if a soldier was posted as a lookout.

George chose to run.

He crouched like a tiger and counted in his head to ten, calming his nerves. When he got to ten, George bolted from the bushes. His legs pumped hard as he sprinted to the barn, expecting a bullet to find him at any moment. It was the longest minute of his life. When he reached the barn, he yanked the large red door open and closed it behind him, breathing heavily.

No shots followed him. He had reached the barn undetected!

He pondered his next move and knew what the most successful option would be. George could return to the British army based at Beaverdams and get a team of soldiers to reclaim his house, alerting the British to the American's expanding territory in the process.

He pulled out the letter from his overcoat and thumbed the seal. It was still intact. Clara's name was on the front. He needed to at least get this to her. George knew in the depths of his heart that Clara would not last much longer without him. She needed him as much as he yearned for her. She was very attached to him. Even when they first met, Clara had said that they were soulmates. He believed it to be true.

George scanned the barn quickly. The horses neighed and snorted in acknowledgment. He stepped quietly through the barn, looking for a spot where Zee regularly worked. It had to be somewhere she would intuitively find the letter and give it to Clara. He spun around at a sudden noise and saw the tool room at the back whisk a gust of wind into the barn as the door rhythmically slammed shut. He had never fixed that loose door. George silently crept towards the back where the saddles were, wondering if Ewart was here or in the house. The creaks and shifts of movement in the barn were from the wind, nothing else. George assumed that Ewart had either run off or was a prisoner in the house. It certainly appeared like no one was in the barn.

George stopped and scanned Zee's tool room. He approached the rough wooden table. On the workbench, a small pocket hung open for tools and such. It was the perfect spot. George slipped the letter into the pouch just as the large red barn door opened.

⚓

"Surrender!" one of the soldiers hollered into the darkness of the barn. "This is the American Army. We are not here to harm you, but you must surrender." They heard a movement at the back. A door was hitting something repeatedly. "Make yourself known!" The soldier shouted again.

The two men advanced into the barn cautiously, with their weapons at their sides. They were jumpy and uncertain whether it was another boy or an animal. They weren't going to shoot a boy and would just turn back if it was an animal.

The wind howled through the large barn as the men stepped warily into the damp darkness. "Make yourself known!" the lead soldier growled. The door kept hitting something, grating on their nerves. They both jerked involuntarily as the horses nickered at them. "Dammit! We can't see anything. There's no windows in here at all."

The back door kept hammering onto something rhythmically. Then something fell, and the men both raised their weapons instinctively.

"Surrender!" the lead soldier shouted in panic. "Or we will shoot!"

The wind howled in response.

The men advanced closer to a small workshop in the back and flinched involuntarily as the door continued hammering louder and louder as they neared the area. Both men raised their weapons to eye level.

A gust of wind blew in their faces as they flanked the workshop archway. The lead soldier nodded to the other man, gesturing for him to take up position for support.

"We are coming in," the lead soldier declared. "Hands up in surrender! Or we will shoot!"

A horse whinnied again.

The door slammed again as the lead soldier jumped into the workshop, his rifle raised.

The wind gusted at him.

There was no one inside the workshop.

He waved his partner in as they both crouched inside the workshop.

A large, red, broken door slapped against the outside of the barn. The lead soldier straightened as the door continued its barrage against the frame of the old barn. The wind blew strongly into the workshop, continuing the barrage of wood against wood.

The lead soldier narrowed his eyes and advanced to the door, nodding to his partner. As he reached the door, he aimed his rifle towards the entrance and cautiously grabbed the swinging door. A gust of wind blew in his face, and dirt flew from a nearby bush. He instinctively aimed towards the bush as a flock of sparrows flew out in surprise.

He straightened and gazed outside at the approaching sunset. The skies were swirling with orange and pink clouds as the sun shone directly in his eyes. He flinched as more birds made their hasty retreat.

"There's nobody here," he stated, grasping the door and pulling it closed. He inspected the broken latch and turned to his comrade. "Grab something to close this stupid door! I've had enough of this endless slamming!"

CHAPTER 19

The morning sun streaked into Zee's bedroom as her eyelids slowly opened. The house was quiet and felt surreal. Her groggy mind momentarily forgot what had happened the day before, and she moaned, rolling onto her side.

Her mind began slowly awakening, and then she remembered with a start that the Americans had invaded their homestead yesterday. Zee sat up quickly.

She blinked and watched the clouds momentarily obscure the sun. Her home had been converted into an American field hospital overnight. An American doctor had been called in and had arrived before she had fallen asleep. It had been the longest day in Zee's life. The doctor had inspected the two patients and praised the work that Zee had done. The American doctor had even said that she had saved the boy's life and, most likely, Samuel's as well.

Zee stretched and then relaxed wearily against her bed frame.

A thousand thoughts ran through her mind, some angry and some caring. She was furious that her home was taken over but grateful to have saved Tommy's life. His little brother, Eric, had stayed the night, falling asleep by his brother's side.

As the events of the previous day unfolded in her mind, she felt like the day was somehow not real. It seemed like a fable. Slowly, she began analyzing yesterday's events and accepting it as reality.

Zee, unexpectedly, found herself thinking about the handsome Sergeant. She knew it was wrong, but something about Jesse made a big impression on her. He was a tall, slim man, almost emaciated, but strong and willful. Almost like herself, she thought. Zee had lost all of the pregnancy weight and worked herself so hard that her frame was very slim now. Zee's stubbornness was what made it possible for her to take care of an entire farm.

But yet, she was powerless against the armed takeover.

She was furious at Jesse for taking over her home, but she didn't fear him. Sergeant Eastman was one of those men who had integrity. She could feel it right down to her toes.

It didn't help that he was so ruggedly handsome. His hair was a dark brown, and his matching dark eyes had bored right through her body, making her skin tingle every time he looked at her.

When he had stretched out his bloodied hand, she had to restrain herself from instantly shaking hands. His demeanor was commanding but friendly. He wasn't much older than herself, she deduced. Zee could sense a roughness about him as if he had survived many hardships and still somehow came out as a good man.

She shuffled to the end of the bed and stretched her neck up, wondering why her mind couldn't stop thinking about him.

"Jesse Eastman," she whispered, letting her hands fall onto her lap. "Why are you here?"

Jesse heard the floorboards creak and jerked awake, instinctively grabbing his weapon. He smelled her before he could see her. It was Zee. He had spent the entire day yesterday working closely beside her, saving Tommy and Samuel's life. He couldn't get the smell of horses and flowers out of his head. Jesse placed the weapon silently down and watched her pad softly into the kitchen. She was clearly trying not to awaken everyone.

Jesse laid still and just observed her. She was a tall woman. He guessed she was 5 foot 10 inches, maybe a bit shorter, but still quite tall for a female, or a man for that matter. Some of his unit soldiers were shorter than her.

He grinned abruptly, remembering how she had instructed his unit to save the wounded. Zee Collard was a woman with a backbone.

Jesse continued laying on his side with a hard pillow under his head, watching her long arms filling the coffee container and placing it on the stove. She briefly flung her hair to the side as she leaned forward to grab the coffee grounds from the cupboard. Her small butt was shaped like a lovely upside-down heart, and Jesse felt his penis twitch involuntarily.

He hadn't been instantly attracted to a woman in a very long time. Jesse wondered if he had ever been attracted instantaneously to anyone before. Most of the women in New York City that he had slept with were interested more in him than he was in them. Jesse had sex with two women when he was in the city. He had reasoned at the time that he was a young man and needed sex, like any other man.

He was right, partially. Jesse enjoyed sex, but he had always wished for a wife whom he was undeniably attracted to. A special woman and not just anyone. He wanted to relate to her on a deeper level. Maybe he needed someone who was a lot like himself.

Jesse shifted and stretched, yawning uncontrollably. His back hurt from the endless days of fighting and living on the edge of survival.

Zee turned immediately and stared at him through the kitchen archway. "You're awake," she stated softly. "I am making coffee. Would you like some?"

"I would love some coffee," Jesse answered, shuffling to a sitting position, then slowly stretching his body to standing. Several other soldiers started stirring as Jesse padded tiredly to the kitchen, running a hand through his matted hair.

"You look like you could use a coffee," Zee said, throwing wood into the stove and lighting it.

"It has been a rough few weeks, yes," Jesse replied. "I am immensely grateful for your hospitality, Zee."

Zee grinned lopsidedly, charmed by his response. "Coffee should be ready soon," she stated, leaning against the counter, eyeing him appraisingly. "Looks like you could use a big meal of eggs and potatoes for breakfast."

"I haven't had eggs and potatoes for breakfast in months," he responded. "Last time was at Queenston."

"You fought at Queenston?"

"Yes."

"Were you injured?"

"Nope," he replied. "I was captured by the British army, along with my friend Samuel. We were held as prisoners for a while."

Zee nodded and placed a pot on the stove, grabbing a burlap bag of potatoes from the cabinet. She looked up as Jesse sat at the kitchen table. "How long have you been friends with Samuel?"

"Almost three years now," Jesse replied. "He's saved my life a few times, and I've saved his. He's like a brother to me." His stomach growled as he watched her cut up the potatoes and plunk them into the boiling water. "Thank you for saving his life and Tommy's."

"Why did you care so much about Tommy?"

"I couldn't live with myself if I had killed that boy."

"Oh," Zee replied, watching the potatoes slowly return to a boil. "Well, I'm glad you had the sense to bring him here. Tommy and Eric had helped me plant this year's crop of corn. With no men in the family and a house full of children and women, I needed those boys."

"You don't have a husband?" Jesse asked without thinking.

Zee stopped and narrowed her eyes at him. "No, I do not," she answered. "My father was called into the war. We haven't seen him since June of last year."

"I'm sorry."

Zee titled her chin up. "I miss him." She grabbed several cups and poured hot coffee into them. "I was able to run the farm on my own," she stated proudly. "Barely, but I did it."

Jesse stood slowly and grabbed one of the cups. He sipped the hot brown liquid graciously. "Oh, this coffee tastes good. Thank you."

Zee smiled. "You're welcome."

Several other soldiers wandered into the kitchen, following the aroma of fresh coffee. They each grabbed cups as Zee frowned at Jesse. When they left the kitchen, she addressed Jesse. "So, I am a caterer to all your soldiers now?"

"No," Jesse answered. "We can bring our own food and supplies in. One of my men can cook. I'd rather have you working as a valuable nurse."

Zee drained the water from the blanched potatoes and dumped them into a sizzling pan. "You think I will be your nurse prisoner, then?"

Jesse chuckled. "I didn't say any such thing. I would appreciate the help, but we can always bring in more soldiers to do the job."

"So, you are taking over my home permanently as a field hospital?"

"Nothing's permanent in this war," Jesse replied quickly.

Zee quietly stirred the potatoes and grabbed another pan for the eggs. "This war is stupid," she stated. "My father is an American. My grandfather was a loyalist who fought at Germantown. You guys are fighting your own people here."

"Are you from Philadelphia too?" Jesse asked, his interest in this woman increasing with every minute.

"No," she answered, cracking several eggs into the cast iron pan. "I was born right here. In this house."

"You've never left?"

"Nope," she replied. "My family needs me too much."

Jesse examined Zee appraisingly as she fried four eggs. "I would have expected a beautiful woman like you to be married off to someone right away."

Zee froze, then quickly recovered, flipping the eggs over and speaking tartly. "My parents tried. I'm too willful. Strength is not a good wife trait, apparently."

Jesse stood, gulping the rest of his coffee down, and approached the stove for another.

"I will make another pot," she said, changing the subject of discussion. "You are hungry and thirsty."

"I haven't eaten well in over two weeks."

"Why?"

"Long story," Jesse replied, unsure if he could trust this woman completely. "I have lived to tell too many tales."

"You aren't that old," Zee replied. "I would guess you are my age."

"I'm twenty," Jesse replied. "But I have been through more than most men my age."

"I'm sorry to hear that," she replied. "I turned twenty last April, too."

Jesse laughed. "You were right, then. We're both the same age."

Zee grinned as she placed four eggs and a large serving of fried potato hash on a plate. "Yes, that we are." She shoved the plate towards him. "Eat. I'll make some more coffee and get you a glass of fresh cow milk."

"I appreciate this, Zee," Jesse said, grabbing the plate and returning to his seat at the table. The aroma of fried potatoes and eggs wafted up to his nostrils. He picked up the eggs with his hands and started eating.

Zee laughed. "Wait! I will get you a fork!" She rummaged through a kitchen drawer, returning with a fork, and placed it in front of him.

"Sorry," he replied, glancing up at her. "It's been a long time since I had a good meal."

"I see that," she said, chuckling.

Jesse devoured the breakfast like an animal and gulped down the two glasses of milk while Zee prepared another pot of coffee. She turned sideways as he placed his plate on the countertop. "Your soldiers will just have to be satisfied with fried potatoes. I don't have enough eggs today for everyone."

"Thank you, Zee," he replied. "I'm sure they'll be happy with whatever you offer them."

⚔

Tommy had regained consciousness that evening. Zee spoon-fed him a watery beef stew and gave him lots of water to drink.

The boy was thirsty, drinking almost four cups of fluids. Tommy had lost a lot of blood, but the color was slowly returning to his face.

He scowled angrily at Jesse from across the room. "Those Americans tried to kill me."

"Jesse shot you, yes," Zee answered. "But he also saved your life bringing you here, and he carried you across town in his own arms."

"Why would someone do that?" Tommy asked incredulously. "Shoot me and then try to save my life?"

"I don't know," Zee answered. "He said that he couldn't live with himself if you died."

Tommy frowned and laid back tiredly.

"Rest up, Tommy," Zee said. "The doctor says you should recover fine, but you'll need a lot of rest."

Tommy's eyes blinked tiredly, and he lay back on the pillow.

Samuel was sitting behind her on the large front room sofa. "Tommy doesn't understand war. Every soldier has his morals. Jesse's just happens to be higher than the average man's."

Zee turned to face Samuel. "I suppose you are right," she replied, getting up to look at his wrapped shoulder. She placed a gentle hand on his forehead to check for signs of fever. "You seem to be doing well. No signs of infection. How's your shoulder feeling?"

"Doctor says I should be back to normal in a week or two," Samuel answered, looking down at his sling. "Just will take time to get my shoulder working again, that's all."

Zee frowned. "I don't understand war," she stated, sitting down beside him. "It inflicts suffering on the innocent and the brave, without much sound reasoning except for some political rhetoric."

Samuel nodded in agreement. "I don't understand it either." He smiled momentarily at the welcomed female attention. "Thank you for fixing me up. I appreciate it, Zee." He paused. "You Canadians aren't too bad after all."

She smiled. "You Americans aren't so awful either."

Samuel sat up straighter. "Jesse didn't expect a house full of children, you know. He told me that he just wanted to save my life and the boy's."

Zee smiled. "I'm starting to understand Jesse a bit more."

"He's a good man."

⚓

Jesse stood on the front porch outside. The cool May evening caressed his thoughts as the gentle gusts blew in his face. He turned and gazed inside the house, looking through the large bay windows. He saw Samuel talking with Zee as she sat beside him on the large sofa.

Jesse instantly felt a pang of jealousy. He wanted to go inside and steer Zee away from his philandering friend. Jesse took two giant steps and stopped himself. He had no right to be jealous over Zelda Collard, he told himself. She wasn't his possession, nor did Jesse even know that she was attracted to him. He stepped back slightly. That wasn't entirely true. Jesse strongly suspected that she was attracted to him.

He had caught the way she had gazed at him several times. Zee had this sweet, glossy look in her eyes whenever they talked. Maybe it was his mind playing games with him, but Jesse sensed an instant chemistry between them. It was like nothing he had personally ever experienced before.

The first time they had met was definitely chaotic and they both never had a moment to reflect on everything. But now that he thought about it, Jesse noticed her smiling whenever he was close to her. Maybe she just smiled a lot.

But Jesse could smell her every time she was in the room! Then, his heart always did a funny flip-flop in his chest. Zee must like him, he thought. He was almost sure of it now. Jesse grinned and felt almost as if there was an invisible magnet pulling them together.

Or maybe that was only what he wanted, he thought. Maybe Zee didn't feel the same.

Jesse continued staring as Samuel continued chatting with Zee on the sofa. He could not hear the details of the conversation; only a hum of human voices filtered through the exterior stone walls. Jesse strained his ears and realized it was a futile, immature effort.

He turned away and faced the midnight air as the full moon shone before him, illuminating the fields in front of the house. Jesse pondered about the coincidence of meeting her father, George Collard, outside Fort George, and he wondered again what had happened to the man. Jesse hoped that George was still alive and prayed that he knew enough to stay away from the occupied house. Jesse did not want to become embroiled in a homestead war.

He ran his fingers through his hair and sat down on the porch swing, deliberating on his future and the outcome of this war. Every day seemed to bring new reasons to support his grievances against this war. Shooting Tommy had badly affected Jesse. That could have been Zee's brother or a young woman's child.

Jesse Eastman was no murderer, but the war was molding him into just that, and he didn't like it. Jesse was a good man; he knew this deep inside his soul. Nothing would ever change him, not his father, not the Western Frontier, and definitely not this war.

The door creaked open, and Jesse turned his head abruptly.

Zee stood at the entrance, closing the door behind her quietly. "It's a beautiful night," Zee said softly. "Full moon."

A few frogs croaked in the midnight moonlight. "Yes," Jesse answered. "The moon is bright tonight."

Zee walked over to the porch railing and leaned against it. Jesse instantly stood and offered his seat to her. "Here, take my seat."

Zee giggled. "It's a two-seater swing," she said, taking two strides toward Jesse. "It'll hold both of us."

Jesse instantly became uncommonly nervous and sat back down on the swing as Zee sat beside him. "Are you sure?" he asked hesitantly, cursing himself for the slight crack in his voice.

"Yes," she replied calmly. "I couldn't care less what others think. I feel comfortable enough around you. We saved lives together."

Jesse shifted on the seat to allow her room, unsure of what he should say next. His mind was preoccupied with Zee's unique scent of flowers and horses. It was a strange, intoxicating mixture of farming and femininity.

The moonlit night blanketed them with a moment of silence. All they could hear for several minutes were the mating calls of the frogs in the darkness and the crickets in the fields. The moon cast a bluish glow on everything. The bushes, the trees, the porch, and the grass all danced together in a vibrant blue nightlife. The air was rich with moisture, and the sky lit up with a thousand stars.

They both stared with fascination at the beauty of the midnight symphony.

Zee's mind churned with a million deep thoughts. "Samuel thinks highly of you," Zee stated quietly.

"He does?"

"Yes," Zee replied. "He said that's why he would always be by your side." Zee folded her hands on her lap and looked down at them. "You have a devoted friend there."

"We've been through a lot."

Zee stared out into the moonlit wilderness, wondering what drew her so strongly to this man.

"We were part of the Overland Astorians," Jesse continued. "We almost died traveling the Mad River. Spent over a year in the wilderness before finally coming back home. We almost died of starvation twice."

"Oh my," Zee replied. "That's why you were so hungry with those eggs I made. I had no idea."

"I suppose so," Jesse laughed. "We spent a few weeks eating rabbit and lynx when we escaped Queenston and arrived back at Fort George. The wilderness seems to be a crazy lure for me." He stopped and wondered if he should be telling her all this. "We were starving when we got back to Fort George. I felt it all come back to me, and I refuse to eat my boots again."

"What?"

"Oh, nothing," Jesse said, laughing. "Just another day of survival in the Northwest." Jesse paused briefly, certain that she had no idea what he was talking about. He tried explaining further. "We just had one day of meals at Fort George, and they sent us out again. I haven't eaten well in over two weeks, and I wasn't too keen on starving again."

"Oh, well, I can see to it that you are well-fed here, then."

Jesse blinked and gazed sideways at her. "You would do that for me?"

"Of course," she answered, turning to look directly at him. "You saved Tommy's life. No average soldier does that."

Jesse watched her eyes glow in the night and felt his heart flip flop again. The silence of the moonlight descended upon them once again, and Jesse could not stop gazing into her bewitching multi-colored eyes. "Your eyes," he stated.

"I know, ever since I was young, I was an outsider," she said. "The doctor said it's very rare to have two different colored eyes. It doesn't affect my sight. I can see fine. It's just that people look at me differently, as if I am somehow deformed."

"You're not deformed," Jesse stated. "You're quite beautifully unique."

"Thank you," Zee glanced down demurely at her folded hands, unsure of what to say next.

Jesse placed his right hand along her chin and lifted her face to meet his. Zee's eyes glittered in the night. He shifted closer and pulled her chin slightly towards him, kissing her soft, full lips.

She groaned lightly, a sensual utterance from the belly of her soul, as she kissed him back.

The porch swing slightly swayed as they continued kissing, the moment almost seemingly suspended in time. Jesse placed his other hand along her waist and instinctively pulled her towards him. She molded right into him as they embraced without breaking the kiss.

Her tongue slipped into his mouth, and Jesse thought she tasted like milk and honey. He swirled his tongue into her mouth as she melted in his arms. His body instantly reacted quite strongly. His penis hardened immediately, the blood rushing to his groin almost painfully. He kissed her harder and deeper, urged on by a primal desire void of thought or reason.

Zee could feel her body soften in his embrace and wondered about all the uncontrollable sensations that were hijacking her body. She wanted to feel him all over and experience his skin on hers. Zee wanted to see him naked in the moonlight and kiss him all night, right here on the porch. The thoughts were seizing her rational mind.

Jesse felt her urgency and matched her intensity, roaming his hands all over her body through her clothes. The fire within them was lit and quickly spreading without any further thought.

A loud door click broke the stillness of the midnight air. A man stood at the front door and coughed uncomfortably.

In an instant, Jesse tore away from Zee and stood straight up, staring awkwardly at the intruder.

"Sorry, Sergeant," the soldier said. "I was just coming out to tell you that we were all going to sleep for the night. I didn't mean to interrupt."

Jesse grabbed the door, slightly embarrassed at his lack of control. He glanced back at Zee. He smiled sheepishly as her face blushed a bright pink, and she looked away briefly. Jesse composed himself and turned to his team member. "Thanks for letting me know. We were just preparing to come in for the night." He outstretched his hand to Zee and guided her back into the house.

CHAPTER 20

After weeks of promises to send troops to the Collard household, George stood stubbornly at the Beaverdam's commanding room door with Lieutenant James FitzGibbon. George had been reinstated as sergeant and had mixed feelings about the war now. He looked around the rough log structure and noticed a strange lady with a soiled white dress standing across the desk from all the men.

"Who's the woman?" George asked.

"This is Laura Secord," FitzGibbon answered, waving towards her as an introduction. "A group of Indians found her. They brought her here."

"Why is she here?"

"Mrs. Secord overheard American commanders detailing a plan to attack Beaverdams," FitzGibbon replied. "She trekked almost 20 miles through bush and enemy lines to forewarn us."

"That's quite the hike," George replied, shifting his weight to his left foot nervously. He loosened his shoulders in defeat, knowing the answer before he asked the question. "What about my family and my household? When are we going to take it back from the Americans? I've been here for two weeks now, waiting to assemble a team."

"We need all our resources in Beaverdams right now," FitzGibbon replied. "Mrs. Secord could not give us an exact date for the planned assault on Beaverdams, so we must be prepared. We have sent some scouts out to report the American's movements, but for now, there's no way I can send a team to battle directly on your homestead." FitzGibbon leaned on his right hip as if to say the matter was concluded.

George narrowed his eyes slightly and felt his blood boil. He would go back by himself if he had to.

FitzGibbon relaxed his stance slightly, knowing George Collard was one of Upper Canada's best soldiers. He didn't want to lose him. "Look," FitzGibbon said in a more conversational tone, stepping towards the front door and grasping George's arm lightly. He gestured outside to keep the conversation more private. "If we storm your household, there may be civilian casualties, and that may include your family. Do you really want to risk a frontal assault on your home?"

"The Americans have taken over my home!" George yelled a bit too loudly. "How would you feel if it was your home?"

"I understand, George," FitzGibbon responded. "I really do, but your presence here is much needed. If we manage to ambush the American's plans, then this war may start coming to an end. Your family is safer if the Americans withdraw." FitzGibbon walked casually with George to another log structure. "I know it's not ideal, but we did send scouts out to survey your household. It appears the homestead is now operating as an American field hospital. They are caring for the injured and dying there."

"And forcing my wife and daughters to nurse the Americans!" George exclaimed.

"There has been much worse around here," FitzGibbon responded. "Your family is still alive. Your oldest daughter appears to have taken the brunt of the nursing work."

"Zee?" George said aloud.

"Is that her name?"

"Yes, Zee Collard."

"Well, Zee Collard is holding things together for now," FitzGibbon said, trying to calm George's emotions. "For now, the situation is stable. Let's not make it unstable." FitzGibbon stared directly at George's face, analyzing the man's intentions. If George Collard left to recover the Collard farm on his own, then he'd have no choice but to reprimand him.

George's eyes softened. "You may be right."

"I am right," FitzGibbon stated. "I haven't been a Lieutenant for this long, for no reason."

George stopped at the front door of the secondary log structure. "But we have such a small regiment here," George stated. "How will we thwart a large-scale American attack?"

"The Mohawk warriors were the scouts sent to Fort George," FitzGibbon replied. "They will be the ones who can force the Americans to surrender."

"How?"

"With the simplest emotion in mankind," FitzGibbon stated, removing his sweaty commander's hat and peering straight into George's eyes.

"And what's that?" George asked, genuinely confounded.

"Fear," FitzGibbon answered simply.

True to his word, on June 24th, 1813, approximately 500 American soldiers and the commander Boerstler surrendered to FitzGibbon. With very little loss of life, the plan was a success.

Over 400 Mohawk warriors fought in the shadows along an enclosed, wooded section of the trail near Beaverdams. As the Americans advanced under Boerstler's command, they were ambushed and threatened repeatedly over three long, terrifying hours. When FitzGibbon arrived with only 50 of his own troops, he attempted to negotiate a surrender. It took a bit more persuasion, but eventually, the surrender was complete.

George was relieved. He would be able to go back to his home now. George was granted a team of fifteen soldiers to dissolve the Collard Farm military hospital.

⚕

"There's more coming," Jesse shouted, opening the door to the oncoming American unit carrying wounded soldiers.

Samuel grabbed the door with his good arm. "Tell the unit to come in!" he urged. "I will keep the door open."

Jesse stepped around a wounded soldier with a bleeding leg wound on the front porch. The injured soldiers had just arrived thirty minutes ago with news of a large surrender at Beaverdams. Jesse walked briskly to the American unit that was limping towards the field hospital. Jesse raised his hand and motioned. "This way, men! You've reached the correct field hospital. You're safe here. We will tend to you. Whoever can walk, go right into the front room. An American doctor will attend to you." Jesse watched several men pulling a makeshift stretcher with a neck-injured man on it and directed his instructions to the man in front. "We'll need to have him on the front porch. Keep him on the stretcher. We don't want to move him too much."

The injured soldier moaned as they carried the stretcher onto the deck. Miraculously, the man's eyes were open, but a bright red gash spread around his neck, spilling blood over his shoulders and down his arms.

Jesse bent down. "You'll be in good hands," he said reassuringly. "We'll have the doctor see you in a moment."

Zee stepped onto the porch. Samuel continued to hold the door open for several other injured soldiers who were still able to walk. One man had his ear blown off, and another was holding his bloody left arm. It was a motley crew of injuries ranging from life-threatening to minor, and the sight had Zee swallowing against the bile rising in her throat. She always thought she was a tough girl, but this war was entirely something else. Zee had never experienced war before, and its bloody aftermath was not easy to witness.

She stood motionless and stared at the carnage making its way into the house and onto her porch. Words couldn't come to her mouth. She began to speak and then stopped. It seemed every word didn't seem right somehow. Her thoughts jumbled from outrageousness for having her home invaded in such a bloody mess to gross disgust for her selfishness. She was half American. It all seemed like needless suffering for two countries who were so closely related to be fighting like this.

Zee sat heavily on the porch swing as she watched Jesse speak reassuringly to the bloody man on the stretcher. She had grown quite fond of Jesse in the last few weeks. They had kissed again several times but had never managed a private moment together for longer than a few minutes. Her mind swirled with conflicting emotions about Jesse. She pondered why she was attracted to him so strongly and still could not understand it, other than his demeanor, which was so calming and masculine. It was futile to resist.

At that moment, Jesse peered over his shoulder and met her eyes. He nodded his head and summoned her wordlessly.

Zee instantly stood and walked over to his side.

"This man has a neck wound," Jesse said. "Please call the doctor and have him attend to this man first. I need you to assess the rest of the soldiers based on urgency. Start by numbering them so the doctor knows which one to start on next." Jesse placed a reassuring hand on Zee's arm. "Your expertise is valuable to me. I trust you can stitch minor wounds, and I can help you sterilize items, whatever you need."

Zee nodded. "Yes, Sergeant." She turned and walked back into the house like it was all a dream.

Jesse sat waiting by the stretcher until the doctor appeared several seconds later. "Here, doctor!" Jesse said, his voice unusually high-pitched. "Neck injured. We're trying not to move him."

The doctor rushed over and began examining the patient. He barked out many orders, and the surrounding men scurried around for the requested items. Jesse walked into the house, and the scent of blood wafted up to his nostrils. He looked for Zee and found her in the kitchen with an injured soldier sitting with his bloodied arm on the table. She looked up and met Jesse's eyes.

"There's a bullet lodged in this man's forearm," she said, her voice sounding oddly calm. "He needs the bullet removed and stitches. If you can hold him down, I will remove the bullet and wrap the wound tightly to prepare for stitches."

Jesse grabbed the man's arm and pinned him down as Zee started the minor surgery. She pulled a pair of forceps from the boiling water and began pushing the bullet out of the wound like a sliver. Zee dabbed the blood away methodically every few seconds so she could see the bullet. She positioned the forceps into the wound. "Hold him still. Firm grip."

Jesse laid his weight on the man's arms. "Look away," he instructed.

The soldier turned his head as Zee inserted the forceps, fished around for a good grip, and then finally pulled the bullet out amidst seething yelps from the patient.

"It's all done now," Zee cooed. "You were great. We will wrap it up, and I will come back for the stitches after the disinfection has done its job." Zee held the bottle of whiskey over the wound. "Bite this," she said, offering him a rolled-up piece of fabric.

The man chomped down on the fabric as the whiskey seared through the wound, and he let out a blood-curdling scream. Jesse immobilized the man's arm from flailing and held him firmly.

"It's alright now, Jesse," she said. "You can let him go." Zee wrapped the wound tightly and patted the man's soldier. "You did well. I'll be back to do the stitches after I see to all the rest of the patients."

Jesse slipped his hand into hers briefly and squeezed her hand lightly. "Thank you," he whispered. "I know this is hard for you."

Her eyes warmed at his touch. "I know it means a lot to you," she responded. "Let's get the rest of these men fixed up."

The week had been long and tiring. Zee felt like her muscles were rubber, and her mind was turning to mush. She cradled her son in the early morning and sang softly to him in her bedroom. After the hospital chaos in her house, Zee relished in the solitude of her bedroom. She couldn't even keep track of how many minor surgeries she had completed. She just wanted out of this house. Zee wanted to run away with her baby and flee from all this suffering.

But her family was here.

Her momma wasn't in any shape to run things. Most days, Clara was a patient herself. Her mind was degrading, and her energy was faltering. Clara lay in bed most of the time and barely awakened on some days.

Zee was afraid for her mother. She didn't know what to do to help her. The little comforts she tried had failed. Zee had little energy left at the end of the day but still managed to always cook a wholesome stew or soup for her family. The American army had begun cooking their own food and even brought in supplies. The Collard homestead was no longer a home.

Zee hummed the last part of the song to Xavier over and over again. The monotonous repetition lulled Xavier to sleep. Zee watched his baby eyes blink heavily, and finally, his head lobbed into the crook of her arm.

A soft knock sounded at the door. So quietly that Zee wondered if she had imagined it. At first, she froze and just listened.

Then she heard it again.

She quietly placed Xavier in his bassinet and pulled the door open a crack.

Jesse's gentle eyes seared through her body. "I'm sorry for interrupting you," he whispered. "Can I have a word with you?"

Zee jutted her chin out and then relented. She would do anything for Jesse. "Come in," she whispered back. "Be very quiet though. I just put Xavier to bed. He was fussing a lot." She opened the door wide for Jesse to enter.

The room was relatively small but decorated surprisingly feminine, with lace curtains and several vases of dried flowers. A few masculine touches adorned the walls and dressers. A painting of wild horses, several carvings made out of bull horns, and a used horseshoe with a bouquet of dried colored leaves added a unique touch.

"I love your room," Jesse commented immediately, gazing across the room. "It speaks volumes about the kind of woman you are." He quietly closed the door behind him.

Zee smiled. "Thank you."

Jesse smiled back, glancing at the sleeping baby boy. "He's quite a darling, isn't he?"

"Xavier is honestly a gift from heaven," Zee answered. "He's changed me so much."

"I didn't know you before," Jesse replied. "But it seems your baby brother has a wonderful mothering effect on you."

Zee looked down immediately. She was awful at lying. Her eyes always betrayed her.

"What is it?" Jesse asked, a veil of concern washing over his face at the sudden silence.

"Xavier is my baby," Zee murmured, almost too quietly.

Jesse leaned forward, wondering if what he heard was correct. He blinked and touched her knee, sitting on the bed beside her. "He's your baby?"

"Yes."

"Why does everyone think he's the youngest sibling?"

Zee hung her head down in shame.

"You don't have to tell me," Jesse said quietly. "I am just curious."

"I got pregnant with one of the farmhands," Zee replied almost soundlessly.

Jesse nodded and grasped her hands, letting the silence blanket their delicate conversation.

"I'm not the kind of woman many men would like to marry," Zee stated.

"I would," Jesse blurted out before he could think of the hidden meaning behind the words. He stammered. "I mean, if I were a suitor, I would be interested." He exhaled and looked up at the ceiling, rolling his eyes. "Now I've just made us both uncomfortable." He chuckled quietly. "You're a gorgeous, interesting woman with many talents beyond your years. How could anybody not appreciate that?"

Zee looked into his kind, brown eyes and squeezed his hands. "Thank you," she replied. "Nobody has ever said such wonderful things to me before." She jutted her chin out again.

Jesse reached over and wrapped his arms around her shoulders, hugging her tightly and murmuring into her hair. "We've never had much chance to talk, given everything that has gone on." Jesse buried his face in her hair. "You smell as beautiful as you always do." He relished in these brief moments with her. It was like the only sunshine in his day, it seemed. But he knew that it would come to an end sooner or later. He could not keep her and her family prisoner for much longer. It wasn't humane.

Zee loved the feel of his manly scent surrounding her and melted in his embrace. She wanted him more and more each day but didn't know how to tell him. Her mind wandered, and she wondered how he felt. "Why did you come knocking this morning?" Her heart thumped, hoping the answer was what she wanted to hear.

Jesse pulled away briefly and looked into her entrancing eyes. "I wanted to set you and your family free from this prison of medical emergencies."

"What do you mean?" she asked, appalled yet thrilled at the chance at freedom. A streak of disappointment crossed her face, and her eyebrows frowned slightly in response.

Jesse cupped her chin, knowing he had hit a nerve. He had to step carefully and explain things to her in detail. He inwardly chuckled, knowing that he had grown to become quite close to her. "I do not want to keep you and your family against your will in this American hospital anymore. It is not right." He frowned. "I can help you all escape into the barn, and then you'll be free to go." He searched her eyes and noticed the darkness of disappointment again. He added quickly. "To be honest, I don't want you to go. I am becoming quite fond of you. But I don't want you to be held as a prisoner here anymore, either."

Zee's heart soared at his last words. He was falling in love with her as she was for him. He didn't seem to know it, Zee mused. She steeled her nerves and straightened. Zee Collard could never let this man go. He was better than any man she had ever met in her entire life. She didn't care if he was American or part of the army sent to destroy her country. All that mattered was the man behind the armor. Jesse Eastman was the man for her, and no amount of hell or heaven could steal him from her. Zee followed his blinking eyes and spoke strongly. "I will remain with you wherever you go, Jesse Eastman. You aren't getting rid of me that easily."

Jesse's lips curled up into a boyish smile, and his eyes lit up with surprised joy. "You continue to surprise me every day, Miss Zee Collard."

Zee chuckled. "I hope that's a good trait."

"It definitely is," Jesse responded and leaned towards her for a kiss.

Her soft lips opened and allowed his mouth on hers. She tasted like sweet honey with a slightly salty taste. Jesse's hands encircled her body and pulled her into him as they molded into one effortlessly. Her lips were supple and soft as he kissed her passionately. His tongue darted inside her mouth, and she moaned, releasing a deluge of hormones into his penis. His erection awakened in an instant, and he shifted uncomfortably as Zee began to rub her fingers along his back, pulling him impossibly closer. She turned and laid back, pulling him with her onto the bed. Her eyes glittered with mischief, and Jesse felt his penis poke into her thigh.

Zee curled up towards him and ran her hands over his thighs, meeting his erection.

Jesse momentarily held his breath as her hand pressed onto his erection, smoothing over it. "I'm sorry, it happens when I'm around you."

"Don't be sorry," Zee replied. "I like that." She blushed momentarily at the words and chuckled softly. "It means you really like me."

He held himself on his elbows over top of her, gazing down at her lustfully. "I think you're right." Jesse lowered his mouth and kissed her lips again. The sensations traveled up his body, into his arms and legs, even his brain. His mind felt cloudy and full of passion. He didn't want the kiss to end.

Zee moaned underneath him, and it sent his senses instantly spiraling. He grasped her buttocks and gently squeezed them. She groaned again and began kissing his ear.

"Shh," he whispered. "You'll awaken the household."

Zee muffled her groaning against his uniformed shirt. "Yes, you're right," she breathed.

Jesse peered down at her and searched her eyes. He could feel something special happening between them. It was like a slow, glowing fire that just continued getting warmer and warmer. The more he understood Zee, the more he began to love the woman she was. He had never felt love for a woman before, but he was sure this was what he was feeling.

He watched her squirm underneath him. Her lovely face was surrounded by the morning sunlight streaming through the windows. If he could capture this moment and suspend it in time, he would.

Jesse smiled. "You look so beautiful right now."

Zee opened her eyes, the green one glittering emerald in the sun, and the blue shone with a darker aqua ring. "Jesse," she murmured. "I want you inside me."

Jesse felt his penis jump in response and willed his erection to calm down. Jesse smiled and kissed her gently on the lips. He pulled away slowly and lavishly, extending the kiss to its maximum effect. Finally, he slowed it down and pecked her lips softly. Jesse gazed into her eyes as Zee abruptly reached into his pants and palmed his penis.

He stiffened and held his body up like a board for her to explore with her feminine hands. It was the most exquisite feeling in the world, having this special woman touch him everywhere.

Zee watched his reaction with every touch. His eyes closed, and his body was stiff, but his throat let out a muffled moan from deep inside his masculine body. She unbuttoned his pants and began pulling them down.

His penis sprang free, and she smiled, tentatively rubbing her cheek against the hard ridge.

Jesse moaned again, a deep guttural groan escaping from somewhere inside his body, and then shuddered from the incredible sensations. He watched her loving his penis as he shucked the remainder of his pants off. He leaned to the side as she explored his body. She ran her hands along his scrotum and raised her hands up into his shirt. Jesse immediately shucked off his shirt as well, throwing it on the floor. He peered at Xavier, who was sleeping peacefully. He turned back to Zee and watched as she pulled the nightgown over her head, revealing her gleaming nakedness to him. Her round breasts bopped onto her chest, and her small blond mound between her legs summoned him. He grasped her a bit too roughly and shifted her back onto the bed, laying fully on top of her. Jesse pushed a knee in between her legs and opened her thighs.

Zee groaned heavily, and Jesse clasped his hand over her mouth. "You must be quiet, my love," he whispered. "I don't want any of the other soldiers knowing or Xavier waking up." He removed his hand. "Do you understand?"

Zee nodded obediently. "Yes, Sergeant," she replied provocatively.

That sent him over the edge, and he pushed his penis between her legs, feeling her moist entrance beckoning him.

"Jesse," she whispered sensually. "I want to feel you inside me."

He slid his groin closer until finally, he felt the tip of his penis moistened by her vagina. Jesse could hold back no longer and plunged into her wetness, sliding slowly but steadily until he reached the deepest end of her cervix. He panted hard and breathed the words out. "You feel so wonderful."

Zee was beyond words. Her eyes were closed, and her hair was splayed all over the pillow as she panted for more. "Yes," she whispered quietly in his ear, over and over again.

Jesse pulled slowly back out and felt her vagina grip him like a suction. He pushed back into her depths as a deluge of hot fluid coated his penis. He clenched his teeth for control and squeezed his eyes shut. Jesse couldn't look at her beautiful body anymore. He would just immediately ejaculate if he did.

He slowly kissed her lips and laid his weight fully onto her. She moved with him and kissed him back, angling her thighs into his groin at every pump of his hips. Her skin felt exquisitely soft, and her vagina was so warm it was almost hot. He continued slowly kissing and pumping his hips slowly into her. Jesse found his rhythm and continued his steady thrusts into her vagina. At every push, he felt her tightening a bit more, and her body became tenser with every thrust.

Zee suddenly groaned, and Jesse instinctively cupped his hand over her mouth. He felt her vagina squeeze his penis, almost milking him and knew that he could no longer hold back control anymore. Her legs began to shudder, and Jesse inhaled sharply, then pushed back into her vagina, pressing past the clenching entrance. He pushed harder until he reached her depths again and held it there, panting on her shoulder.

"I want your seed," she whispered.

Jesse obeyed instantly without thinking and groaned rebelliously. His sperm shot into her depths and flooded her vagina in several long streams, pulsating inside her warmth. His hips instinctively rammed into her, desperately trying to reach as far as possible. He suddenly pulled back, realizing what he had just done, and pulled out.

He kissed her lips and smoothed her hair, slipping his body alongside her. Jesse cradled her head into his chest and kissed the top of her head. "If there's a baby in there, I won't let you raise him alone," he murmured. "I'm sorry, I should have pulled out. I should know better."

"No, don't be sorry," Zee replied. "I wanted all of you, Jesse, every single drop. I adore you, Jesse. It was perfect. I wouldn't change a thing."

Chapter 21

"I need to check on my horses," Zee said to a group of soldiers standing around in her home.

The soldiers looked at one another for answers and shrugged. One of the soldiers said noncommittally. "One of us should go with you."

Zee glanced uncomfortably at Samuel, then searched the room for Jesse. She couldn't see him. It seemed that he wasn't in the house.

Samuel stood and waved at the men. "Sergeant Eastman will escort Zee to the barn." Samuel opened the front door and walked out. He returned seconds later with Jesse.

Zee tried to stop the smile from spreading across her face. Her eyes glowed, and it appeared that Jesse was stifling a grin as well.

"You have to check the horses?" Jesse asked.

"Yes," Zee replied. "And the goats and cattle. It's been too long. I have to make sure they have enough hay and oats."

Jesse waved her to the front. "Let's go then."

She followed obediently as a small group of soldiers watched. The house was filled to full capacity. Over twenty-five soldiers, doctors, and cooks inhabited the home now. It was no longer a home; it was a cramped hospital now. Zee was glad to get out, even if it was only for a few hours.

They stepped onto the wet grass and walked towards the barn, conscious of several pairs of eyes on their backs from the house. It was impossible not to feel the alluring chemistry between Jesse and Zee. The two often locked eyes and had this curious, glazed-over look on their faces. Zee tried her best to hide it but she was steadily falling in love with Jesse. Since they had made love a few days ago, neither had managed to find another opportunity to touch each other, except for a quick goodnight kiss every night. Jesse made sure he felt her lips on his mouth every midnight before bed, and Zee was grateful for the nightly affectionate embrace.

It was a calm, hot summer day, and the light breeze lifted Zee's hair as she walked. She swung her arms casually as they trekked up the slight incline to the barn. Once they were out of view, Jesse linked his hand into hers and continued the trek to the red barn.

"I like how warm your hands always are," Zee commented, deep in thought.

Jesse smiled. "I like your hands too." His mind was curiously foggy when he was with her. Jesse daydreamed of her often when she wasn't around. His admiration for her grew every day. "You are a strong woman. Your hands are a little bit rough but still feminine. Perfect, in my opinion."

They reached the barn, and Zee opened the large door. The horses whinnied outside upon hearing the door. Zee and Jesse stepped into the hot, muggy barn. Several goats and horses shuffled into the large barn, excited to see Zee again. She had come to the barn more regularly than anybody knew, but this time, she had wanted Jesse to come with her. Zee wanted to introduce Beauty to him. "Beauty!" she called out and clicked her tongue.

The large grey mare galloped across the field and slowed as she neared the barn. Zee opened the back door wider to greet Beauty. The large horse whinnied and snuggled her large snout against Zee's arms. She looked at Jesse and wondered if he loved animals, too. "This is Beauty," she said, stroking the mare's neck.

Jesse reached out immediately, stroking the mare's neck. "Aren't you a beauty?" he said, smiling. "Just like your namesake."

Zee chuckled and grabbed a saddle. "Did you want to go for a ride? I have a bay gelding as well."

Jesse's eyes lit up. "I would love that. I just wouldn't want to go too far. The war is closing in around us."

Zee nodded. "We won't go far," she said, motioning with her hand. "Grab that saddle over there, and let's go."

Jesse hoisted the saddle expertly off the wooden rack as Zee grasped the reins of the gelding. When she stopped in front of Jesse, she was pleasantly surprised that he knew how to saddle a horse.

He grabbed the pad first and laid it onto the gelding's back, then Jesse returned to the saddle, hoisting it over and cinching the straps underneath. The horse obediently stayed put, swishing its tail occasionally, knowing he was going for a ride.

"This is Harry," Zee said, impressed at Jesse's skills. "You seem to know horses well."

"Harry," Jesse replied, clucking his tongue. "Well, I was part of the Overland Astorians, remember? We traveled quite a distance on horseback and returned back home the same way. I was indebted to those horses for bringing me back alive."

"Oh, yes," Zee responded. "I suppose you would have spent a good amount of time in the wilderness."

"An understatement," Jesse countered. "I barely survived."

"And then you came home to a war?"

"Yes, precisely."

"Were you forced to join the war?" Zee asked.

"Sort of."

Zee finished saddling her own horse, put one foot in the stirrup, and hoisted her body over top of Beauty, settling comfortably onto the mare. She looked down at Jesse with a questioning frown.

"I could have paid for someone to go instead of me," he replied simply.

"Why didn't you then?"

Jesse mounted the gelding and grabbed the reins expertly. He looked straight at Zee. "Because the war needs men like me." With that, he trotted out of the barn, leaving Zee to catch up.

Zee smiled and galloped to meet him outside. She pointed to the bushes near the rear of the property. "We can go this way. There's a small horse trail." She galloped ahead of him to lead the way.

As they neared the bushes, she slowed to a trot and entered the thick shrub on a well-worn path. Jesse followed behind as the forest beckoned them. Once inside the forest, a symphony of nature crooned. Several different species of birds sang, some flew away, and a few squirrels scurried up the tree trunks. A deer bolted in the distance.

"What a beautiful land!" Jesse exclaimed. "Have you lived here all your life?"

"I was born here," Zee answered. "Never had a good enough reason to leave." She chuckled and pulled the reins in, slowing the mare to navigate the rough portions of the path.

Jesse watched as Zee handled her horse exceptionally well. He was impressed with her wide range of skills. "You've been working on a farm your entire life?"

"Yep," Zee answered immediately. "Nowhere else I'd rather be."

Jesse grinned as Zee guided the horses through the forest, teaming with life. "I think I would feel the same about this area. It sure is beautiful!"

"I was thinking of planting some fruit trees, but Pappa said fruit is always too much work."

Jesse paused at the mention of her father. "Mr. Collard is proud of you," Jesse stated. "Most likely, he is. You've taken care of everything since he left."

Zee felt the hairs on her head stand up. "Do you know my pappa? You speak of him as if you know him."

Jesse rode his horse quietly behind her for a few minutes before answering. "The truth?"

"Preferably."

"Yes," he confessed. "I met George Collard during the war twice."

Zee stopped her horse and looked back at Jesse. "You've met him?" she asked astonishingly.

"Yes, I met him when I was a prisoner of war in Queenston and one other time."

Her face brightened. "How is he? Does he look okay? Was he injured? We know so little! Nobody has sent word or anything for a year."

"He's fine," Jesse replied. "He wasn't injured."

Zee frowned at the sudden lack of information. "You must tell me more."

"I only met him twice."

"When was the second time?"

Jesse coughed nervously. "Just over a month ago."

"You saw him recently?" she asked excitedly.

"Yes, we recognized him from Queenston. George gave us his water canteen at Queenston. The kindest man we had encountered so far."

Zee ran the sequence of the events through her mind. "Where did you see him the second time? He was supposed to come back for a visit, and we feared he was dead!"

"He is alive and well," Jesse stated, trying to avoid the questioning.

"Is he nearby?"

Jesse exhaled. "I suppose you should know the truth."

Zee inhaled sharply. "Please."

"I almost shot him," Jesse answered, quickly describing the events. "He surrendered to myself and Samuel. I questioned him, and he told us about the Collard farm, his wife, and seven children. We let him go."

Zee's heart twisted in her chest and then soared. "You didn't tell me."

"I'm telling you now."

Zee's heart crumbled. She could not be angry with him. Her Pappa was alive and well! She examined Jesse's face and realized she was deeply in love with him. He had released her father! She smiled. "You are a good man, Jesse. I don't know how else to convey this, but Pappa means a lot to my mother and this family. We desperately need him back." Zee circled the horse towards Jesse. "Thank you, Jesse."

Jesse sighed heavily in relief. "Like I told you," he replied slowly. "The war needs men like me."

"You are certainly right about that, Mr. Eastman," Zee said, climbing off her horse. "We can rest the horses here for a bit, and then we'll go back." She approached Jesse as he disembarked. Zee reached over and hugged him fiercely. A deer pounced from the woods in the same instant, making her flinch.

Zee and Jesse froze, staring through the trees for several minutes. When they were certain nothing was out there, she turned back to Jesse, holding his arm. "You are a valuable man,

Jesse. Don't let anyone ever tell you differently. Integrity and values are what defines the men from the beasts in war."

🜨

George watched the sunrise on the horizon. It had been a full five days of assembling a scouting team, and they were due to arrive at the homestead in another hour. His heart hammered in his chest with worry.

The cautionary words of FitzGibbon rang in his head. Do you really want to risk a frontal assault on your home?

George didn't want any of his children or his wife to catch a stray bullet in the fight to reclaim his home. He also couldn't just sit and do nothing. He had to see what was going on with his own eyes. If the conditions were right, they would take back the Collard farm. But if they weren't, he'd have to decide what to do next.

His family's safety was more important than anything.

He entered the woods with his team quietly and methodically. His heart raced at the thought of seeing his wife and children again. As abruptly as the thought entered his mind, it was replaced by fear. A rustling sound echoed far away in the woods. He saw a deer pounce through the trees and immediately crouched down, cautioning his team to do the same. He had hunted in these woods many times. The deer only pounced when there were people or predators nearby.

He strained his ears and heard a faint, familiar female voice. He briefly pondered the source of the voice, then almost stood straight up when he realized who it was. It was Zee! His mind rejoiced and then instantly recoiled when he heard a muffled male voice speak back to her. He couldn't make out the conversation, but it didn't sound like she was in distress.

George silently moved closer, then froze. He noticed a movement to his right. George held up his hand for his team to be still. He squinted through the forest and surveyed the area as he had done so many times before. The green leaves and bushes obscured his sight as he scanned the forest for the sight of his daughter. Then George heard her voice again. He could barely hear it, but he was almost certain that she was laughing glee-fully. George stayed rooted to the spot.

A horse's hooves stopped abruptly as a squirrel raced up a tree.

George strained to hear more but could not. He peered through the bushes and caught a ray of sunlight glinting off her head of blond hair. His heart raced as he glimpsed the random sight of his daughter. George smiled with long-awaited grate-fulness. It was her! She was strong and healthy, standing tall.

He watched the scene unfolding as his heart yearned to race through the trees and embrace his daughter. But he knew he could not. He had to know who the man was. George searched the area where she stood. Then suddenly, the mosaic of trees revealed a man nearby. The man wore an American uniform.

George instinctively gripped his rifle, his knuckles turning white. His temper boiled, and he fought to control his reflexes.

Then Zee chuckled again, saying something softly to the man. Suddenly, as clear as the sunlight could offer, George saw his eldest daughter hug the American affectionately and then kiss him.

George's body froze as he analyzed the events unfolding before him. He exhaled as silently as he could, gripping the rifle tensely. He peered through the trees but could see no more than vague figures in the distance.

He heard a few female murmurs and chuckles. George's emotions dueled between rage and love. He couldn't believe his daughter was kissing an American. Out of all the men she could pick! Zee, of course, would pick an American soldier, the worst choice right now.

George pursed his lips. He, himself, was an American. Nothing wrong with Americans, his mind countered. But something was definitely sinister when it was during a war! George strained his ears to listen and heard Zee's voice exclaim something indiscernible. He stopped and a chill ran over him as he noticed the tone of her voice.

It was full of joy.

His heart fluttered open, and George immediately felt a warm rush of parental love for his daughter. Zee may be captive, but she was obviously very happy.

George inhaled and knew what he had to do.

His family was okay. Zee was falling in love. Finally, he thought. After all those years of matching her with unsuitable men, she had finally found a man on her own. He released the grip on the rifle and watched the pair kiss again in the woods.

His team stood motionless behind him.

George held his hand up again to order them to stay.

His heart told him what he needed to do.

He must leave and return when the Americans are gone.

George waited hidden in the bushes for what seemed like an eternity until, finally, his daughter and the American rode the horses back to the barn.

George let out a sigh of relief and frustration as he commanded his team. "My family is fine. We're heading back. I won't risk my family getting shot in the crossfire." He waved his men on as they headed back to Beaverdams. "Let's get out of here. Zee has everything under control."

⚓

They had returned to the barn in no time. Zee had asked Jesse to help with the hay and oats for the animals. They fed and filled the water troughs for the animals for over an hour, then finally entered the barn.

"One of the troughs needs some fixing," Zee said, opening the back man door, which was flapping in the wind again. "I have some tools in the back." She entered the shop as Jesse waited. She rummaged through her tools until she found the hammer and nails, then felt her hand brush lightly over something white. Her eye immediately focused on the strange item, and she wrinkled her nose. It wasn't something that belonged here. She grasped the object roughly and saw that it was a letter!

She stared at the offending object as if it was a bomb. She quickly scanned the inscription on the front, and it was her father's writing! She smiled gleefully and stuffed the envelope into her pocket without any further motion.

"Did you get the hammer?" Jesse asked, walking into the shop.

"Yes," Zee replied, turning abruptly. Zee grasped the hammer and shoved her hand deep into her pocket, making sure the letter was hidden from sight. She turned towards the back door. "Let's fix the troughs and get back to the homestead before anybody starts worrying."

"Good idea," Jesse responded cheerfully and followed Zee out of the barn.

CHAPTER 22

Zee sat down quietly on the chair beside her mother's bed and opened the letter. "Momma, wake up." She lightly shook Clara's shoulder. "Momma, it's important. I found a letter from Pappa."

Clara's eyes immediately blinked open. "What?"

"I found a letter," Zee whispered. "In the barn."

"In the barn?"

"Yes," Zee whispered. "He must have been watching the house and left the letter for us. I want to read it with you." Zee fingered the seal and handed it to Clara. "Open it."

Clara sat up in her bed, rubbing her eyes. "Is it really a letter from George?"

"Open it, and we'll see."

Clara ripped open the seal and pulled out the folded letter. She read it aloud.

My sweet Clara,

This war is troublesome, and I yearn to be back home with you. I am fighting a war I didn't ask for.

The Americans surrendered during the Queenston battle, and I am unharmed. I want you to know that I am strong. I have persevered more than any other man here because I have a family that needs me. Do not doubt my strength and conviction, Clara. If you ever think of such thoughts, expel them from your mind. I will not die without seeing you again, my love.

I miss you more than words can describe. Every night, I lie here thinking of you and my children. But most of all, it is you, Clara, that my heart beats for. You are my one and only love. My heart yearns to see your loving smile again. I hope that day will be in the very near future.

I can't wait to see you. I will be requesting some time off to go home, hopefully soon. I am alive and well, still at Queenston. They will be sending me back to Fort George in the next upcoming weeks and hopefully, then I'll be able to go home for a few days and kiss your wonderful lips again.

Darling, don't worry. I will be back home soon. I love you so much, my dear Clara.

- George Collard, November 20, 1812

Clara looked up, her eyes wet with tears. "My George," she said, swallowing hard.

Zee smiled broadly. "He's alive and well!"

Clara immediately started sobbing heavily.

"Momma!" Zee exclaimed. "This is great news! We finally heard from Pappa! I know it's tough emotionally, reading his words, but he's alive and well!"

"No," Clara stated in a weak voice, thick with emotion.

"What do you mean?" Zee asked.

"George is dead," Clara mumbled, sobbing heavily.

"What?" Zee asked incredulously. "How can you say that? We have a letter in his own handwriting!"

Clara sniffled and pointed at the bottom of the letter. "Look at the date," she said ominously. "November 1812. Over six months ago." Clara burst into a river of tears and collapsed onto the bed, releasing the letter.

Zee grasped the letter before it fluttered to the floor and reread the letter, staring at the final date. "Momma," she said quietly. "He is not dead. Listen to his words! He said not to doubt his strength and conviction."

Clara couldn't hear her daughter from the sobs shaking her body.

"Oh, Momma," Zee said, patting her mother's shoulders. "Don't think the worst." She sniffed the air and could smell her mother's sweat. Zee frowned and tried to soothe her mother, but she knew it was futile. Her momma would get something in her head and never believe a single word another person could say.

But Zee knew that Pappa was alive! Jesse had seen him recently. Zee opened her mouth to tell her mother then clamped it shut. Momma would question her about how Jesse knew about George Collard and then Zee would be pressed to reveal her relationship with the American Sergeant.

Zee smoothed her hand along her mother's shoulders. "He's alive, Momma. Trust me."

Clara blinked through the tears. "You don't know that."

"He's alive, Momma! You must believe it!"

Clara curled herself into a ball and sobbed into her knees, overcome with grief.

After several minutes, Zee shook her head bewilderedly and quietly rose to leave the room. Clara grabbed the blankets and pulled them up to her face, sobbing into the thick cotton bedding. Zee glanced back and closed the door quietly, hearing the door click close.

She would tell her mother soon.

Jesse could sense something had disturbed Zee. Her mind had been in a faraway place for the past few days. He wished he could read her mind and know what she was thinking. Jesse wished he could convey his feelings for her.

Every day that passed by, he felt his heart grow warmer and warmer. Today, he had awakened and immediately wondered what life would be like without her. If the Americans continue having losses like Beaverdams and Queenston, they might be ordered to leave. What would he do then?

He didn't want to leave Zee Collard behind. Ever.

He wanted to take her with him to America. But he instinctively knew that she would refuse. She was proudly Canadian. He felt honored to be the man whom she had chosen. Or had he chosen her?

Jesse gazed out at the descending sun and marveled at the beautiful sunset glowing like a fire in the sky.

A movement caught his attention, and he quickly glanced behind him.

Samuel waved and quietly sat down on the front steps with Jesse. Samuel looked up and admired the glowing colors of the sunset, flitting back and forth along the darkening clouds. Samuel spoke first. "Do you love her?" he asked.

The question caught Jesse unaware. He had been asking himself the very same thing. Just hearing it spoken was like a nugget of truth hanging before him. "I ask myself this every day, it seems," Jesse replied. "I am not sure that I know what love is. I have never experienced any such emotion before."

Samuel nodded and remembered feeling the same way many years ago. "I felt like that once," he said slowly. "I didn't know it was love until she was gone. Then it was too late."

"Did she die?"

"No," Samuel replied. "Her family moved, and she left with them."

"Didn't you try to stop her?"

"No."

"Why?" Jesse asked sincerely.

"Because I was too stupid," Samuel said. "Believe me, I still regret it to this day." Samuel exhaled and rubbed his beard. "I should have told her that I loved her. I should have asked for her hand in marriage. But I was too young and inexperienced to know what I was feeling."

Jesse rubbed his stubbled chin thoughtfully. "You think I should tell her?"

"If you love her, yes. If you don't, then you should stop what you're doing. You will only hurt her and yourself."

Jesse nodded and roamed his eyes along the vast landscape. "How do I know if I'm in love?" Jesse asked thoughtfully.

"Good question," Samuel replied, laying his pistol down thoughtfully. He mindlessly started disassembling it. Samuel laid the parts on the porch, cleaning the gun quietly beside Jesse. He contemplated the question, then looked up as if the truth had suddenly become apparent. "I suppose you should ask yourself the questions I never did." Samuel methodically began cleaning his weapon and mumbled out the responses without much thought. "Do you think about her every day? Do you look forward to seeing her every day? Is there a terrible twist in your gut when you think of her being gone one day?"

Samuel mused and finished cleaning the weapon. He examined his thoroughness and accepted it as good enough. "These are all questions only you can answer. Nobody else."

Jesse watched his friend reassemble the pistol and was astonished by his own response. "Every one of my answers is yes," he said with a low voice. "Now, what do I do?"

"You will know what to do, Jesse," Samuel replied. "I will be here for you. I will try to do what I can." Samuel glanced at Jesse, knowing from the bottom of his gut what might happen.

Jesse stood. "Thank you, Samuel," he said. "You are the best friend anyone could ever ask for."

♙

The moonlight was bright again. It was only a half-moon but still brighter than the brightest star. Jesse stepped lightly down the hallway and laid his hand along the bedroom doorknob. He turned it quietly and stepped into the dark room.

He could smell her before he even saw her. "Are you still awake?" Jesse whispered.

"Yes," Zee replied from the darkness of her bed. "I've missed you," she added.

"I've missed you too," Jesse responded, taking two large strides to the bed. "May I join you?"

"To sleep?" she asked.

"Yes," he replied. "I can leave before dawn and return to my bed." He sat gently down on the bed.

"That would be lovely," Zee responded, moving her blankets over and shuffling her body to make room for him on the small bed.

Jesse pulled his trousers off and removed his shirt, laying them in a neat pile on the floor. He left his underwear on and climbed into Zee's bed. Her warmth immediately surrounded him, and it felt like a secure sense of home, something he had never felt before. His home was always filled with strife and conflict.

Jesse shifted his body closer and wrapped his strong arms around her shoulders, pulling her into his chest. She murmured satisfyingly and nuzzled her head into his chest hair. Jesse felt his heart flutter as he cuddled her intimately. He knew he had to tell her his feelings but had no idea how to start such a conversation.

"I love the way I feel when I'm with you," Zee murmured.

Jesse kissed the top of her head. "I do, too," he stated dumbly. His mind didn't seem to want to articulate his feelings just yet.

Zee could sense something in his demeanor. "Is there something wrong?" she asked, a small quiver in her voice. "Will you be leaving?"

"No!" Jesse answered quickly, chuckling. "I wouldn't do such a thing." He stopped himself and backtracked. "I mean, I wouldn't want to. It would tear me apart inside if the Americans forced me to leave. Beaverdams was another American surrender. I don't know which way this war is going to turn. I wish it would end."

"It will end one day," Zee stated quietly.

"Yes, it will."

"Will you go back to America?"

Jesse inhaled and answered what his heart told him. "I would not leave you, Zee." He shifted his body a tiny bit, pulling her closer. "I could not."

Zee smiled broadly into his chest as her nostrils filled with his manly scent. Her heart blossomed open like a flower splaying open for the sun. "I love you, Jesse." The words had escaped her mouth before she could stop them. It was what she felt in her heart, but now she feared he did not feel the same. She held her breath and waited for the inevitable disappointing response from him.

Jesse sighed and kissed her head again. "I have never felt this way before, Zee. Some mornings, I think we are one and the same; that's how close I feel towards you. I yearn to see you every day." He stopped and grasped her chin, looking into her eyes. "If this is what love is, then I wish for us to never be apart." He bent forward and kissed her lips softly.

Their tongues met in a sweet, lovely mixture of man and woman. Her mouth was sweet and sexy, his mouth salty and full of musk. They kissed for an eternity it seemed, before either wanted to pull away, but eventually, Jesse pulled back and gazed into her eyes.

"I want to run away with you, Zee," Jesse said, his tone serious. "We can escape this war and go live in the wilderness of the Canadian forests."

"You really mean that?" Zee asked, poking her head up in surprise.

"Yes, I do."

"We will marry?"

"Yes."

Zee settled into his chest again, warmed by his loving words. She contemplated what he was saying to her and rolled the thoughts around in her mind. "What about Xavier?" she asked. "I cannot leave my baby."

"We will take him with us."

She snuggled closer and inhaled his scent, analyzing all the possible outcomes. "We may die in the forest," she whispered.

"No, we won't," he answered. "I've lived in the wilderness too many times now. I know how to kill animals for survival now. We can create a camp near a lake and fish."

"There are lots of lakes around here," Zee agreed. Her mind swirled with all the possibilities. She kissed his chest thoughtfully.

The silence of the dark night fell over them as they both reviewed the consequences of their future actions.

Finally, after several minutes, it was Zee who spoke. "I cannot leave my entire family here. My momma needs me. My siblings need me."

Jesse felt his heart recoil inwards at the rejection.

Then she added. "We will just need to find another way."

Jesse smiled and kissed her head, relief washing over him. "Yes, we will find a way. I don't ever want to lose you."

CHAPTER 23

Zee awoke early and felt the bed empty beside her. They had made love slowly all night, with both of them barely sleeping at all. Jesse was insatiable, and Zee met him with every urgent desire. Her legs ached, and she groaned from the pleasant afterpain in her groin. She smiled at the memory and could still smell their sex on her sheets.

She turned and inhaled heavily with the sheets bunched up to her nose. "I love you, Jesse Eastman," she mumbled into the sheets.

He had left early at 4 am, as he had stated. But this time, he said he would return to her bed every night. She grinned happily and sat up swiftly, shuffling her feet into her slippers.

Zee immediately felt the urge to urinate and rushed out of her bedroom. She stumbled hastily, throwing on a coat, and ran out the back door to the outhouse. The bright morning sun warmed her shoulders as she raced to the outhouse.

She pondered her future with Jesse and wondered what her pappa would think. Would he be angry that she had chosen an American? Or would he be content that she had finally found a man on her own? Probably both, Zee concluded.

She hoped her family would understand, Zee thought. However, the problem remained that Zee was the primary caregiver of her mother. She could never leave her mother. Zee had to stay at the house and take care of her mother. Her siblings could probably survive just fine, but Momma was Zee's greatest concern.

The promise of a happy life with Jesse in the forests of Upper Canada tugged at her heartstrings. She had finally found her husband. He had proposed to her last night! Jesse Eastman wanted to marry her and accept Xavier, too! It was a wonderful wish come true. Zee felt immense joy fill her heart, but her mind was still conflicted about her responsibilities to her family.

She opened the outhouse door and walked back to the house, feeling the warmth of the sun on her face. Zee felt her heart thump with butterflies when she saw Jesse on the porch, waving at her. A huge grin spread across her face, and she quickened her steps. She wanted to hug him immediately but knew that he didn't like displays of affection in front of his team members. Zee calmly controlled her emotions, but nothing could erase the smile on her face.

Once she reached the porch, Zee now saw that he wore a frown on his face. Immediately, a shiver ran over her spine. Something felt wrong.

"Zee," Jesse stated gravely, reaching for her hand.

"What is it?" she cried, immediately sensing something terrible had happened.

"You must come inside," Jesse said. "It's your mother."

"What?" Zee shrieked. "What's wrong with Momma?"

Her twin brothers rushed abruptly out of the house with tears in their eyes. "Zee!" Jacob shrieked in a high tone. "Momma! Something's wrong with Momma! Charlotte found her on the floor!"

"Did she faint again?" Zee asked, momentarily hoping it was just another fainting spell. An evil tendril of fear slid through her veins, and she prayed it was not something worse.

"We don't know!" Sam yelled. "Charlotte and Betty chased us out!"

Zee rushed into the house and ran into the hallway. She stopped suddenly. Her mother lay prone on the floor with Charlotte and Betty bent over her. Zee's throat constricted as the hairs on her head stood up.

Charlotte immediately looked up at Zee with tears streaming down her face. She was holding Clara's arm as Betty was trying to shake their mother awake.

"Momma! Wake up!" Betty shrieked. She looked up and saw Zee standing in the hallway. "Zee! It's Momma! She's fallen again, but this time, she won't wake up!"

"Get some water!" Zee shouted as several soldiers crowded into the small hallway.

Jesse stood close behind Zee and spoke to his soldiers. "Awaken the doctor," he commanded. "Now!"

Several men rushed up to the second story as Hanna and Elise ran down the stairs. "What's going on?" Hanna shouted.

Zee crouched over her mother and felt around for her pulse. At first, she couldn't feel anything, so she bent down and curled over Clara, placing two fingers firmly on her mother's wrist. A very slow, weak pulse beat onto her fingers. Zee immediately opened her mother's mouth and began mouth-to-mouth resuscitation. She blew oxygen into her mother's mouth frantically as the doctor suddenly appeared by her side.

"What happened?" the doctor asked.

Charlotte stood and answered immediately. "We just found her on the floor. She's fainted before, but this time, she won't get up."

"Do something, please," Betty begged.

The doctor knelt beside Clara's body and felt her pulse. "Keep breathing oxygen into her, Zee," he said. "I'll try to get her heart started."

"But I felt a weak pulse!" Zee cried.

"Well, she doesn't have a pulse any longer," the doctor replied gravely as he began pumping Clara's chest with quick, short thumps with his palms. He bent to check her heart and shook his head. "Nothing," he stated. "Let's keep trying."

Zee continued blowing oxygen into her mother's mouth. "Come on, Momma," she whispered briefly and continued the resuscitation as the doctor worked on Clara's chest.

A tense few minutes passed as the entire family crowded into the hallway with Jesse and his soldiers looking on. Samuel stood stiffly beside Jesse as they all watched the emergency unfold.

Then, the doctor sat down on his knees, placing his ear once more on Clara's chest. There was no movement, no breathing, and no heartbeat. "Zee," the doctor stated gravely.

Zee stopped and looked across at the doctor, tears forming in her eyes. "No!" she yelled. "I felt a pulse!" She grabbed her mother's limp arm and placed two fingers on her wrist again. She felt around Clara's body, frantically looking for a pulse, but could find none. Zee placed two fingers on Clara's throat and waited.

There was no pulse.

"No!" Zee yelled. "Momma!" She hollered at Clara, shaking her. "Pappa is alive! You can't die!" Zee gazed around at everyone who looked down at her with sympathy. Finally, Zee curled over her mother and collapsed in grief, clutching Clara's limp body. "Don't do this! He needs you, Momma. We all need you." Zee's tears flowed freely down her face and mixed with her sweat as she hugged her mother's dead body. "I'm so sorry, Momma. I should have told you. I should have told you."

Several moments passed before Zee felt a calm, soothing hand on her shoulder. She jerked her head up and looked into Jesse's eyes.

"I'm so sorry, Zee," Jesse said, his voice heavy with emotion.

Zee gazed again at everyone. The soldiers all stood with sad faces. Her siblings were all crying. This cannot be happening, she thought immediately. Her mother can't die.

"Come," Jesse said, stretching out his hand to hers. "Let the doctor deal with your mother."

Zee looked at Jesse and gazed down at her mother's body, then glanced back at Jesse. "Momma's dead," she declared, almost to herself.

Jesse bent down and grasped Zee's shoulders. "I'm so sorry," he said calmly. "Come with me, Zee. I will make you a coffee."

Zee straightened and then slowly stood, allowing her lover to console her. Jesse wrapped his arms around her and pulled her away to the kitchen. Everyone noticed the affectionate hug, and Jesse could not keep the concern from his voice. "I'm so sorry," he repeated in her ear as they made their way to the kitchen.

Jesse pulled out a chair for her. "Sit, my dear," he said softly.

Zee sat down in the proffered chair and watched Jesse rummage in the cupboards for the coffee. Everything felt so surreal. It felt like the foundation underneath her feet had somehow become unstable. A wave of dizziness assaulted her. Zee smoothed a palm along her forehead and exhaled heavily.

Suddenly, there was a cup of water in front of her.

"Drink," Jesse instructed. "You've been through a lot."

Zee grabbed the water and gulped it down. She hadn't realized that she was so thirsty. The wave of dizziness passed as quickly as it had appeared. Zee watched Jesse grind the beans and stuff it into the metal coffee container. He glanced at her several times with heavy emotion splayed over his face. Then, he added water and placed the coffee on the iron stove.

At that moment, she realized that he was the one. He was the man whom she would live the rest of her life with. Jesse Eastman was her future husband and the father of her next child, and many more to come. The realization hit her with a ferocity, and her heart melted. She knew that she must do everything to keep this man, no matter the odds. Clara had died of a broken heart. Her mother and father were always very close. It tore at her heartstrings to know that such a travesty had happened. Her Pappa was alive, and she knew this. But the heartbreak was too much for her momma. Clara could not live any longer without him, just like Zee could not live without Jesse in her life.

She continued watching Jesse rummage in the kitchen until finally, he sat down and placed a cup of hot coffee in her hands.

"I didn't tell her," Zee said softly, almost to herself.

"Tell her what?"

Zee sipped at the hot liquid. "I was going to tell Momma that you had seen Pappa alive," she whimpered. "But I forgot. I knew she'd question me about my relationship with you so I delayed telling her." Zee blinked and swallowed. "Then I forgot. I just forgot, Jesse." A river of tears cascaded down her cheeks.

Jesse wrapped an arm around Zee's shoulders and shifted his chair closer to hers. "I don't know if any of my words will suffice at this moment, but I will do what I can physically to be there for you and your family." Jesse kissed the top of her head and kept his arm around her shoulders.

Zee felt the warmth of his love surround her. She looked at him as if seeing him for the first time. "Momma died of a broken heart," she said quietly. "She could not live without my Pappa. They were very close." Zee sipped and swallowed some coffee. She gazed into Jesse's kind brown eyes. "I always wanted what they had, a genuine love. Not just something arranged but a heart-pounding, life-or-death love. I always wanted that."

Jesse hugged her closer. "Zee Collard," he replied softly. "You have that with me if you choose it."

Zee began to cry heavily into his shoulder. She could not contain the emotions any longer. She had waited all her life, against all odds and against societal influence, for this man. The tears poured out of her like a river bursting its dam. She had lost her mother, but she had gained an understanding that nobody could ever take away from her.

CHAPTER 24

Samuel lifted the cup to his lips and sipped the strong coffee, surveying the hills before him. The sun rose lazily above the landscape and scattered rays amongst the clouds, turning everything into orangish tones. The land was beautiful and serene this early in the morning. It was a pity that this war continued on without end. Samuel, Jesse, and most of the soldiers in the unit didn't want this war any longer. The fight had gone out of them.

Samuel had begun to slowly realize that the people they were fighting were so closely related to himself that it just seemed futile.

The storm door creaked open, and Jesse stepped out onto the porch with a coffee in hand. He sat quietly on a small wicker armchair, the chair creaking with his weight.

"Good morning, my friend," Samuel said quietly, turning towards Jesse. "In contrast with yesterday's events, it's a beautiful morning." Samuel waved his hand over the horizon at the magnificent sunrise.

"It is that," Jesse agreed. "Sometimes the worst darkness reveals the brightest sunrise."

"True," Samuel replied.

Jesse and Samuel sipped their coffees in silence for several moments before either spoke. The thoughts in Jesse's mind whirled to a final conclusion. He knew what he had to do. Jesse had slept with Zee all night, not even awakening until 5:30 am. He did not have sex with Zee. He just held her and kissed her all night. She had informed him of something that had been troubling her and then fell into a deep sleep on his arm. Jesse's heart had thumped crazily knowing that he must now move mountains for her. He analyzed everything, turning it over and over in his mind, then finally settled on a plan. But it would revolve around Samuel's assistance.

"Samuel," Jesse started. "I need your help."

"Anything," Samuel replied. "I told you that before." He turned to face Jesse. "What do you need?"

Jesse peered over the rim of his coffee cup and took another sip. "Let's go for a walk, away from prying ears."

Samuel stood as Jesse followed him towards the barn.

Jesse spoke first. "I need you to take over command for me." He paused and waited for the reaction. When he received none, he continued. "I'm leaving with Zee and her son Xavier at midnight tonight." The summer morning air wisped through his hair as he paused again. Jesse analyzed Samuel's reaction. Again, his friend's face was calm, and even a hint of a smile graced his friend's face. "It is much more important than just assuming command, though. I must request a personal favor from you."

Samuel sipped the remainder of his coffee, then dangled the empty cup in his hand. "What is it?"

"I need you to promise me that all the children will be kept safe and away from harm. They need to be fed and taken great care of. All six of them."

Samuel nodded knowingly. "You love Zee, then?"

Jesse peered down at his toes as they walked. "Yes," he answered. "I will do anything for her."

Samuel nodded again. "I thought so," he stated bluntly.

The sun rays streaked across the field and they both momentarily admired the scenery, both heavily in thought.

"I would stay and fight until the end," Jesse said slowly. "If I believed in this war. But I don't any longer."

"Neither do I."

"But I have a reason stronger than that now," Jesse stated quickly. "Zee is pregnant with my child." Jesse gazed up at the barn. "She told me last night that her monthly curse had not come." Jesse kicked at a clay mound of mud on the grass. "I'm going to be a father, Samuel." He looked sideways at Samuel. "I must leave with her and her baby, Xavier." He exhaled heavily and straightened his shoulders. "All those times we had to survive in the mountains have prepared me for this moment. I will take my new family and some horses to the forests near Lake Huron. We will return when the war is over. I will be back. I can promise you that. You will be an uncle to my children someday."

Samuel quietly mused over Jesse's plans. For several minutes, the only sounds were their boots crunching on the grass. When they reached the barn, Samuel sat down on the grass, looking at the house in the distance. "I will take good care of Zee's remaining family, Jesse. You can count on that. I have nothing keeping me here, so I will take over command and help end this war so we can all go back home one day. But promise me something." Samuel asked, pausing briefly. "Make sure that you are doing this for you as well. I know you've always wanted to find a good woman. Is she the one?"

"Yes," Jesse answered immediately. "She's the woman I've been waiting for. We will be marrying," Jesse tipped the coffee cup up and drained the last bit of liquid. "I see in her what I see in myself, Samuel. I've never experienced that before in my life. If I don't do something now, I know deep down inside that I would live every day of my life afterward, regretting my decision of not acting accordingly. I must leave with her tonight."

Samuel nodded. "Then, I must honor that." Samuel mused briefly, thinking about possible scenarios. "I may tell the team that you had been killed in a skirmish going into town for supplies." Samuel waved his hand and clucked his tongue. "And that Zee was with you."

"That may work," Jesse replied slowly. "Whatever you have to do, that is fine with me. I don't want to be pursued, if at all possible. I can fix things when I get back to Philadelphia."

"Will she move to the US?" Samuel asked.

"I think Zee will follow me to the ends of the earth."

Samuel smiled. He was happy for his friend. If anybody deserved happiness, it was Jesse. "Well, that seals it then." Samuel reached forward and hugged Jesse. "Make sure you find me when you get back. I want to meet my new nephew."

Jesse chuckled. "Or niece."

⚑

The midnight moon shone brightly, illuminating the barn and the fields in a blanket of bluish, dark light. The nocturnal songs of the crickets masked the sounds of the horses leaving the stable. Zee had packed enough food and staples for a few weeks. She slung the supplies over the pack horse's back and then saddled Beauty. Zee handed over the reins of the bay gelding to Jesse. "Harry likes you," she whispered. "He was a tad difficult breaking in when I first got him, but he is a strong, young horse, and I'm certain he will learn from his new master."

Jesse smiled and patted the horse's strong neck. "Harry," he said softly. "We meet again." Jesse lifted the saddle calmly onto the gelding's back, then led him out of the rear doors. Zee, Beauty, and the pack horse walked behind him as quietly as possible.

When they were outside in the moonlight, Zee stepped forward and hugged Jesse. "I love you more than any man I've ever known. I hope you know that."

"I know that," Jesse responded, kissing her briefly on the lips. The moonlight and the symphony of crickets enveloped them in the midnight darkness. The baby on Jesse's back began to squirm. "Are you sure Xavier will be alright on a horse with us?"

Zee chuckled softly as she mounted her horse, then stretched her hands outwards for the toddler. "Xavier has been on rides with me since he was born."

Jesse reached up and handed Xavier to her, helping to strap the infant around Zee's back. He made sure the boy was wrapped securely in a warm blanket. Xavier was half asleep and murmured from the movement as if somehow knowing that he must remain quiet. "There, that should do," Jesse stated, inspecting his work. He looked up at Zee and was astonished that she appeared more beautiful to him every day. It was as if Zee was an apparition from heaven in the moonlight. "You are the most beautiful woman, inside and out, that I've ever met, Zee."

Zee smiled, and her heart thumped with love. "And you are my handsome husband."

Jesse grinned, feeling the love emanating from her. Momentarily, his eyebrows crinkled in concern. "Are you sure that you don't want me to take Xavier?" he asked.

"For now, I must have him close to me," she replied. "At least until we have gotten far enough into the woods. When he gets to know you more, he will come to you."

Jesse patted the small boy's legs through the blanket, high up on the horse. "Xavier, you will be protected at all costs. Don't you worry." Then he turned and mounted the bay gelding. "Come on, Harry," he commanded. "We have a lot of ground to cover in the next week and some precious cargo to protect." He trotted behind Zee and the pack horse, reaching the tree line in no time.

The quiet caravan then stepped silently into the woods with the moonlight guiding them.

PART III

THE BATTLE

CHAPTER 25

Sir Gordon Drummond squinted across the dark waters at Fort Niagara as the boats quietly entered American territory. The only sounds were the sloshing of the water against the hulls of the boats. The fog eerily wafted in front of them, obscuring most of the American mainland. It was the perfect camouflage.

Drummond nodded silently at his team. They all knew what was expected of them. Thankfully, the British troops believed in victory again, and it was mostly because of Drummond.

Sir Gordon Drummond had arrived at Newark a few weeks ago, at the beginning of Dec 1813. After many months, the war of 1812 had taken a turn for the worse. Drummond had been summoned to replace Brock and Sheaffe. Without Brock, the troop's morale was suffering, and Sheaffe had proven himself to be an inefficient leader.

Previously, when Fort George was taken in May 1813, the Americans had briefly commanded the entire Niagara Peninsula, but the British had been successful in slowly driving most of them back into a narrow territory around Fort George. When many of the American troops were redeployed to Sacket's Harbor to take part in the attack on Montreal, it left the American defenses in Niagara weak.

Major General Francis de Rottenburg, the British Lieutenant Governor of Upper Canada, had been alarmed by the defeats on Lake Erie and the American concentrations in the east. The British had managed to defend Montreal successfully and repel the American attack. But General de Rottenburg still ordered the Niagara troops to retreat to Burlington heights on the west end of Lake Ontario, fearful of another attack.

Drummond disagreed.

He was born in Quebec and had fought his share of battles, earning a status similar to Brock. Drummond commanded the troops at Burlington to advance to Fort George rather than retreat.

Drummond picked at his rough hands and questioned whether he was wrong to do so, considering that so many innocent lives were consequently lost.

The Americans had hastily retreated from Fort George. But something terrible happened when they had left. The Americans had set the nearby town of Newark ablaze.

The town was completely burned to the ground, with women and children dying in the cold winter.

Drummond exhaled heavily, and a small facial tick began twitching on his upper lip as he remembered seeing the charred remains. He tried over and over again, unsuccessfully, to calm his rising temper. It was contagious, and his troops felt the same anger bubbling inside of them, all 562 of them. Drummond stepped off the boat silently in the midnight darkness with the mass of British soldiers alongside him. They scurried into Fort Niagara on the American side and ran stealthily throughout the dark village of Youngstown. Several men silently crept towards the gate ahead of him. Drummond stood in the dark waiting.

A Canadian soldier approached the sentry, faking an American accent. "Let me in, it's cold tonight."

The sentry responded with several exchanges with the Canadian, then finally opened the gate.

The ruse had worked!

The Canadian soldier swiftly rammed his bayonet through the sentry's body. Another British soldier caught the sentry's body before he fell to the ground. Several half-asleep backup sentries died in their sleep as they opened their eyes. Blood dripped from the Canadian's swords as the lead soldier waved the rest of the unit inside.

Scurrying soundlessly, hundreds of angry Canadian soldiers infiltrated Fort Niagara under the cover of night.

Drummond followed and crept into the heavy stonewalled fort. "Bayonet the whole of them!" Drummond whispered angrily at his troops, stepping forward into the fort. "This is for Newark!" He raised his bayonet and led the charge.

The Canadian troops yelled and viciously attacked the American garrison at Fort Niagara, mercilessly bayoneting hundreds of sleeping Americans under the cover of night.

George wasn't happy with the murders of the American soldiers at Fort Niagara and did not partake in the savageness. He calmly sat on a rock after the taking of Fort Niagara and watched the Niagara River stream by. George gazed across the river at the Upper Canada side and wondered when this war would be finally over. He felt content in knowing that Zee was still at the Collard farm and everything was in her capable hands, but every once in a while, a shiver would spill down his spine, and his mind would worry.

He wondered what she would do. He knew his daughter well enough to know that she never followed orders too well. Would she risk her life to escape with the American man?

His mind churned over the possibilities. There was nothing he could do about it now. He was on American land, and the war was turning in Canada's favor. George had no choice but to focus on fighting until this war was over. That was the only sure way to free his family.

⚓

Jesse lifted the heavy log from the pack horse's sleigh and dragged it to the foundation he had cleared for the cabin. The structure was already mostly built. He proudly placed the log onto the front wall of the house he was finishing. Sweat formed on his brow, and he wiped it away hastily, standing briefly to survey his work. Three walls were erected, and a roof to keep them all dry. The fourth wall he was finishing this week, he told himself.

"Don't work yourself to the ground, sweetheart," Zee said softly, sitting near the fire with Xavier. Her round belly protruded out in front of her as she mindlessly smoothed her hands over her swollen abdomen.

Jesse straightened and smiled. "Don't worry about me," he replied, laughing softly. "Keep roasting that deer meat, and call me when it's done." Jesse bent over and positioned the log onto the previous log, using clay mud to secure it. It had been a warm start to the winter, but a recent snowfall had coated everything in white and then melted, creating a mess of sticky clay mud. He had been working on the cabin slowly since September, collecting fallen wood, dragging it onto the pack horse's sleigh, and assembling it all. He had entered a small town near Lake

Huron and bought nails, hammers, and materials for building the roof. It was slow, methodical work but he had successfully built the cabin to its present state.

Zee walked over with Xavier. "Let me help."

"No," Jesse said firmly. "You need rest."

"I'm pregnant, not an invalid."

Jesse frowned. "Please listen," he replied softly. "There are no doctors nearby. I don't want you to have any problems with the pregnancy. That's my baby inside you."

Zee shifted from foot to foot, holding Xavier's hand. She inhaled heavily and let out an exasperated sigh as she watched Jesse build their home. A thought crossed her mind as she bent down to pass him some nails. "I wish Samuel didn't have to tell everyone that we were both dead," Zee said thoughtfully. "Charlotte, Hanna, Betty, and the boys must be very upset."

"Elise would be too," Jesse responded, looking up.

"Elise never liked me much," Zee laughed.

"Still, she wouldn't have wished you dead."

"True," Zee replied. "I hate knowing that they are grieving over me."

Jesse wiped more sweat from his brow. Even though it was winter, the physical work was challenging. "It won't be for long. We will explain when we come back."

"That may be a long while."

"When the war is over, we will return," Jesse stated.

Zee handed him more nails. "I don't know how Pappa would react to the news," she said, sitting down tiredly on a log. "He may want to kill every American he sees."

"I will deal with your Pappa when we get back."

"You are very sure of yourself."

Jesse straightened. "I am," he stated firmly. "My love, I have been through hell and back. Nobody will send me back there."

He wiped his hands on his dirty pants. The pants were an old pair of George's that Zee had given him, along with many other items. He chuckled at the irony. "I will make peace with your Pappa, and I will return his clothes too."

Zee chuckled. "I suppose he would need some of his clothes back."

"I can't exactly walk around in an American uniform."

"No, you can't," she replied, staring up at the fading sun. "I hope we can survive the winter and be back soon."

Jesse grasped her arm gently and pulled her into his embrace. "Everything will be fine. Trust me, Zee. I will do whatever is necessary for our survival."

Zee looked into his eyes and kissed him.

Jesse kissed her back softly. He worried if they would survive, too. He just couldn't let his worries invade her thoughts. Jesse ran his hand along her rounded belly. The immediacy of her growing pregnancy filled him with urgency. He would ensure their survival for certain.

Jesse had hunted the deer last week and they were still filling their bellies with the delicious dark red meat. They also picked up some potatoes, peas, coffee, and milk for Xavier from town.

Zee smiled and sniffed the air. "I need to change Xavier's bottom." She broke the embrace and returned to the fire, hoisting Xavier up on a log and wiped his bum, then wrapped a clean towel through his legs and tied it in knots.

Jesse smiled, watching them both. He finally felt that he understood what love was.

It was exactly this. It wasn't romantic gestures and candlelight at a dinner table for him. Love was survival in the woods with the people he felt an immediate bond with, the people he would kill for.

He smiled and continued hauling another log into place. It would be January soon, so he had to finish everything soon. He would pick up the wood stove in town tomorrow and then the house he built would be their nest for the foreseeable future.

CHAPTER 26

In early 1814, American Lieutenant Colonel Winfield Scott was promoted to Brigadier General. After the wins at Fort George and Chippawa, he was an asset to the US Army, and his people began to look up to him. At six foot five inches tall, most men had to look up physically to meet his eyes. He had gained a considerable physique from the harsh fighting and would most likely tip the scales at 230 pounds of muscle mass and sheer determination.

Scott sat down and patiently waited for General Jacob Brown to discuss their next strategy. Fort Erie was taken, followed by Chippawa, although the latter was a somewhat unsatisfying success. The British forces at Chippawa had remained mostly intact and had hastily fled to Lundy's Lane. But regardless, Chippawa was still an important victory for the troop's morale.

Brigadier Scott was unsure of the outcome of Niagara. He felt they could win this. However, he also knew Brown was not in favor of this war. Jacob Brown was a good General and had won many battles with his meticulous planning, although the General's heart was not completely invested. Working closely under Brown, Scott knew this more than anybody.

Brigadier Scott was certain he could command the forces better than Brown, but similar to tensions with Van Rensselaer at Queenston, Scott tried to keep his sharp tongue in check. Scott was rising quickly in command during this war and along with his law background, he was ambitiously contemplating a future career in politics. He had to be careful whose toes he stepped on and make certain that his next actions counted towards his goals.

"General Brown," Scott announced as Brown entered the commanding station at Chippawa. "What will be the next move?"

"I am hesitant to send troops full force," Brown answered and stood with his hands splayed on the table. "I want to assess Lundy's Lane first."

Scott grimaced. He felt this was a mistake. They knew Drummond had been called in from the UK, and British forces were much stronger now. The US Army needed to show their strength now.

"I want you to go on a scouting expedition to Lundy's Lane," Brown announced, tapping his fingers on the table thoughtfully. "I need to know what kind of force we are dealing with."

"I can tell you right now," Scott countered quickly. "The British are much stronger with Drummond."

"That's not enough!" Brown stated firmly, glaring at Brigadier General Scott.

Scott held the man's glare for several seconds. Anger bubbled in his throat. He would be risking his life going to Lundy's Lane. Scott needed a full army behind him.

"You will go to Lundy's Lane and report back," General Brown commanded, slamming his hand down loudly onto the table.

Scott stood slowly, rising to his full six feet five inches, and glared heatedly at Brown. "I will assemble my team and leave tomorrow," Scott barked. With that, he turned on his foot and stormed out of the post. Scott willed the anger to leave his body and stomped toward his team with instructions.

⚓

George sipped his strong coffee and looked up at the bright summer sun near the cemetery on the hill. It was a beautiful July afternoon, and the air was heavy with the smell of humid grass, although a strong gusty wind blew at the top of the hill. Despite the heat of the sun, George felt a cold chill run up his spine. The small cemetery was to his right, in front of a small church, and he looked down upon the gradual slope of the hill leading into the forest. Something was spooking him, and he didn't know what. The regiment had arrived yesterday at Lundy's Lane, four miles north of Chippawa. The orders were to maintain contact with the Americans.

His commander, Riall, had suddenly ordered them to withdraw when he noticed movement from the Americans to the north. But Drummond had arrived today and countermanded the order from Major General Riall.

Lieutenant Governor Drummond's orders were clear. The British Canadian troops were to drive the encamped Americans from the west side of the Niagara River. Period.

It was 4:30 in the afternoon, and George had just sat down on Lundy's Lane Hill. He suddenly felt extremely grateful for the cup of hot coffee in his hand. He wondered how many more days he would live to smell another coffee or breathe another breath of the Niagara humidity. His left hand had developed a tremor a few weeks ago, and he fought to calm his rising anxiety. His coffee cup quivered, and he stilled it with his right hand.

George scanned the terrain and exhaled slowly as he prepared his mind for battle again. After many months of fighting on the American side, the unit had finally returned to the Niagara peninsula. George was glad to be on Canadian soil again. Fighting defensively settled much better in his mind. His goal, after all, was to protect his homeland.

A sharp wind blew in his face, raising goosebumps on his neck. He gazed down the hill.

The landscape surrounding them was an imposing site. The Canadian troops sat atop a sloping hill, with a commanding view of advancing armies with the river laying to the west. Strategically, it was an excellent position.

The wind gusted in his face strongly again as if to whisper a warning. George inhaled deeply. Drummond's words had been final. They must force the Americans to retreat.

George shook his head but admitted to himself that he liked Drummond. The new Lieutenant Governor of Canada was sometimes hot-tempered and very similar to Brock. Since Drummond had arrived, there was an electric positivity within the troops. George appreciated the firm command of Drummond. But George did not want to engage in more fighting. He was weary and hungry.

George would do as instructed, regardless. He trusted Drummond.

It would soon be 5 pm, and George stood. Hopefully, they would get fed soon.

♙

Brigadier Scott stepped through the forest with his troops, advancing towards Lundy's Lane. He was sure they were on the right track, and they would soon see the British lines. Scott had convinced Brown to send troops immediately upon any gunfire, although Brown was still adamant it was only a scouting march.

Scott wasn't so sure. He was keen on instinct, and what it told him wasn't good. Scott wasn't normally a jumpy man, but his nerves were getting the better of him today. It felt like something was wrong, and he couldn't shake the feeling.

The forest was thick with overgrown bushes and trees in July. So much so, that they had to slow their approach to make their steps as silent as possible. The forest floor was covered with moss, ivy, and riverbank vines, as well as thousands of other types of vegetation. It looked like a rain forest beneath the canopy of the trees. But Scott barely noticed the beauty of the area. He was too concerned with the drumming of his heart.

A soldier behind him suddenly stepped on a branch, and it cracked in half. Scott froze and glanced behind him at the soldier. He knew noise was inevitable, but they had to strive to be as quiet as possible. Scott was almost certain that Lundy's Lane was heavily enforced. He knew it in the pit of his stomach. All those troops they had banished from Chippawa were here, most likely with reinforcements.

He turned his gaze around to the front and waved the troops forward. The forest was incredibly thick and they could barely see 10 feet in front of their position. Scott grabbed a low-lying branch and quietly moved it to the right, allowing the next soldier to grasp the same branch.

After hours of creeping through the forest, their stealth paid off.

Scott knew they were closing in on the British lines and stepped forward with his rifle aimed. His troops followed suit.

But they still couldn't see anything. No British movements, no encampment, nothing. All they could see were vines, ivy, and tree trunks with leaves that reached up to 40 feet high. Frustrated, Scott cleared another branch away, then suddenly stepped out into a large clearing. Approximately twenty of his troops did the same. The forest had sheltered them so deeply that they hadn't even seen the clearing.

The British artillery team stood right before them, just as surprised as the American scout team. Scott jumped back and rolled into the safety of the forest but it was too late. Cannons and bullets rained down on their position, taking all of the twenty Americans out and many more. The cannons continued slamming into Scott's troops, taking more and more of his men.

Scott raced back into the forest and assembled his remaining troops, his heart drumming loudly in his chest. He realized that he had just skirted death. "Listen," he commanded in a low voice. "We've lost a lot of men, but it's not over yet. Brown will send for the remaining troops. Until then, we need to focus on a new strategy. From the little that I did see, it looks like the British have amassed several forces here at Lundy's Lane." He paused to take a few deep breaths. "The left flank is open." He lifted his brow and turned his eyes to the side, making a split decision. "Major Jesup!" He pointed at a regiment commander. "Lead your 25th regiment to the left flank and attack there. I think I saw a British General to the left. Let's hit them where they don't expect it." Scott waved his hand to signify the movements of the troops. "The rest of us will attack the center to keep the British engaged."

The men had fear but a strange excitement glowing in their eyes. They all nodded.

"Now go!" he commanded.

The 25th regiment ran off into the bushes to the left, and the remaining men inhaled a deep breath of courage. Scott crouched towards his men in the center. "We will give them a few minutes to get closer to the left position, and then we start engaging with a force stronger than we presently are." He sensed the fear rising within his troops and attempted to calm the panic with a lie. "Brown will be right behind us."

Scott knew the General a bit too well. Brown wouldn't engage until it was absolutely necessary. Scott prayed that Brown would send the remainder of the troops immediately, but he knew that Brown would only send them when it was impossible not to.

Hopefully, they would all stay alive until then.

⚓

George was loading the 6-pounder as the evening air filled with smoke. They had barely had dinner when the surprise fighting occurred. His regiment was in a state of panic. Many had abandoned their food and amassed towards where the shots were fired. Major Riall was behind him and slightly to his right when George began loading the 6-pounder with gunpowder, followed by the cannonball. George moved away from the side while the gunner aimed the weapon. Finally, after careful consideration, the fuse was lit on the cannon.

The team waited an agonizing several seconds, then the 6-pounder fired with a loud bang. The weapon was one of two 6-pounders. The British artillery at Lundy's Lane also included two 12-pounders, one 5.5-inch howitzer, and a Congreve rocket detachment. With all this firepower, George was certain that they would win this battle.

That was before he noticed the skirmish to his right. He dropped the cannonball and wrapped his arm around to swing his rifle up, but was a second too late.

A bayonet pointed at his face. "Surrender!" a bloodied American soldier shouted in his face.

George dropped the rifle, and it swung to his back. He raised his hands. A group of ten American soldiers crowded around Riall and took him prisoner as well. It was a swift, coordinated attack that the Canadians didn't see coming.

"March!" the American soldier shouted as several other British soldiers joined the prisoner line.

George stepped in line and marched with the others while Riall was led in front by the stronger group of American troops. He noticed a commander within the group, his hat poking out amongst the crowd. The line moved slowly at first, and then a fight broke out in the middle. George had no idea what was going on. Everything began happening too fast. But what he did see was that the American regiment was small and mostly concentrating on detaining Major General Riall. The Americans who were in charge of the prisoners were so low in number George estimated they had not been aware of how many British they were taking.

Someone bumped him from behind, and George sprang into action, using his fists. He struck out hard with his right fist and connected with an American's throat, sending the man reeling. George raised his rifle, but the man had already disappeared. Several other British prisoners escaped, running back up to the hill. George jumped to the right and tripped on a dead soldier, stumbling into the mud. All he could hear was his own heavy breathing for a tense five seconds. The body in front of him wore a British militia uniform, and George shivered involuntarily. He braced himself for another attack, or worse, a bayonet.

Then he heard several shots being fired from behind his position. George stayed down. He noticed the uniforms of a Canadian militia team rushing toward the American troops as they attempted to return to the main body of the American position. The skirmish lasted a brief minute. George was still too close to engage, only six feet away from the prisoner line.

Major Jesup shouted over the commotion, "Bring Riall! Don't let him go! Leave the others!"

George stayed still as a stone, watching the American regiment leave with Riall, another Captain, and several remaining British prisoners. His breath was almost coming out in gasps, and he feared he would be noticed.

The Canadian militia continued its attack, releasing the majority of prisoners. George breathed a sigh of relief as a Canadian soldier held out his hand and helped him up. "That was close," George said thankfully.

"We need to retain as many people as possible," the Canadian soldier answered. "It's getting bloody fast."

Several other Canadians tried unsuccessfully to release Riall, but the American regiment had disappeared out of sight with their prized capture.

George wiped the mud from his hands and sprinted back to the hill with the Canadians. He slowed his approach as he neared the hill. George had to walk carefully and sidestepped the growing number of both American and Canadian casualties littering the landscape.

♠

Scott aimed and fired toward the center of the hill. His men were falling in great numbers beside him, and he cursed loudly. "Brown," he muttered. "By God's grace, get your troops here already!"

Sweat dripped from his forehead as he hunched over, trying to keep his commanding presence from being known by the enemy. He crouched and aimed at the gunner on top of the hill. Scott's shot went wild, and the 12-pounder returned fire, hurling a cannonball just ten feet from his position. Scott ran to the left and ducked as fragments of trees, blood, and mud flew everywhere.

Several strangled shouts sounded from the damaged tree line. Another group of his soldiers had been hit.

Scott darted closer to the center position and crawled to the tree line to get a better look. He watched as Drummond rallied his troops to secure the left, where Riall had been captured. Major Jesup was already back with their prize prisoner. Scott tried to contemplate what Drummond was thinking.

He aimed his rifle at Drummond and found a clear shot, then frowned. It was too far a distance. It would do nothing but show his reconnaissance position.

A large contingent of British and Canadian soldiers were moving to the left. Drummond must not be aware that Jesup was already back, Scott thought. He crawled back into the cover of the forest and stood, contemplating his next move. He leaned against a tree and then glanced back at the British center. The setting sun glinted off the two 12-pounder cannons. Astonished, Scott could see that the two large weapons were momentarily unmanned.

Lying amongst the field between the tree line and the hill were hundreds of bodies, some groaning in agony and others motionless in death. Scott noticed many of his team were completely gone. He grimaced.

Scott exhaled, glancing up again, and watched as the sun began setting, sending a blanket of darkness over the unmanned British artillery. Scott smiled as a new strategy filled his calculating mind.

George felt his kneecap buckle as a bullet fragment hit his leg. He fell hard and felt the whoosh of air above him as the firepower from the Americans increased. He scanned the battlefield and was revolted at the high number of casualties. He could not determine which bodies were Canadian, British, or American in the field. All he knew was this battle was taking a turn for the worse.

George cut his pant leg and exposed the injury on his left knee. He breathed a sigh of relief. It was only a graze. It hurt like hell, but the bullet fragment had just skimmed the outer side of his knee. George ripped a length of cloth from his pouch and wrapped his knee tightly for support. Slowly, he stood, trying to keep the knee as straight as possible.

He gazed over towards the tree line as Drummond appeared on his right. They both stared for several seconds before increased gunfire sent them back.

"Governor Drummond!" a man shouted beside George. "The American troop reinforcements have arrived under Brown's command. Take cover."

Drummond crouched cautiously but continued staring and eyed the tree line suspiciously. "It's not Brown we need to be worried about," he replied. Then he shouted unexpectedly at the wind. "What are you planning, Brigadier Scott?"

♠

Brown's troops had finally arrived, and Scott pushed down the urge to yell at his commander. Scott's troops were severely depleted, hundreds of them dead or dying on the field. He wanted to swing his fists and rail at Brown but knew that this would only deplete whatever remaining energy he possessed. Scott had been running, shooting, and pushing the offensive for several hours. Brown's reinforcements only arrived once nightfall began descending.

Scott crouched with Brown and pointed towards the 12-pounders. "Drummond has sent his troops to reinforce the left from our attacking 1st infantry," Scott stated. "That leaves a window for us. We can take the center and capture those guns."

Brown nodded as several large horses pulled their own 6-pounders towards the tree line. "We have more of our own firepower now, but I agree. If we can capture that hill, we've won this bloody battle."

"I wouldn't be so certain," Scott cautioned. "Drummond is a crazy Canadian. He makes rash decisions, just like Brock."

"Well," Brown replied. "Brock died. Maybe those rash decisions are going to cost him his life as well."

Scott muttered under his breath. "I wouldn't be so sure."

"Miller!" Brown shouted to a man behind them.

Lieutenant Colonel James Miller approached from the bushes. "Yes, sir."

Brown moved to the side as the horses were steered into the correct position for the heavy artillery. "Lieutenant Miller," Brown pointed to the British 12-pounders sitting up atop the hill. "Capture those British guns."

Colonel Miller straightened and replied strongly. "I'll try, Sir!"

⚐

George was positioning the 12-pounder when Drummond instructed him to join the troops to their right to defend the area from the 1st US infantry's heavy attack.

George felt the bullet whisk the air beside his head as he suddenly ducked just in time. He ran and hit the dirt, trying to make it to the right as quickly as possible. He looked back and was astonished by what he saw.

A massive musketry attack was bombarding toward his abandoned position at the 12-pounder cannon. "Lieutenant Colonel!" George shouted as he squirmed his body down across the ground. "The Americans are taking our artillery!"

But his voice was drowned out by the sounds of American gunfire. George scrambled, clawing at the grass and dirt until he joined his troops to his right. He watched with several others as hundreds of American soldiers raced up the hill and captured the cannons. Everything began happening so fast that George fought to make any decisions at all. A soldier beside him fell from a hail of bullets, and George crouched down, lifting his rifle towards the captured artillery.

Drummond was suddenly standing beside him. "Get down!" George shouted. "Brown's troops have taken over our position on the hill!"

Drummond shouted a command, but it was drowned out by the bullet that slammed into his throat, sending the Governor flailing to George's side.

George took the brunt of the Governor's weight. George's knee screamed in pain as he hit the ground with the commander.

His heart beat thumped in his ears as he scrambled to check his commander's wound. "Lieutenant Governor!" George shouted, laying the commander beside him.

Drummond lay on the ground with his eyes closed. Time seemed to stand still as George worked quickly to tie up the wound on Drummond's throat. He gently shook his commander as his knee seethed in pain again. "Lieutenant Drummond! What are your orders?" George shouted.

Drummond's eyes fluttered open, and George exhaled a sigh of relief.

"Lieutenant," George stated more calmly. "You've been shot in the throat. It is bleeding, but I have tied a scarf on it. We need your directions!" George pointed to the abandoned 12-pounder cannons. "Brown's troops have taken over our artillery, sir. What should we do now?"

Drummond miraculously sat up, his eyes refocusing. He narrowed his sight at the captured artillery and began to speak with a rasp in his voice. "We charge to recapture those guns." He glanced around at the group of worried faces surrounding him. "I'm fine! Let's get those cannons back!"

George looked up at the astonished soldiers as Drummond stood with the bloody scarf tied around his neck.

"You heard the man!" George shouted. He stood back briefly and aimed at the mass of Americans running up the hill, discharging his weapon. "Recapture the artillery!" George shouted as he swung his rifle and joined the charge.

Scott watched as his troops secured the artillery. Suddenly, from the left, he could see Drummond returning to the captured British artillery with a thousand men. Scott buttoned his jacket and ordered his remaining troops in the forest to counterattack without authorization. He could not find Brown in the chaos, but it didn't matter in his mind because they were winning. They could not allow the captured artillery to slip from their hands.

Scott held up his bayonet rifle and charged through the center with his troops. As soon as he cleared the tree line, his large frame pounded the ground, and he bounded up the hill. Several tense moments of fighting passed, and then Scott raced towards the hill. Out of the corner of his eye, he could see a massive British attack roll down the hill. He instinctively crouched, but it was too late. Gunfire erupted all around them. A bullet slammed into his shoulder, sending him flying in an arc. As he was flying, another bullet caught his side, sending a gush of blood shooting into another soldier's face.

Brigadier Scott slammed down hard on the ground and fought to catch his breath. He willed himself to get up but couldn't move his arms. Something was stopping his determination. Confusion melted into his brain as the weight of what felt like a hundred tons centered on his chest. He tried again to get up but could only look up at the midnight stars glittering down on him.

Then Scott's mind went blank.

✠

George watched as the American commander went down, and several American soldiers dragged their leader from the field. He was sure it was Scott or Brown. He had certainly hit someone important. George reloaded with his heart pounding heavily. The deafening roar of the exchanging gunfire made his ears ring harshly. He could barely hear anything anymore, but he could see. Drummond was in the fray, fighting with the bloody rag tied to his throat. George attempted to stand, but his knee abruptly buckled from the exertion. George fell backward onto a patch of muddy grass as bullets flew overhead from the attacking Americans.

Midnight was approaching soon, and the fields were illuminated with an eerie purplish dusk. The carnage lay before him. Blood and bodies littered the slope up to the hill. So much so that if he attempted to run down the hill, he would trip on the massive amounts of injured and dead soldiers. Emotions welled in his eyes. George just wanted to go safely back to his family. That's all he wanted.

He tried to stand and felt his knee click loudly as his kneecap popped out of the socket. George screamed loudly, crumpling to the ground. Sweat dripped from his face as the pain seared into every bone of his body. He inhaled sharply several times, trying to avoid unconsciousness.

A shiver of dizziness invaded his brain. He sat on the ground, bravely trying to stand. Finally, he managed to come to a full stand and aimed his rifle.

He discharged his weapon and reloaded when a bullet slammed into his chest. His arms went flying back, and his body flung high into the air and landed on a mound of dead soldiers.

George's heart raced to understand what had just happened. The realization dawned on him quickly. He was shot.

A tear escaped from his eye as he gazed up at the twinkling night sky.

He just wanted to go safely home to his family.

That's all he wanted.

Then, the stars faded to blackness.

Drummond held the rag on his throat as blood seeped through his fingers. He noticed the Sergeant who had tended to him lying injured on a pile of bodies. "Help this man!" Drummond shouted. "Take him to a medic if he's still alive!"

A team of bleeding soldiers gathered around the body of George. They checked his pulse and then lifted him carefully away, several of them stumbling from their own injuries.

Drummond surveyed the scene. It seemed that almost every one of his soldiers was injured in some way. So many were dead. He estimated over 500 lay severely wounded or dead. It was difficult even to distinguish the Americans from the Canadians.

Then, he saw another significant movement to his left. A group of American soldiers were carrying away another commander. This was most likely Brown, Drummond thought.

The blood eased through his fingers as Drummond fought to stay standing himself.

Then, the most miraculous thing happened next.

The Americans began retreating down the hill, leaving the captured artillery and disappearing back into the tree line.

Drummond had never felt so much relief before in his life. With both of their commanders shot or even possibly dead, the Americans were exhausted, and several of them stumbled down the hill. Drummond didn't even have the strength to send his troops to follow them. He sat wearily down on the hill with a group of bleeding, exhausted soldiers surrounding him.

"They're retreating, sir," a soldier stated as he wiped a bloody hand across his forehead.

"I see that," Drummond responded as weariness took over. He pressed his fingers against the cloth tied around his neck wound.

"What shall we do?"

"We do nothing," Drummond responded with a rasp in his voice. "We just tend to our injured and dead. The rest of us will just wait here and defend our position." He nodded to the retreating Americans. "I don't trust them not to come back."

Drummond settled with a small regiment on the hill for a long night of guard duty as several men began collecting the wounded.

CHAPTER 27

A loud knock hammered on the front door, almost splintering the wood. Samuel bolted upright as fear ran down his spine. He raised his loaded weapon and approached the locked front door cautiously.

The house was quiet. Samuel peeked out the side window and could see the early dawn rising. It must be 4 am, he thought. Whoever was coming at 4 am was not bringing good news.

"Who is it?" Samuel shouted at the door. "Make yourself known!"

A muffled response came back. "It's Sergeant Greaves from the 21st US Infantry. We have orders for everyone to withdraw to Fort Erie."

A silence descended on the house as Samuel opened the door. "What happened?"

"Lundy's Lane was a massacre on both sides," Sergeant Greaves replied, with several splotches of blood across his uniform. "We're retreating from Niagara."

"I'll get my team out of here then." Samuel nodded towards the interior of the house. "There is a family of children still in the house. Nobody is to harm them."

"Yes, sir."

Within the next hour, Samuel gathered his team, the injured occupants, doctors, and nurses, and fled the Collard homestead. When they were far enough away from the large white house, Samuel turned around and whispered to the rising sun. "The Collard children are safe. I've done my job, Jesse. It's time to go home."

Ⱥ

"Pappa?" a girl's voice sang over him.

He could feel someone tending to his wounds as strange visions swam in his head. The walls were almost blindingly white, and George could barely see. Then Clara was suddenly there!

He tried reaching his arms to embrace her, but he still couldn't move them. He strained to call her name. "Clara!" he mumbled as his voice crumbled into a mess of garbles.

Clara wouldn't move. She just stared at him from the end of the hallway. She didn't talk to him either.

Confusion clouded his mind as he tried to piece the events of the past few days together, but all he could remember was the bloody field of bodies. The ringing in his ears was so strong it made his head hurt. A fierce headache swamped his brain, and he felt exhaustion melt over his body again.

Then Clara moved closer. His heart burst with love. He would be able to touch and hold her once again!

"Pappa," a girl's voice whispered in her ear. "Stay with us."

Then, the world vanished in a cloud of whiteness.

Ⱥ

Zee awoke with a start and tried not to rouse her new baby. She had a disturbing dream and her emotions jumbled up into unexplained knots. The darkness of the night reminded her of how quickly time had passed juggling her new family. With her heart hammering in her chest, she cuddled towards her sleeping husband.

Jesse groaned as Zee's arms encircled his warm body. Her hands curled around his hips as she snuggled closer. "I had a disturbing dream, honey," she murmured.

Jesse replied sleepily with his eyes still closed. "What was it about?"

"I can't remember all of it," she replied. "But someone died. Someone I loved dearly."

Jesse rolled towards her and wrapped his arms around her body, pressing himself into her. "Oh, sweetheart. It's alright. We're home, sweetheart, and everything is okay. I'm not dead."

Zee nuzzled her head into his chest and inhaled his manly scent. It had a calming effect on her. "No, it wasn't you in the dream who died," she replied. "It was someone else. All I can remember is that I was very distraught."

Jesse ran his palms over her hair and pulled her in closer. "It was just a dream, sweetheart."

"What if it wasn't?" she replied. "What if my family back home is in danger?"

"Samuel is a very capable soldier," he countered. "I trust him with my life and the lives of your loved ones." He kissed her forehead and gazed into her eyes in the deep darkness of the night. "I know it's hard on you. It was a difficult decision to leave, but we had to do it for our own growing family."

Zee felt tears well in her eyes as the troubling dream still lingered in her heart. "I hope they will understand one day. The last year passed by so quickly with us together."

"Don't fret. We will go back when it is safe, my dear."

"Are you certain?"

"Of course," Jesse said, pulling himself up to his elbows. He shifted his weight and pulled her into his lap. He could see the shadow of Zee's head lying on his thighs and her arms resting on his legs. "I will always support you and your family. I know how important they are to you. Don't ever let your mind trick you into thinking otherwise."

Zee exhaled worriedly. "What about your family?" she asked, curling herself around his legs like a little girl. "Don't you feel the same about them?"

Jesse paused and looked up to the ceiling. "My family is complicated," he stated. "The Eastmans are a rich, influential, large family. Wealth creates many problems. I love my mother and my siblings dearly. Don't ever think I don't." He exhaled roughly in exasperation. "I just can't live with them for long."

"Is that why you joined the war?"

Jesse remained quiet for several seconds, weighing his answer. "Possibly," he answered. "It was probably part of the reason." He smoothed his hand along her hair rhythmically and gazed down into the blue-blackness of the room. "I also truly believed in the war at the time."

"You don't anymore?"

"No."

Zee raised herself onto her elbows and hugged his chest. "I wish the war would end," she murmured into his shoulder.

"So do I." Jesse bent to the side and gently kissed the top of her head. "Once it does, we will return."

Zee kissed his shoulder in response as a surge of loving hormones cascaded over her body. She loved this man with all her might. Some days, it felt overwhelming, like a tidal wave had overcome her senses. There was nothing in the world that could compare. The ferocity of the emotions frightened her at times. She couldn't imagine what she would ever do without him if he died or was injured.

Zee shook her head. It was silly thinking in such a way. Of course, she would repair and heal his injuries. If he died, she would do anything and everything to secure her family's future. There was no question about it. She would persevere, no matter what.

"Something is churning around in that mind of yours," Jesse said as he began playing with a strand of her hair. He twirled it around and then combed his fingers through it aimlessly. "Do you feel better from your dream now?"

Zee kissed his neck. "I feel better, thank you, my love."

Jesse pulled her chin up towards him and shifted his body. He bent forward and kissed her lips softly. He pulled away briefly and searched her eyes, then pecked her lips again. "You are so beautiful, inside and out. I don't know what I ever did to deserve you."

Zee stretched her neck and kissed him back, his male aroma filling her senses. "I feel the same about you," she replied. "I spent so many years being an unsuitable partner for every man my parents picked."

"I guess we are both unsuitable for most of society." Jesse grinned. "That's what makes us so special together."

Zee chuckled. "I suppose you're right." She kissed his lips again, tasting his muskiness. "I love you," she murmured in between kisses.

Jesse ran his hands alongside her breasts for several minutes, eliciting groans from deep within her. Finally, he lifted her and rolled Zee over onto her back. He crouched over her and kissed her lips softly as her legs splayed apart underneath him. "I love you, Zee."

He felt her breath quicken and her hands flutter towards his penis. Jesse positioned his hips and entered her vagina gently. He kissed her lips again as the darkness enveloped them in a heavy blanket of early morning shadows.

The morning came quickly. Zee felt like she had just fallen asleep, and suddenly it was daylight. She rolled over into Jesse as he sat over her, smiling.

"Good morning, beautiful," he said.

"Oh my, good morning, my husband," she murmured in reply. "You're awake early."

"I have several things I need to get done today, my sweet," Jesse said, kissing her shoulder in between words. "I need to chop a lot of wood. We have almost run out completely."

Zee ran her hands along his biceps and kissed his arm. "You go do what needs to be done, and I will take care of the babies."

"Did I ever tell you how happy I am that you are my wife?" Jesse asked, grinning.

"You tell me that almost every morning," Zee replied, chuckling.

"Well," Jesse stated, rising to a crouch and hopping over her on the bed. "Don't you ever forget it." He pulled his underwear and pants on, then slid his arms into a plaid shirt.

A baby started crying as if on cue.

"Oh, Janey!" Zee cried, straightening out of bed. Jesse helped her slide a nightgown on and then kissed her briefly before she ran towards the small bassinet. "Sweet girl," she murmured as she picked up her baby daughter. "My, my, you have a loud voice for such a little thing."

Jesse watched in loving adoration as Zee breastfed the infant. He loved his wife and kids so incredibly much that it was astonishing how he had lived all his life never knowing such profound happiness. Jesse left the cabin quietly and entered the woods near the back of their property.

Zee and Jesse had purchased the land for almost nothing the day they had arrived in the small town. They got married by the priest the very same day.

The cabin was close to Lake Huron, and the town was only a thirty-minute horse ride away. He had finished building the cabin entirely in December and Zee had delivered Janey at the end of March. Zee was a good mother, and no problems existed during the childbirth, which he was eternally grateful for.

The friends they had developed in town had offered him a good sum of money to start building more cabins by the lake. He was surprised at first and mused about the work but soon agreed to the proposition. He had built their home so well, it seemed, that many of the townsfolk were eager to create their own paradises near the beaches of Lake Huron. Jesse had agreed to start building in the summer, and his mind began envisioning his future unfolding before him.

Jesse smiled and approached the pile of wood shavings with the stump and axe chiseled into it. Jesse could hear only the wind blowing through the trees. The smell of summer humidity on the forest floor was heavy, and he had already started breaking out in a sweat. He grasped the handle of the axe and pulled it out, searching for suitable driftwood.

A joyful feeling spread through his body, and he inhaled a deep breath of country air as he picked up a large log. He positioned it on the stump, then swung the axe down.

The satisfying crack of wood echoed in the forest as the log split.

His life couldn't be better, he mused. He had everything he had always wished for.

🜨

Zee laid Janey on her back and wrapped a fresh cloth around the girl's bottom, fastening the corners. She laid the girl down in the bassinet and cooed her to sleep. Xavier came running in and grasped his momma's hand.

"I want berries!" he shouted gleefully. "You said!"

"Shh," Zee scolded as she held his small hand. "You'll wake the baby." She led him away from the bassinet and whispered, holding her two fingers to her lips. "Yes, I did tell you we would pick berries today."

"Yippee!" the toddler whispered in contained excitement.

Zee laughed and dressed them both for the outdoors. The forest here was sometimes so humid that it felt so much hotter outside. She dressed Xavier in shorts and pulled on a pair of Jesse's hunting shorts over her tall legs. Zee felt a strange joy wearing his clothes, even though the pants didn't fit in the waist. The gap was so large that she had to cinch it with a sash.

She smiled in the broken mirror, then checked on Janey one last time. When she was certain the baby was sleeping, she grabbed a rifle for security, held Xavier's hand, and left the cabin. She walked with Xavier to the place where they had seen the wild black raspberries growing.

It wasn't far from the house but was distant enough into the woods that she began to worry about Janey. She glanced back and looked down at her son. "Okay, the raspberries are here," she said to Xavier, pointing at the thorny bushes. "Be careful not to touch the thorns. You have to pick them like this." She demonstrated and plucked a black raspberry off and dropped it into the small bucket. "Only pick the black or dark red ones. The pink ones will be too sour, and they still need to grow."

"Yes, momma," he responded gleefully and reached towards the bushes.

The bushes shifted, and Xavier jumped gleefully to another bush before she could stop him.

That's when she realized they were not alone.

The brown mass of fur immediately bolted for her son. Zee had zero time to react. She yelled at Xavier, "Stop! Don't run!"

Xavier looked behind him and saw the brown bear in the berry bush. His eyes widened, and he yelled, running into the clearing. "Momma!"

Zee lifted the rifle quickly and fired at close range, the shot reverberating loudly throughout the forest.

🜨

Jesse straightened when he heard the shot. A sudden fear rammed into his spine. He dropped the axe and began to run towards the cabin. As he approached the cabin, he could see the door was closed firmly, and he could hear Janey crying. He bolted into the house and grabbed the baby girl, searching everywhere for his wife and adopted boy.

They weren't anywhere in sight.

He immediately panicked and ran outside with Janey in his arms. Directly to his left, Xavier ran towards him from the bushes, and Jesse sighed a deep breath of relief. "Where is your momma?" Jesse asked as a sudden fear gripped his throat. "What happened?"

Then he saw Zee twenty feet behind Xavier, walking back to the cabin with a smoking rifle in her hands. Jesse ran to Zee in a panic. His long strides reached up to her in no time. "Honey, what happened?" he asked, his heart beating in his throat at the thought of them being harmed. "Are you okay?"

Zee let the butt of the rifle hang towards the ground. "We are fine, sweetheart," she answered as Jesse hugged her and Xavier while Janey cried at the top of her lungs. "Shush, baby," she cooed. "Give her to me."

Jesse took the rifle from Zee and exchanged it for Janey, searching the woods for answers. "What did you shoot?"

"A brown bear," Zee replied over the baby's screams. "He's over yonder in the raspberry bushes."

Jesse peered behind them and could see a mass of fur sticking out from the bushes. "Is he dead?"

"I don't know," Zee replied calmly. "I think I shot him good. Nobody messes with my family." She chuckled as the tension of the moment dissipated.

"I will load another shot and take a look," Jesse replied. "You both get safely into the cabin, please."

Jesse reloaded the rifle and watched his family safely enter the house, with the door closing behind them. He stomped through the bushes and approached the animal, the rifle pointing directly at the mass of fur. He waited several seconds and patiently watched for any signs that the animal was breathing.

After a few moments, he concluded that there were no signs of life and approached the dead animal.

Jesse bent down and grasped the bear by the neck and felt a gush of sticky blood as he wrestled with the body to see where it was shot. After several minutes of confused inspection, he realized why there was so much blood.

Half the head of the bear was missing.

Zee had blown the bear's head into pieces.

Jesse chuckled and smiled. "That's my woman," he said proudly.

CHAPTER 28

"Pappa," the girl's voice called to him again.

He fought to open his eyes but still could not see. Was he blind? Was he dead? He tried to lift his arms or even move his fingers, anything. He urged his mind to move just one small finger and focus on that one task. George strained to connect with his physical body.

But it was of no use.

Not one finger moved.

His mind clouded, and then he felt a massive pain in his chest. It felt like he had a ton of weight pinning him to the bed. The pain radiated into his forehead, and a sharp headache shot through his skull. He groaned and suddenly felt the bed spinning.

His mind clouded over, and he could see once again! Clara stood at the end of the hallway, waving at him with a large smile on her face. She looked strange, almost ethereal. Her dress was white, and her hair was so blonde that it was nearly see-through. He didn't understand, nor did he care. This was his wife, the woman he had fought so hard for! All he had wanted during this entire war was to return home, and he did it. He was finally home!

George ran to wrap his arms around her and felt his body swing upwards eerily. His stomach churned.

Then, just as suddenly, the pain returned to his chest, and he felt pinned to the bed again. He remembered the fighting at Lundy's Lane, and the ringing in his ears started again. All the bodies and the blood that had littered the hillside came back to him. A shiver ran up his spine as he remembered the horrors of Lundy's Lane.

"Pappa, wake up," the girl shouted at him.

Then he felt a wonderful cold cloth on his forehead, and several small hands were shifting him upright in the bed.

"You have to eat," the girl whispered in his ear. "Wake up, Pappa."

The girl started crying.

George felt his own emotions tug at his heart. He felt a tear escape from his eye as he could feel the girl curl up beside him, and several other children moved him back to a laying position.

As much as he tried, he still could not open his eyes.

He suddenly felt very tired and his body relaxed into a deep restorative sleep as the world once again faded into blackness.

George remembered when he had first met Clara. She had been the most beautiful woman he had ever encountered. He was smitten by her looks but even more so by her kind and caring personality.

It was a long time ago, and they were young adults. George had the exuberance of youth in his physique and his face. They laughed and swung on her parents' porch swing as he reached for another kiss. Clara smelled like flowers and cinnamon. His

270 J. A. BOULET

eyes glittered, and his heart warmed in his chest. She was everything he had always dreamed about.

Clara smiled at him and held his hands in hers, smoothing the tops of his palms. He leaned over and kissed her lips. It felt like he was floating on a cloud in heaven. His hopes soared. She had told him that she had loved him. He was the luckiest man alive!

He bent to kiss her again, but Clara's hand stopped him. She laid two delicate fingers on his lips and spoke softly in his ear. "You must go home now," she cooed.

He grinned. "I want to spend eternity with you. I don't want to leave."

"I love you more than anything in the world, George," she said softly, rubbing the tops of his palms. "But you must return home now." Clara stood up languidly. "We will see each other again one day. Don't worry."

Clara turned into her parents' old home and blew him a kiss, then disappeared.

George fluttered his eyes open and immediately saw Charlotte folding the cool cloth on his forehead. His daughter jumped as if in shock. "Pappa!" she cried with tears of joy. "You're awake!" She jumped happily from foot to foot and shouted behind her. "Hanna! Elise! Betty! Boys! Come! Hurry! Pappa is awake!"

The children rushed into the living room one by one, laughing and crying.

"Pappa!" Hanna shrieked. "You're alive! Oh, thank heavens!"

"We thought we lost you!" Elise cried, tears streaming down her face.

"Our prayers are answered!" Betty yelled.

"Pappa!" Jacob and Sam sang in unison.

George opened his mouth to speak, but only a croak came out.

"Get Pappa some water, Elise!" Charlotte shouted.

Elise rushed into the kitchen and returned with a cup of water, tipping it to Geroge's lips. He drank hesitantly at first, then finished the rest greedily. "You are thirsty!" Elise cooed.

George stared wondrously at all his children and smiled. "I'm home?" he asked, the words coming out as a low moan.

Charlotte understood. "Yes! You're home, Pappa!" She curled over him and hugged him gently.

Hanna, Betty, and Elise hugged his legs. Jacob and Sam rushed over to his other side.

"Be careful!" Charlotte yelled. "He was shot in the heart!"

"I was shot in the heart?" George croaked.

"The doctors said the bullet just missed your heart," Betty answered. "They said you'd most likely live, and they were right, thank God."

"The soldiers brought you home two days ago," Charlotte added. "You've been asleep ever since. We were afraid you'd never wake up." Charlotte broke down into tears and kissed her father's cheek. "I didn't want to lose you too. We've lost enough."

George coughed, and Elise returned with another cup of water. He drank it greedily.

"Go easy," Elise said soothingly. "The doctors said to feed you water and soup broth slowly. Your stomach is fragile. Did you want beef broth?"

"Yes," George answered, his voice clearing up a bit.

Hanna ran to the kitchen and returned with a cup of clear, warm soup broth. "Here," she offered.

George took the cup with shaky hands and sipped the warm liquid as his children stared at him with loving admiration. When he was finished, he gave the cup back to Hanna and directed his question to Charlotte. "Where's your mother?"

The children all looked at each other with worried stares. Charlotte spoke softly. "Pappa," she started, her voice cracking. "Momma isn't with us anymore."

George felt goosebumps run up his spine all the way to his head. "What do you mean?"

"Momma died last year," Hanna said softly, her voice breaking into a soft cry.

Charlotte hugged her Pappa and mumbled into his chest. "The doctor said she died of a broken heart. I'm so sorry, Pappa. Nobody told you."

George felt the warmth of his daughter on his chest, and his heart felt like it was shattering into pieces. He couldn't speak or form any rational thought.

"We need you, Pappa," Jacob said suddenly.

Hanna sniffled. "That's why it's so important that you live. After Momma and Zee left us, we only have you."

George inhaled deeply and felt his ribs ache. He grunted from the pain and frowned. "Zee, too?"

"Yes," Elise answered. "She left with Jesse, and they never came back. The soldiers told us that they were both killed in a skirmish, whatever that means."

George stared incredulously at his children, one after the other. He remembered the American Army Sergeant Jesse Eastman. He couldn't process all this information at once. It was too much. He blinked and felt all his children's eyes on him. "You all have been through a lot," he said.

Charlotte lifted her head up and straightened. "Yes, we have."

George stared up at the ceiling and shifted his aching body. He gained his life back but lost his beautiful wife and eldest daughter. He had a purpose, though. His children needed him. He must live. "It will be alright. I'm here now," he said slowly. "I will heal, and we will put our family back together."

Charlotte, Hanna, and the rest of the children beamed happily.

It was the right thing to say, George knew, for his children's sake. But what he felt was something entirely different. His broken heart ached so badly that he could not even envision a life without Clara or his daughter, Zee.

An unexpected evil thought of revenge began slithering through his veins, looking for a spot to root securely. George was tired and needed to recover. His eyes fluttered closed, and he whispered gently to his children. "Pappa needs to rest. We'll talk more later."

Chapter 29

Jesse lit the wood stove and cuddled with his baby daughter on the rocking chair while Xavier played at his feet. Wet snow was falling against the windowpane outside. He watched as the sticky snowflakes struck the window and slid down, almost melting immediately. Spring was finally here, and he couldn't believe it was already 1815. Time had passed so quickly.

Zee had cooked a scrumptious dinner of wild bear stew, and his stomach was pleasantly full and warm. The bears never learned to stop eating the raspberry bushes, but Jesse couldn't complain because it had supplied them with plentiful meat to store over the winter. The ground had frozen over, and the meat kept well in the cold basement cellar he had dug under the kitchen.

The cellar ladder creaked, pulling him out of his reverie.

Zee poked her head up from the cellar.

"Was there any berry syrup left?" Jesse asked, turning his head around.

Zee nodded, holding a jar of dark red syrup like it was a prize. "I found the last one!" she replied, beaming proudly. "It will go perfectly with the custard." A cold blast of air filled the house as Zee dropped the cellar floor door closed. She smiled and shuffled into the small kitchen, pulling the prepared custard rounds from the stove and placing them onto several small dessert plates. She opened the canned syrup and poured it over top of the custard rounds, one by one. "I'm so glad I canned all those remaining wild raspberries in the summer," she commented. She looked up at Jesse and her children at the fire. Her heart warmed, and she chuckled. "You look like the best father ever, sitting by the fire with the kids."

"That's because I am," Jesse countered.

Zee smiled. "Slightly overconfident, too."

"Of course," he jested. "No husband of yours could ever be anything else."

Zee chuckled and rubbed her belly. Her third pregnancy had just begun showing. "Is it already 1815? I can't believe it. Time has gone by so fast. Before we know it, we'll have three children to introduce to both our families. They will be shocked."

"They definitely will," Jesse stated. "Especially after they realize that we are still alive."

"Did you hear any news about the war?"

"Nothing new since the United States and Britain signed the Treaty of Ghent back in February. Things are beginning to get back to normal," Jesse responded. "The war is certainly over."

Zee smiled and finished arranging the custard plates, bringing them to the table. "When will we return?" she asked.

"We'll start preparations next week," Jesse replied. "Are you sure you'll be okay to travel?"

"I am four months pregnant," Zee answered. "It will be perfect timing."

Jesse nodded as he gathered up the children and sat them at the table. "After we see your family, we will take a trip to

Philadelphia as well," he said, strapping Janey to a highchair. "Momma made a wonderful dessert, Janey." He cooed.

The little girl squirmed and squealed with delight as the custard was placed in front of her. Jesse began spooning the custard into her mouth as Janey opened her lips happily. He tasted a tiny bit of the custard himself. "Oh my, that tastes good, my love," Jesse mumbled and winked at Zee.

Zee smiled and gave Xavier his own spoon. "Don't make a mess," she instructed the boy and turned to gaze at Jesse with love shining in her eyes. "I'm glad you like it. I'm so pleased Momma taught me how to cook."

"I heard you put up a fight," Jesse said, chuckling.

"Of course," Zee countered, laughing softly. "Everything earned the hard way is a much better lesson."

"That's true," Jesse stated as he spooned the remaining custard into Janey's mouth. When Janey was done, he wiped her mouth and then devoured his own custard greedily.

"Don't inhale it," Zee jested.

"You be careful, my beautiful wife, or I'll start inhaling you." Jesse winked at her and laughed. "Seriously, I'm looking forward to going on the trip back."

Zee laughed. "I'm looking forward to it as well." Zee ate her own custard delicately. A thought crossed her mind. "I'm excited to meet all your family, too! If they're anything like you, I'll love them."

"They're nothing like me," Jesse laughed loudly, spooning the last mouthful into his mouth.

⚓

George grabbed his cane and stood up from his bed. His left knee had never healed properly from the Lundy's Lane battle.

He grimaced and shuffled down the hallway towards the kitchen. In the mornings he used his cane, but as the day progressed, he just limped around stubbornly.

News of the Treaty of Ghent was still the talk of the neighborhood. The United States Congress had ratified it in February, and it was a huge relief off of everyone's minds. The war had taken its toll on so many people. George was deeply satisfied that the war had finally ended.

He had heard that Lt. Governor Drummond had somehow miraculously survived the neck wound from the Lundy's Lane battle. But even more surprising, Brigadier Scott was still alive and healing up as well. News was circulating that Scott was contemplating a career in politics.

Those two commanders were the toughest men George had ever known, he mused. He had nothing but pride and admiration for them both and was happy to learn that they both survived. Brown survived, too! George shook his head in astonishment. The indomitable spirit of both sides still amazed him.

Charlotte turned around in the kitchen as George entered. "I have a pot of coffee on, Pappa," she said, smiling. "How are you feeling today?"

"I'm feeling pretty good except for my broken knee," he replied.

"The doctors were more worried about your heart, I suppose."

"Yes," George agreed. "It's a miracle I survived."

"My tough Collard father?" Charlotte stated, chuckling. "Of course, you survived. That is why you earned a medal of bravery. One of the last men standing." Charlotte hugged her father warmly.

"I suppose," George said, grabbing his coffee and sitting down at the kitchen table. It was a new kitchen table that he had built himself. The old table had too many blood stains from the surgeries on it. He smoothed his hands along the wood grain and felt his emotions bubble up in his throat. The Americans had infiltrated his home with their gang of soldiers and terrorized his children.

"Pappa?" Charlotte asked, noticing the sudden silence. "Are you okay?"

He sipped his coffee slowly. "Just upset that all my children were forced to witness all of the atrocities of war right here in their own home."

"Don't think that way, Pappa," Charlotte stated soothingly. "There were so many worse things that could've happened. Many children died. We survived, and the American soldiers were nice to us."

"I don't know how you can say that."

"Well, they weren't mean to us, Pappa."

"But they performed surgeries on the kitchen table!" George countered.

"Yes, that did happen," Charlotte answered. "All I'm saying is that much worse happened to other families. We are all lucky to be alive." Charlotte began stirring cream into her coffee. "Actually, one of the sergeants, the replacement one, Samuel, he was really nice to us. It felt like he was caring for us after Jesse and Zee were gone. I don't know, maybe I am wrong, but it sure felt like he was making sure we were all protected."

"Hmm," George scoffed.

"Don't be angry, Pappa. The war is over. Let's put this all behind us."

George looked down into his coffee cup, and he knew that he should let it go. A heavy suspicion surrounding the deaths of Jesse and Zee had begun circulating in his mind. No bodies were ever recovered. It was only the statement from the replacement sergeant, Samuel, about their demise, but nothing else had ever been found.

George scratched his full beard thoughtfully and remembered seeing Jesse and Zee in the forest back in 1813. They were kissing and obviously in love. George had made the split decision not to kill Jesse because his daughter had finally found love.

George wondered if they had run off and married. It was possible, he mused. George tipped his coffee cup up and drank the warm liquid as he pondered the possibilities. He wondered if it was just his mind hoping that Zee was still alive. But it would definitely make sense for Jesse to provide a cover story so they could run away together.

If his suspicions were true, his oldest daughter was still alive.

George placed the coffee cup onto the table a bit too hard.

"Pappa!"

"Sorry," George mumbled as he stood. "My hand is still shaky." His mind reeled at all the possible conclusions. What if Zee was still alive? What if they had children? That would make him a grandpa. He had learned from his children that Xavier had disappeared as well. He hadn't even known that Xavier existed. Charlotte had told him that Xavier was her brother, but he knew the timing was not right. Clara was not pregnant when he had left for the war. He knew Clara was devoted to him, body and soul, so it was not from a different man. It was most likely Zee's child, and Clara had covered it up. That was definitely something Clara would do to protect Zee. He wondered if Xavier was really his grandchild. Maybe he would never know.

Charlotte had mentioned that the sergeant had not said anything about Xavier's death initially. It was like they had forgotten about the baby during the cover-up. His daughters had enquired, and Samuel had just stated that whoever was with them had also died in the firefight. It all sounded a bit suspicious.

George limped to the living room and plopped down onto the new sofa. He had replaced that piece of furniture as well. There was so much blood covering everything in the house it had taken months to return the house back to any semblance of normality.

At least the homestead was recovering. His life would never be normal again, though. The nightly war dreams kept reminding him of what he had lived through. He was alive, and his children were his life now. George was immensely grateful for this. His family was his strong purpose in life now.

He had lost his wife, daughter, and a possible grandson, but he still had the rest of his children. George fought briefly with thoughts of revenge almost every day. The madness inside of him must be contained, he thought, for the future of his children and himself.

Ŧ

Jesse reined in his horse and yelled ahead of him. "This looks like a good clearing to stay for the night," he hollered to Zee as she slowed her horse. They had been traveling for several days now. Zee had Janey strapped to her back, and Jesse had Xavier on his back. A rough sled full of supplies was pulled behind one of two packhorses as the caravan slowed to a halt.

Jesse dismounted and approached the other packhorse, removing the tent supplies. Zee dismounted as well and stretched, removing Janey from her back pouch. They set up quickly and had a fire blazing in no time. The weather was pleasant and aided in making the expedition a pleasant one.

They were traveling slowly and taking things easy but surprisingly making good time.

"I am so excited to see Pappa again," Zee said, throwing potatoes and dried meat into a pot.

"If he made it back from the war," Jesse stated.

"Oh, he would have," Zee replied. "You don't know my father. He's tough as nails."

"I only met him twice," Jesse said, throwing another log on the fire and chasing Xavier playfully with a stick. "I sure hope he made it through the war. I heard about the Lundy's Lane battle. It was a bloodbath." He grabbed Xavier as the toddler squealed gleefully.

"Maybe he was lucky and didn't fight in that battle," Zee responded.

"Maybe," Jesse muttered as he struggled to contain the wild toddler in his arms.

Janey squealed and ran towards her father and brother. The little girl jumped and then fell over a log. Janey's face scrunched up into tears, and she started wailing. "I've got her, sweetheart," Jesse said, scooping up Janey in his left arm. He chuckled, balancing Xavier with his right arm. "Hurry and get the food cooking before these two tire me out."

Zee laughed. "I'm trying. The stew should be ready soon." She plunked a bag of cut carrots and onions into the pot. "I'll make some coffee."

"Thank you, sweetheart," Jesse replied. "Do you know how beautiful you look right now?"

"Thank you, my sweet," Zee replied, her lips curving into a sexy grin.

"When you smile like that," Jesse stated, his left eyebrow lifting. "I want to strip you naked and have my way with you."

"Shh," Zee scolded. "Not in front of the children."

"They're not old enough yet to understand."

"Yes," Zee chuckled. "But they'll certainly grow up learning an eclectic vocabulary."

"They'll grow up learning how much their parents love each other."

"That's true," Zee agreed, grinning.

A gentle wind blew through the late April countryside. In the clearing, several spring flowers bloomed alongside the tall brown grass blades. Pink and purple tiny flowers dotted the landscape as the forest canopy grew taller in the distance.

The smoke from the fire rose in a column, sending birds flocking away. Zee inhaled the fresh scent of the meadow flowers. "What a beautiful spot," she said admiringly.

"Just like my wife."

Zee giggled. "I will never tire from your attentions, but my body is getting tired of traveling already." She stirred the stew thoughtfully. "When will we be arriving at the Collard Farm?"

"If everything goes well, we should arrive tomorrow afternoon."

"Good." Zee sat down heavily on a log and cradled her growing belly between her hands. "I'm tiring easily. I don't know why, but this pregnancy feels different from the others."

"Your belly looks bigger than before," Jesse pointed out. "Are you sure you aren't seven months pregnant instead of five?"

"I'm sure it's only been five months," she replied. Zee rummaged in a pack and found a water flask, tipping it up to her lips, and drank. "I'm so thirsty. It seems I have gained more weight than last time, and my belly is sticking out farther."

"Maybe we have two babies in there," Jesse offered.

"Oh, I hope not!"

"Why not?" Jesse countered, smiling devilishly. "I would be thrilled to have a big instant family of four."

Zee wiped her brow and pushed herself up. "The coffee is ready," she said, digging in the supplies for two cups. She pulled the cups out and filled them both with steaming hot coffee. "Can we stay with Pappa for a while before going on to Philadelphia?"

"We can stay as long as you like," Jesse replied. "We have three months to complete the entire trip and get back home. I promised the neighbors I'd start building their cabins by midsummer."

"Are you sure you want to settle at our property along Lake Huron? We could go anywhere now that the war is over."

Jesse smiled. "I love the home we've made. If we decide later on to move further south, we can. But for now, let's just enjoy our home and visit our relatives twice a year. The housebuilding work will provide for us nicely."

"That sounds like a nice yearly adventure," Zee replied, gazing up at the tree line. The wind calmly breezed through her hair as her thoughts centered on returning home tomorrow. "I'm looking forward to seeing Pappa," she said thoughtfully.

♇

"Pappa," Charlotte said, frowning and trying to place the saddle on the horse correctly. "I'll never be like Zee."

George grabbed the saddle before it slid to the side and straightened it. "I don't expect you to. Nobody can ever replace Zee. She was a special young woman."

Charlotte looked up at the forest tree line sadly. "I miss her."

"I miss her too, sweetheart." George grabbed the reins on the two horses and walked them towards the field in the afternoon sun. "I still hold onto the hope that she ran away with that Sergeant Eastman."

"It did seem like they were in love, Pappa," Charlotte confessed. "They looked at each other often, and Jesse touched her waist a lot."

George nodded. Many of his children said the same things about the daily interactions between Zee and Jesse Eastman. As he pieced together the events in the home military hospital, it renewed his hope that they were somehow alive and well. George grinned. It just didn't feel like he had lost his stubborn Zelda. He felt the void from his loss of Clara, and his heart felt damaged every day, but he didn't feel the same about Zee.

He wondered if it was just his grief speaking through his emotions, lighting up hope to see something better on the other side.

His feelings of revenge had calmed down, and George had a cap on his emotions now, but he was still wary and jumpy, always making sure to have a rifle ready. He had taught all his children how to shoot, and surprisingly, it was Betty who had become quite a target shooter. The girl was only sixteen years old but showed a lot of interest in hunting small game. George was proud of all his children.

Charlotte pointed towards the tree line. "It's windy today," she stated, pointing at the swaying bushes. "Do we really need to go out for a ride?"

"You need to get used to doing some of the farm work," George argued. "We will be back shortly."

As they mounted the horses, a movement caught George's eye. He swung his rifle to the ready and silenced Charlotte with two fingers in the air.

Charlotte knew better than to protest and watched fearfully as Pappa aimed toward the tree line.

A bead of sweat instantly formed on George's brow, and the sounds of distant cannon fire filled his ears. He scanned the tree line for movement and felt the pain in his chest returning. It felt eerily like he had been transported back onto the battlefield.

"Pappa," Charlotte whispered.

George looked at his daughter in a haze. She was a fully grown eighteen-year-old woman now. He turned his head and strained his ears to hear the cannon fire. It was silent. There were no cannons. George lowered his rifle and frowned. His mind was playing tricks on him again. He looked down and felt ashamed of his madness.

"Pappa," Charlotte said again, her voice laden with emotion. "I don't believe it."

He looked at her, confused. "What is it?"

Charlotte pointed. "I think that is Zee with some others."

George's eyes darted in the direction of her outstretched finger, the hope rising in his chest like a painful ache.

"You were right, Pappa!" Charlotte shrieked. She snapped the reins, and her horse started galloping. "Zee!" she shouted exuberantly.

George galloped to catch up to his daughter as tears began spilling down his cheeks. "My dear Zelda," he muttered as his heart pumped madly in his chest.

"Zee!" Charlotte yelled louder.

Zee looked across the field at the galloping riders and was astonished to see her younger sister, all grown up, riding a mare. "Charlotte!" Zee yelled as her tired horse ambled onto the Collard Farm countryside. Behind her, the packhorse pulled the sled of supplies slowly. Another pack horse followed with a strap of supplies across his back. At the end of the caravan, Jesse stood erect on his horse with Xavier tied to his back.

Charlotte reached Zee first and jumped off her horse with glee. "Oh my God! Zee! You're alive!" She reached up to help Zee unstrap her baby daughter and dismount. "And who is this sweetheart?"

"This is your niece. Her name's Janey!" Zee replied, kissing Charlotte on both cheeks and handing the small girl to her.

George pulled up and had trouble seeing because of all the tears welling in his eyes. He sat on his horse, like a statue, partially not believing that it was true.

Zee looked at her father. "Pappa!" she yelled with heavy emotion in her voice as she dismounted excitedly. "You made it through the war."

"Of course I did," he replied, his voice cracking with emotion. He swung his legs off the horse gently and joined his daughters.

'Oh, Pappa," Zee cried out and hugged her father warmly. "I'm so sorry about the story Samuel told everyone. It was the only way we could leave the war to raise our family."

"I knew it in my heart," George replied. "A parent always knows." He wiped the tears away with the back of his hand. "I'm just so glad you are unharmed and happy." He looked down and noticed her bulging belly. "Are you pregnant?"

"Yes," Zee stated proudly, rubbing her belly through the fabric of her dress. "Another one or two, maybe. We'll see. My belly is so much larger this time."

Jesse dismounted and joined his wife. As he neared, Jesse eyed George Collard and could tell that he was a changed man. George walked with a noticeable limp, and a deep intuition told Jesse to approach with caution. This was an embattled man of war, and it was obvious.

Jesse stopped in front of George and put out his hand in greeting. "I come in peace, Mr. Collard," he said peacefully. "I married your daughter."

George stood erect and swallowed, trying to will the tears to stop pooling in his eyes. "You did?"

"Yes, I did," Jesse answered. "I built a house near Lake Huron for our growing family. You are welcome to come visit anytime."

George's tough façade melted away. He reached out his arm and shook Sergeant Eastman's hand, feeling his damaged heart tingle with joy. "I have a granddaughter and a son-in-law?"

"Yes," Jesse replied. "You have a granddaughter and a good son-in-law." He chuckled. "I adopted Zee's other baby, Xavier, and we've got some more on the way."

George looked at Zee and hugged her fiercely. "I was right about Xavier then?" he asked. "He's your son? Not Clara's?"

"Yes, Pappa," Zee answered sheepishly. "Xavier was born in 1812, right after you left. His biological father is Ewart." She looked down, embarrassed, then looked over to Jesse. "Jesse has been a good father to them both."

George looked over at Jesse and shook his hand again. "You're a good man."

Zee smiled and glanced towards the house. "Are all the others okay?" She motioned at the house with her chin. "Jesse had made a pact with Samuel to protect my brothers and sisters until the war ended."

"He did that?" George asked with a glint of gratefulness in his eyes.

"Yes, sir," Jesse stated.

George looked at Jesse and saw him in an entirely different light. "Thank you," he muttered almost inaudibly. "Thank you for protecting my family." Several tears welled in George's eyes, and he struggled to contain them this time. Nothing worse than a grown man crying, he mused.

"Pappa," Charlotte said lovingly. "Let's all go inside and introduce everyone to my lovely new niece." She held up Janey in the air and kissed her small cheeks as the little girl began to squeal happily.

"We are here to visit for as long as you'll have us, Mr. Collard," Jesse stated, leading the larger packhorse forward. "We have three months before we need to get back home."

George waved them towards the house. "You are welcome at the Collard farm anytime, my son." He grabbed the other packhorse's reins and started walking towards the house with a joyful smirk on his face. Everything was going to be alright, he mused.

Zee watched her father amble towards the house and followed, slipping her hand lovingly into Jesse's rough palm. "Let's go reunite with the rest of my family, sweetheart," she said, kissing him lightly on the cheek. "I love you, Mr. Jesse Eastman," she whispered in his ear.

THE END

Final Note to Reader

On November 5, 1814, American forces evacuated the Niagara Peninsula. The region, including Fort Niagara, remained under British control until the signing of The Treaty of Ghent on December 24, 1814. It was later unanimously approved by the US Senate in February 1815.

The Treaty was the beginning of more than two centuries of peaceful relations between the United States, the United Kingdom, and Canada. It restored the prewar 1812 borders between Canada and the US, amongst many other key considerations. Many people still believe that Canada won the war, although it remains documented internationally as a stalemate war. British Canada excelled from a military standpoint, but the United States excelled on the Naval front and solidified their rights as an independent nation. Both sides were eager to end the war peacefully with the treaty. Great Britain agreed to relinquish claims to the Northwest lands of the US, and America gained strength as a foreign power.

It was a hard fight for both countries to arrive at this conclusion, though. Many more battles raged than those depicted in this novel and caused much hardship to both sides. The battles were scattered all over North America, from New Orleans to Montreal. In August of 1814, after a British victory at the

Battle of Bladensburg in Maryland, British troops marched onto Washington, DC. In retaliation for the burnings of Newark, York, and Port Dover, the British Canadians set ablaze various US government and military buildings, including the White House. The British occupied the US Capitol for only 26 hours. As luck would have it, four days later, a heavy thunderstorm, possibly a hurricane, extinguished the flames but also resulted in further destruction to the buildings.

I chose not to include many of the other significant battles of the 1812 War and kept my focus solely on the Niagara Peninsula. There were so many other battles, in fact, even in the Niagara Region alone, that I experienced extreme difficulty picking which ones to include in my novel. As a historical fiction writer, I always run the risk of including too many battles. The cost of war is high, and families suffer the most. My stories are plotted on the families involved in the conflict, not the war itself.

Many Canadian soldiers were similar to George Collard, born Americans who had fled to Canada following the Revolutionary War. Some historic farms in the Niagara area have ancestors going right back to the loyalist settlements. These people had relatives still living back in the United States, and their lives were heavily intertwined with those of Americans. I attempted to portray this as vividly as possible in this novel. George Collard, Zee, Jesse Eastman, and the majority of my characters are all fictional, with the exception of the following historical non-fiction individuals:

Wilson Price Hunt – head of the Overland Historians and a St. Louis merchant.

Robert McClelland – Pacific Fur Company partner from Pennsylvania and part of the Overland Astorians.

Major General Sir Issac Brock – (October 6, 1769 – October 13, 1812) Brock's remains are interred at the base of a 185-foot-high monument that still stands today at Queenston Heights Park in Niagara-on-the-Lake.

General Stephen Van Rensselaer – American General during Queenston battle.

Brigadier General Winfield Scott – American General who replaced Van Rensselaer and later became the top Commanding General of the US Army between 1841 - 1861.

Major General Sheaffe – replaced Brock until December 1813.

British Lieutenant Governor Gordon Drummond – replaced Brock and Sheaffe in December 1813. After the war, he took over as Governor General and Administrator of Canada in Quebec City. Postwar, Drummond was promoted to Knighthood in Great Britain.

General Jacob Brown – commanded over Winfield Scott during the Lundy's Lane battle. He survived his injuries at Lundy's Lane and ordered the American retreat.

Laura Secord – a Canadian heroine during the 1812 war. A hiking path called the Laura Secord Legacy Trail exists today, which spans the full 20 miles of Laura's precarious journey from Niagara-on-the-Lake to DeCew House in Thorold to warn British forces of the American's planned attack.

Lieutenant James FitzGibbon – commanded the Battle of Beaverdams, and the American surrender following Laura Secord's leaked American advance.

During the early Western frontier of the United States, many Americans were making plans to open up the Northwest region. The rights to this land later played a major role in the War of 1812. The Northwest was extremely rugged and often inaccessible, mostly inhabited only by native groups such as the Arikaras.

The Northwestern region of the United States would not exist as it is today without these brave first explorers. Individuals from Canada and the United States participated in these early expeditions and formed a group called the Overland Astorians. The group split apart by accident and some of the explorers did indeed eat their leather boots to survive. It was a dangerous expedition that cost several men's lives.

Tensions surfaced between the British and United States over territorial expansion in this area. The British supported the North American tribes who opposed US colonial settlement in the Old Northwest. The fur traders desperately wanted this area to expand their commerce.

Things escalated on the East Coast during the same time period and took a turn for the worse. The British Navy imposed tighter restrictions on US maritime trade with France and stifled all US trade with Europe.

Britain was busy fighting the Napoleonic war with France from as far back as 1803, and as time progressed, the British desperately needed all the help they could get. The line was crossed with the Americans when the British began taking United States sailors from their ships and impressing them into the British Navy, claiming they were British subjects, even though the sailors held American citizenship.

Several southern and western US senators led the decision for war, calling for a defense of American interests and honor. War was declared on June 18, 1812.

Multiple battlefield sites dot the landscape of the Niagara Region today. There are rumors of many ghost stories in several of the small towns and battlefields. The town of Niagara-on-the-Lake is one of those towns. It was built near the site of the old burned-out town of Newark. Many of the town buildings reflect the dates built after 1813, along with a few standing taverns and hotels that were rebuilt from the ashes.

I personally visited many of the sites and was astonished by the eeriness of the sites. Lundy's Lane was one of the sites that surprised me the most. Tucked behind an old church, it is easy to drive by and miss this important landmark. I kept circling the block until I found the entrance. It was a quiet, almost deserted park and graveyard. Amongst the winds blowing at the top of the hill, a concrete memorial sits with cannon balls stacked neatly upon each other. When I neared this memorial, my dog started barking with his hackles up. A chill ran up my spine as I continued through the park. Several mass graves were marked for all the souls that had lost their lives during the bloody Lundy's Lane battle. So many, in fact, that a concrete list of names was erected on the memorial.

I included some pictures of the researched areas that so fascinated me about this area. Hiking through these areas was such a rich source of early Canadian history and highlights the links that intertwine us with the United States of America.

So many parks scattered across Southern Ontario are named Loyalist Park that you'd have to go through an entire page-long list of them. Many early settlers in the Niagara region were displaced Americans trying to make a peaceful homestead.

The War of 1812 is often misconstrued as America attempting to conquer more land. But as it is with all wars, so much more than one reason pushes nations to war. Many historians conclude that American expansion was an idea that occurred during the war, not during the beginning of it. As I've detailed previously, American citizenship and land rights were at stake.

The War of 1812 was a pivotal war for both the United States and Canada. Back then, British Canada was composed of the provinces Upper Canada, which was positioned where most of Southern Ontario lies today, and Lower Canada, which was mostly Quebec. The confusing upper prefix designates the position where it lay above the Great Lakes and above the headwaters of the Saint Lawrence River. Lower Canada was situated farther down the headwaters of the Saint Lawrence, hence the lower prefix. It wasn't until 1867 that Canada became a unified country.

Britain offered Loyalists free land in Canada for their support to the Crown. Loyalists living in the United States following the American Revolution had a very difficult life. They lost their rights; some were imprisoned, and many lost their property. The decision to flee, in most cases, was by pure necessity.

Upper Canada received approximately 7500 Loyalists, the remainder fleeing to the Maritimes in large numbers and Quebec as well. They often married Canadians and raised their families for many generations in Canada. When the 1812 war started, they saw this as an extension of the Revolutionary War. Their biggest concerns were to protect their land, their rights, and, most importantly, their families.

George Collard and his American Canadian family are fictitious but resemble the plight of so many families who were caught in the crossfires of the 1812 war. These men fought with ferocious abandonment because the lives of their children and their future lay in the balance of the war.

Both sides, Canadians and Americans, had many good reasons for fighting. In the end, thankfully, the war was resolved with a peaceful treaty. It was a short but bloody war. The treaty solidified trade, commerce, borders, and citizenship rights.

I personally live in the Niagara region, and upon moving here from Western Canada, I was initially astonished by the numerous battlefields dotting the entire Niagara Peninsula. Museums, statues, parks, and even mausoleums are a common sight. I hiked along these paths and researched the battles depicted in this novel. The British redan in Queenston still stands to this day on the slopes of Queenston Hill, where the Americans launched their attack. It is now a heavily wooded area with very steep hiking paths.

Research and history are many of my favorite parts of my job as a historical fiction author. Many readers are astonished at the amount of research I undertake for each story. For me, it is a wonderful way of combining both my passion for writing and my love for history. I take my job seriously as a historical fiction author. In 100 years, my books will still be available, and I hope my Final Notes to Reader do justice by separating the factual parts of the story from fiction.

I would like to thank my proofreader and biggest fan, Kathy, who awaits each new novel with gusto. She is American, as are so many of my readers. I wrote this book for my American and Canadian readers. I tried my best to remain neutral on both sides of the war. A big thank you to all my readers for reading and reviewing each book I write. I cannot describe the glow that I get when a reader leaves a wonderful review. It is validation and confirmation that I am doing what God intended for me to do: writing stories of the past.

Another big thank you to my two sons for enriching my life with love, support, and happiness. They are always the first to learn of my books, the plot, the characters and they live along the journey as the story unfolds with me. Without family, passion, and love, I have nothing. I am forever grateful to them and for the many other blessings in my life.

I will always aim to live my time on earth to the fullest, and so should you. We only have one body and soul. Don't waste it.

Lundy's Lane Mass Grave Monument